A VISION TO DIE FOR

BY M.R. CHANEY

Prelude

THINGS ARE RELATIVELY NORMAL in Nashville, Tennessee. It's the summer of 2027. The economy is doing fine. Well, things are terribly expensive, but the DOW is over $45,000. So, there's that.

I'm working a normal day job doing normal things for normal people. I don't love what I do, but I don't hate it either.

I live with my girlfriend in a small retro-chic ranch in East Nashville, far too near Five-Points, which has quickly become the new Broadway, to the local's utmost dismay. Just a few years ago, this was the most thriving hippest-trendiest-folksiest part of perhaps the entire southeast. But now, Five-Points is littered with casinos, bachelorette party buses galore, thousands of tourists, and addicts of all sizes and stripes.

To the money men, the new Five-Points is a dream come true. To the locals, not so much. Luckily, some of the nearby areas picked up the slack with some rather odd and wonderful joints.

Perhaps the busiest part of town is along the Cumberland River, which is lined with large casino boats, as well as the casino just north of the stadium, the largest of the bunch.

I'm happy to say that we're getting back to the time of jazz and rhythm and blues. The roaring twenties have come back in more ways than one, included a few speakeasies that sprouted up during the continued lockdowns—no phones allowed.

The one good thing about what's coming is that I'll never again have to hear about Swift Du Soleil or Miley World, which has taken over and rebuilt Opry Land. You don't even want to know what they call the log ride.

My girlfriend is this beautiful starry-eyed dreamer, Jasmine Laine. She fell from the heavens into my arms. Now that I have her, I will never let her go, nor she, I.

She makes me want to do all the things I had once never given a second thought towards. But now, I'm considering everything; marriage, a family, supporting her and the kids. This is weird stuff for me. I've always been a bit of a lone wolf. Sure, I valued love, but love has always seemed to allude me. Not this time. This time it's everything.

She and I just have it. We can feel it. We don't even have to speak it. We don't have to speak at all, but we do. We stay up all night laughing together in the sheets, making love and sharing stories, dreaming about our future adventures and endeavors. It's the first time I've had it all with a woman, and I'm not going to lose that. Nothing can take that from me.

We began living together several months earlier. Months before that, nearly every day at lunch, we'd take the trolly over to East Park to share a picnic under the Sycamore Tree. She'd bring the veggies and salad. I'd bring the sandwiches and dip. We'd hold each other and share endless stories.

What started sweet and innocent quickly became a raucous good time. We've been devouring each other in the sheets every morning and night. We're energized every time we touch. I can feel the waves flowing between us.

She's everything I had ever wanted, but so much more than that. Every moment together feels like eternity. The flowers grow taller and more fragrant, and the light shines brighter every time she enters the room; birds and butterflies sing and flutter. She brings magic to my world. And they want to take that magic away. They want to destroy the magic.

This is Nashville, our city. But it could be any city.

Part One

1. And So It Begins

ON THIS FATEFUL DAY, Jasmine and I awaken in each others arms to the sunrise peaking through the warm bay window. I wrap my fingers through her hair as I cup her head. She turns towards me. Forehead to forehead, we look deeply into each other's eyes, then kiss slowly and gently, yet passionately. The golden sunlight glistens upon her naked body. This is how all of our mornings begin.

I feel her wetness as I enter her smoothly yet firmly. I hold her leg over my shoulder as we embrace with our entire bodies making love, our hands, our heads, our lips, our feet, calves, thighs, and hips. She rolls on top of me. Her hair creates beautiful waves of light as we feel every atom of each other, our energies flowing in ecstasy. I roll her over. Back and forth, back and forth until our morning ritual ends with blissful pleasure.

We lay together in each other's arms, soaking up the moment, playfully engulfed in each other's love until that oh-so-ever-present alarm clock decides to disturb our morning blissfulness, forcing us into our daily routines of the nine to five modern world. Which, in reality, is more like seven to six. But today, all of that will change.

We slowly release with a sweet kiss and begin our days. She looks so beautiful showering and putting on her blouse that I just can't help myself, but she holds back her desires for now. She's right. We have jobs to do—boring, mundane jobs, but they offer us many pleasantries that we often take for granted.

I wish I could spend every moment with her. At least we work nearby and can carpool. But today, we're driving separately so that she can run a few errands in the afternoon.

We kiss each other a quick momentary goodbye and follow each other to Ellington Pike towards downtown Nashville. Neither of us works on Broadway, but still too close for comfort. I'm in an Office Building on 3rd Avenue, right near the Symphony; not the high rise. She's just south.

Jasmine follows along, but takes an early exit.

She calls to let me know she forgot something and has to run home.

I pull into the office garage, park my car, grab my bag, and walk towards the large glass door. Out bursts my co-worker, Ken, along with several other folks who seem quite anxious for some untold reason.

"What are you doing here, Harry? Go home," Ken says in a panic as he rushes by me.

"What are you talking about?" I ask with a slight laugh.

"Haven't you heard?" Ken asks, then stammers. "Look at the news."

"What are you waiting for?" a woman shouts from a crowd pushing to the exit.

I grab my phone and open my browser. My heart stops cold. My temperature drops 20 degrees. Panic sets in. I had lived through 9/11, but I was young then. And this is different, much different. I would try to make my way back to my car, but the roads are already jammed.

All I can think about is her. Over and over, I call Jasmine with no answer. I text her to stay home or to go back. I plead. Where is she?

"Just please stay home," I beg her answering machine as I stand here, frozen in time.

I can't think. I can't move. Where is she? Why am I not holding her? Why didn't we stay in bed for another fifteen minutes? Why aren't we on vacation down in Ecuador or somewhere quiet, where you can live off the land if worse came to worst?

My phone rings. It's her.

"Get home, now," I tell Jasmine. "I'll meet you there as quick as I can."

"What? What's going on?" she asks, worried.

"Just get home. Now. Okay?"

"Okay, but traffic is crazy. It's not moving at all. What's going on?"

"Where are you?"

Jasmine replies, "I'm about to cross the bridge."

"You've got to get home. Go now. Please."

"I can't. I'm stuck."

"I'm coming to you," I tell her.

Wails and panic set in all around. A storm is brewing, but this is no ordinary storm. This is different. This is a storm of the likes which this country has never seen.

Here? Nashville? Why here? Is it everywhere? Is the fate of all humanity doomed? Or just ours?

"Harry? What is happening?"

"Meet me at the pedestrian bridge. Now. Run."

"What?"

"Run!" I shout as I dash down the street towards the pedestrian bridge in a full sprint. I put the phone in my pocket but don't hang up. "I'm on my way."

Booms and Bangs begin to ring out. This storm is not natural. This storm is manmade; a metal horror.

"I'm coming, Harry," Jasmine shouts through the speaker. "I'm close."

Civilians begin ditching their cars and running in opposite directions in full panic—hundreds of them—thousands.

Artillery shells begin thundering upon downtown in an unstoppable rage. I make it to the pedestrian bridge, while civilians run in horror in all directions. Lead and artillery shells start to whistle by. Smoke begins to overtake the city. Attack helicopters storm overhead, smattering thousands of 50 caliber rounds into Nashville's skyline. I sprint up the bridge. Searing cement, metal, and flesh fill my nostrils with acrid fumes I will never soon forget. I'm taken aback as an artillery shell decimates the building behind me and to my right. Lucky for me, I know from the movies to keep my mouth open during explosions. Jasmine surely knows from my screaming it. One man nearby isn't so lucky as his jaw is shattered from the blast pressure, or perhaps his eardrums.

Children and mothers scream in terror. One child stands alone in tears, but I can't help him now. Smoke and debris rain down, but I keep on. Nothing will keep me from her.

"Where are you? Where are you?" Jasmine shouts through the phone.

"I'm almost there," I yell back.

"I'm close."

"I'm here. I'm coming."

I reach near the bridge's crest. I'm out of breath, but I continue sprinting.

I see her—on the other side—my Jasmine, my jewel, my everything. She runs towards me in a golden glow. She sprints with tears pouring forth.

Thousands of others fight their way this way or that, but it's only her. All of the horror and despair disappears as I run for her, and I once again feel the bliss we share with one another.

We lock eyes, and time stands still while we dash towards each other. The hellfire becomes almost majestic as she glows in the smokey air and glimmers of sunlight bounce off her snowy skin. She gleams in the light.

We dash and dash in this eternal moment, feeling as if we're dreaming, running as fast as we can but going nowhere. We're only seventy-five yards from one another. My heart races as we approach. She lights up my entire world. And in one fell swoop, my world is ripped into darkness.

2. Darkness Falls

OUT FROM THE SKY, a large black helicopter swoops down and hangs overhead. Two dozen fully armed men rappel down and land in the middle of the bridge, between her and I, east and west. They wear unidentifiable black uniforms with no visible country of origin.

Jasmine and I run, and we run until these black-clad men raise their rifles, then stand in the center of the bridge forming a wall, aiming down the crowd. She freezes.

"Gibberish, gibberish, gibberish," the black-clad men yell in a foreign language at the civilians trapped on either side.

They plaster the ground in front of the civilians with automatic gunfire.

Everyone runs back down their side of the bridge. I lose sight of her, but I continue climbing my way through the frantic crowd.

The men aim harder at the crowd, and the warning shots get closer. I fight to get to her, but the crowd is forceful.

I see Jasmine. Smoke grenades begin to fill the air with a thick fog as we stare fiercely into each other's eyes.

She's pushed back by the crowd's force. They can't keep us apart.

Gunner trucks and tanks begin pouring in up the bridge from the Eastside. They're not firing, yet.

Myself and a few others fight to cross the dividing line. She and I keep our eyes locked until these bastards start mowing down innocent civilians on both sides, mostly mine, the downtown side.

The man in front of me falls. Bullets spray around me. I hit the ground and take cover behind the dead and the dying.

I look up, and I can no longer see her. She's gone. Is she okay? Is she shot? I have to get to her.

I can't see anything past the bridge's center. The smoke is too thick now. The crowd is panicking. There are too many of them, but that may be a good thing. Perhaps she's safe in the crowd.

A second attack helicopter roars up from the East, shooting missiles towards the skyline. Then it starts shooting machine-gun fire at the people on the downtown side. But not towards the East, at least not towards the East. I feel the heat of the 50 caliber rounds streaming my way as I leap behind a red steel beam. Warm metal fragments spray around me.

The helicopter circles overhead and takes aim upon incoming National Guard tanks and heavy gunners which appear on the streets behind me.

Artillery shells rain upon downtown. My hearing is deafened greatly from the blasts. My vision is scattered from the smoke, dust, and bursting explosions. The air smells of fresh asphalt, iron, fireworks, and molten lead.

Here we are, she and I. Not two-hundred feet away, but worlds apart. I still can't see her. Is she injured? Has she fled? Is she hurting? I must get to her.

Not thirty feet from the bridge, one of the attack choppers crashes down into the Cumberland River.

I stand up. Small drops of blood drip down my feet. I don't notice any pain, only the blood, and a dozen or three holes ripped into the shins of my navy blue pants.

I walk lowly, with raised hands towards the invading line. The black-clad men aim their machine guns at me forcefully, shouting gibberish and signaling me to get down. I continue slowly towards them.

"Gibberish, gibberish, gibberish," these fucking bastards shout. I can tell they're serious now. I slow to a stop and kneel. I beg for them to let me pass.

One tall, dark-haired man with fierce machine-like brown eyes walks my way with his handgun drawn. He steps slowly towards me with a confident strut, obviously showing off to his mates. He stands over me and aims for my head. She's all I can think of. Life, I can let go of, but not her. Will I ever see her again? Is this it?

The machine-like man flails backwards. His blood splatters through the smokey air. The rest of these bastards begin firing upon the incoming National Guard tank, troops, and gunner. They're mowing the paratroopers down.

I make my way, crawling, scratching, and clawing towards the East side of the bridge. The invaders pay me no mind as they fire helplessly at the incoming guard troops.

I stand. I still don't see her. Did she flee in time? Is she still breathing? Or is she now cold and lifeless, as lifeless as this entire universe has become this morning? I run in search of her, but a National Guardsman grabs my shirt by the collar, shakes me, and shouts, "What's wrong with you? Get back there."

"I can't," I respond forcefully, throwing his arms off. "I have to get to her."

"There's nowhere to go," he says. "You can't cross enemy lines. Return behind that line immediately."

"Jasmine," I yell out. "Jasmine? Are you okay?"

There's no response.

The guardsman grabs me and shoves me back towards the molten city. I step to him and take him by the collar. We lock eyes. He knows my pain all too well. And I know I must do as he says no matter how much I want to rebel against it.

I back up slowly. The guardsman waves me on, then turns and begins firing at the incoming storm. An artillery shell flops calmly over his head.

I sprint down the bridge and dive for cover. The shell hits not twenty feet behind me, right next to the guard tank, turning the monstrous dinosaur-esque machine into a sweet useless metal puppy dog. The explosion sends its warm blast outwards, lifting me a foot or two off the ground, and slinging me like a rag doll seven feet down the bridge, rolling another ten with three and a half full rolls.

I crawl to standing. I can hardly see through the dense smoke, but the enemy is upon us, quickly approaching up the bridge from the east with at least one tank and several gunners, plus hundreds of troops. They're much more powerful than the guard line which has been severely depleted with the loss of its tank. The gunner tries to hold them back, but it's hopeless. The firing grows fiercer.

Artillery shells blast the large shiny building up ahead to the left, silencing the screams. Smoke billows out from all sides.

I walk slowly down the burning bridge. Everywhere I look, fire and destruction. The closer I get, the worse it is, the bloodier it is, the realer it is, the worse it smells. Seared flesh, along with putrid metal, rubber, and asbestos lines the air with its unforgettable scent.

The city is up in flames. It's only 9:35 AM, but it looks like the last moment of the sunset before light turns to darkness. If not for the few rays of light shining through the thick dark gray smoke, I would believe twelve hours have passed. That's how it feels. We have all experienced a lifetime's worth of fear and terror in these past thirty-five minutes.

I try to call her. But the service is out. All of the city's power is out. Did she make it down the bridge? Or was she sucked up in the storm?

I make my way down onto the street and rush towards Broadway. The cries, screams, and bloodshed, forever a part of us all now. Men, women, and children run in all directions. Cars slam their way through the traffic until there's nowhere left to slam through. Fire and wreckage surround us all.

Everyone is in shock. Some stand still as lead and fire pour down around them. Others cry and scream. Some search for a place to hide. Many seek shelter in the basement garages. Hundreds run underneath into the auditorium garage straight ahead from the bridge.

I continue my way towards Broadway as glass shards, concrete, and steel crash down in every direction. Mortar shells pound the buildings and asphalt, cratering the streets. And the smell, the fucking smell. The city is seared.

Up ahead, the old Paradise Park and adjoining buildings take two mortar shells to the dome and crumble into monstrous pieces.

One child stands alone in the middle of the street at the crossing of Broadway and 4th Avenue. Cars line both sides, but they're going nowhere. People leave their cars behind and run down Broadway towards safety, but no one's helping her.

I run towards the girl. I'm fifty yards away as a whistling mortar shell passes overhead and begins its descent to earth. I can't help but think that it's headed straight towards her. I run harder.

And just then, a woman grabs the girl and rushes her across the street towards 5th Avenue. But it's too late, I know it. The mortar lands on my side of Broadway, some ten yards from them, but it's a dud, the first dud I've seen. That's one lucky kid.

After a quick pause, I continue towards Broadway, dodging cars, debris, craters, and the raining glass shards from the 50 cal hellfire still being unleashed on the skyline above. Ten thousand civilians must have already died in these last forty minutes. At least it appears East Nashville has been mostly spared, perhaps because our side lacks the same level of firepower the invaders have unleashed upon downtown. And also, hopefully, that our side simply isn't going to fire upon its own civilians.

There must be at least a fifty percent chance that she is okay. Even if she is, what will become of her now? How can I make it to her? When can I contact her? All communication lines are down, and there is no way to breach the dividing line, the Cumberland River, today. Warring is going on all across the river and on what appears to be every bridge.

I look up and see several planes trying to flee the city, each shot down by rockets within seconds of each other, exploding in midair. All routes out of town appear to be shut down.

The invaders have purposely taken the east side of Nashville. My guess is, they didn't have enough men to take the whole city, so they played it safe and only took what they knew they could. But more of these bastards will surely be coming. If history has taught us anything, this is just the initial invasion.

What other cities have been attacked? We know that New York, LA, and DC have been. But why Nashville? And if Nashville, where else? There must be others. They wouldn't simply skip from DC to Nashville, would they? What about Miami, San Fransisco, Seattle, Atlanta, Chicago? These are much bigger cities than Nashville. Is this happening in other countries? On other continents? Europe? Asia? Japan? Australia?

The brunt of the military must be busy elsewhere, in the coastal cities, fighting in DC, New York, Boston, LA, Seattle, Portland; all of the West Coast, I'd imagine; Miami.

Who are these invaders? I don't remotely recognize their language or accent, not that I am any linguistic expert. They are certainly multi-national. You can't tell the difference between them and us, other than the gibberish they speak and that fucking smell.

What is that smell? The essential oil of mule and skunk? I don't know but I sure the fuck can't stand it, nor will I forget it. Nor will I ever forget that they separated us. I will do whatever I must do to get her back.

My fear turns into rage when another mortar shell screams my way and hits far too close to comfort. The last thing I remember is the heat and force slinging me backward like a rag doll into one of the Broadway hoedown hellholes.

Was this morning the last I will ever see of my love? Is this actually happening? Is this real, or could it just be a dream? It all goes black as my body seemingly drifts and sinks into the murky river.

Blackness. A dark, searing blackness. Senseless. Not a smell, feeling, or sound. No light. All is gone.

3. Aftermath

THERE SHE IS, IN A PASTURE, wearing a golden yellow dress. Sunflowers dance to the wind and sun behind her. Birds sing joyous tunes together in ultra-phonic surround sound. Monarch butterflies dance around her dark hair, which looks almost golden in the setting light against her golden dress.

I go to her. She backs away. She keeps backing away. The harder I reach for her, the further she backs away. She's saying something. I can't quite make it out in the distance. I try and try to get closer, but the divide only grows. The ground rips in two in front of me. A deep gorge forms between us. If only I could jump it, but it's far too immense. The ravine opens up and swallows us both at free fall. I can't reach her. She's still trying to tell me something but I can't hear the words, only the sound of whispers.

The sound and vision pulse to a screaming halt. The taste of copper fills my sinuses. I awaken in a totally dark room with a piercing headache. My legs and head are bandaged loosely with gauze.

Dozens of sad and lonely people cower together in fright. Some are injured, some just in shock. Everyone is covered in smoke and dirt. Some are bloody, some not. Some old. Some young. Some crying. Some are almost laughing in madness. All are terrified and devastated. The stench of fear fills this muggy room.

I have no idea where I am, how I got here, how long it's been, or who is here with me.

"Hey, he's awake," a vaguely distressed voice says. "Harry?"

"Yeah. Who's there?" I ask.

"It's me, Ken."

"Ken?"

"Yeah, Harry. We dragged you in here from the street. Are you okay?"

"Where are we?" I ask.

"We're safe," Ken tells me. "That's all I know. In some basement."

"Is it over?"

"No," Ken says woefully.

"Phones?"

Ken shakes, "No."

We are in total silence from the outside world. All any-one's heard are rumors passed along from weary war-torn men and women who have managed to find safety here with us.

Where is she? I'm just sitting in this stupid building with these people I have only vague feelings towards. Ken's okay. We're "friends." I don't hate my boss Evelyn, but she does often suck the joy out of life.

And Carl, his boyish looks and do-goody look-at-me de-meanor have always gotten on my nerves. "Relax, buddy. Quit trying so hard."

I do also recognize the barista from the coffee shop near our office. What was her name? Why is she here? Why are any of us here? It is nice to see familiar faces. It gives me a vague hope that my love is still with us.

I don't much remember the others, and I'm pretty sure I've never seen that "secretary" in my life.

"What time is it?" I ask.

"It's night," Ken answers.

"What are we going to do?" the barista asks, who I now remember thanks to her obvious name tag, Sam.

"We can't stay here," a pepper-haired man responds.

"We'll stay here and wait for help," Evelyn, our wiry-headed boss states.

"That's suicide," Carl says. "He's right."

"Going out there is suicide," Evelyn pushes back.

"I'm not staying," I say. "I have to find her."

"You can't go out there," Ken insists.

"Oh, yeah?" I question

"You can't," our boss Evelyn says fearfully in the candle-light.

"Watch me," I say, then head towards the door.

"Harry, wait," Ken tries to stand in my way.

I storm straight past Ken and through the door. Ken, Carl, and the pepper-haired man follow me outside. Fires blaze all around. The smell of charred rubber, mortar, asphalt, and bodies arouse the nostrils.

I look up and see sparks flying from the 'batman' building as one of the spikes hangs off by steel wires, threatening to smash below. The building still stands, but fires blaze around the 28th floor.

The city would be in total darkness if not for the many fires which cover it with a smokey brightness, lighting the city just enough to see fifty or so feet ahead of us.

The shelling has stopped for the time being, but gunshots continue to ring out as both sides fire upon each other across the river.

In the aftermath of the initial invasion, the city resembles Fallujah more than Music City. All of the honkey tonk signs that aren't shattered to bits look a century old without the neon lights shining bright. Most are strewn about the cratered ground, though several still hang upside down.

Broadway is destroyed. The rooftop bars, which had started as the perfect sniper nests, are now all pretty much flattened. Much of Broadway is gone, all the way up to around 4th Avenue. Some buildings aren't just demolished, they're decimated or even vaporized. The rubble hasn't stopped burning, and it doesn't appear that it intends to any time soon. The fumes simmer in the summer air.

First responders are few and far between, but there does appear to be a few nurses or doctors rushing this way and that to tend to the wounded, or at least comfort them with a large morphine stash.

It's quiet out now, aside from the screaming moans of the dying and wounded civilians scattered across the city landscape, along with semi-auto and some automatic gunfire echoing off in the near distance.

The enemy fires from the stadium top and casino roof across the Cumberland. National Guardsmen snipe back at them from several buildings downtown, including the courthouse, what's left of a couple of smashed-up honkytonks, plus a few hotels and other buildings that still stand.

The Guard continues to roam downtown. They're outnumbered, but their tanks block the invaders from taking downtown. Neither side can cross. It's a standoff.

People are still desperately trying to flee the city, but all I can see are traffic jams for as far as the smokey air will allow. Hundreds of cars rest burning. There must be pileups on every road out of town. There are too many people trying to flee. They're in shock. And now, they too are stuck in this burning city, in this burning country, in this burning world. Hopefully, they can make it on foot.

Remnants of casino ships drift, burning upon the river's surface. The river itself is on fire from the pools of fuel leaking from the fiery ships. I try to catch my bearings as I take in all of the death and destruction. It feels like a surreal nightmare.

Is this really the fate of humanity? Is that all that's left for us? To burn? For our flesh to sear in the summer night?

They can burn down this entire world, but still, our love will shine through the smoke and rubble. We will find each other. No darkness will ever keep us apart. She's out there. I know it. My heart still beats for her. It beats in tune with hers. I feel her. I know she is still here, and we will reach each other.

There is no hope of crossing yet. If I were to swim or try crossing any one of the bridges, I would get shot down before I get a hundredth of the way across.

"I will get to her. If not tonight, very soon," I think to myself as I fall to the ground due to the blood pooling up in my brain from the massive concussion I must have suffered earlier.

4. The Invaders

ONE NIGHTMARE ENDS, another begins as I wake up back in this basement room, surrounded by mostly strangers.

"Who are they?" a stranger's voice pierces through my head. "Why are they here? Why Nashville? Where else have they invaded?"

"Where are the marines?" another voice questions. "Why are the National Guard the only ones here?"

"Does anyone know what happened?" I ask and begin to stand but sit back down as my head swells.

"We've been invaded," a man answers.

"Yeah, but by who?"

"No one knows who it is. All we know is that East Nashville has been taken. That's it."

"We still don't know who it is?" I ask.

"Nobody knows. It could be Russia, the EU, France, Israel. We don't know."

"What about the people stuck in East Nashville?" I ask, my heart aching.

"They're quarantined," Ken says.

"I heard there's a curfew between 4 PM and 10 AM."

"I'll be fucked before that happens here," a man exclaims.

"Let's kill all those bastards," the men all agree in excitement.

"Where are they quarantined?" I ask.

"Some are in camps," the thin pepper-haired man says. "While some are home safe, for now."

"That's what you heard. Nobody knows anything for sure," another voice says, which turns out to be my boss, ex-boss, Evelyn. There are no more bosses now.

Many of the survivors are still too shaken to speak. Sam, the barista, and other women and children gather together for comfort, suffering together in silence.

Silence is surely what I'd prefer, but the men fight on.

"But who are they?" Ken asks.

"Communists," the pepper-haired man exclaims.

"Which communists?" Ken asks.

"Nobody knows who they are," Evelyn responds in as peaceful of a way one could in a time like this. "They could be anyone."

"It's Russia," Carl, the intern exclaims. "Of course, it's Russia. Who else would it be?"

"It's not Russia," Ken states. "They may be communists, but they are not speaking Russian."

"Then what are they speaking?" Evelyn asks.

"It sounds like Russian to me," Carl says.

"Whoever they are, we know they're communist bastards," the pepper-haired man says.

"Yep," another man proclaims. "We should have wiped them off the planet decades ago. Now it's too late."

"Russian communists," Carl continues to insist under his breath. "It's certainly not the Chinese."

"It could be our own troops for all we know," the pepper-haired man states. "They look just like us."

"Fuck you," another man yells.

The pepper-haired man yells back in kind, and the men start to tussle, though it's broken up before it really begins.

"It doesn't matter who they are," the pepper-haired man says. "We're all going to die. Everyone we know and love is going to die."

"No, they're fucking not," I state, in perhaps the deepest tone I've ever taken.

"You really think communists are going to let anyone live?" the pepper-haired man asks.

"They're communists," Carl says. "Not blood-lusting animals."

"They're the same thing," the pepper-haired man shouts in solemn exuberance.

"We don't know that they're communists," Evelyn says assuredly. "They could be anyone."

"Right," the pepper-haired man continues on, ranting and raving until the others stop interjecting and just let him speak.

It's his understanding that communists—whoever they may be—have taken total control of East Nashville on day one. And that's all he fucking knows. Everybody fucking knows that.

No one knows what gibberish language they speak. It seems like a mishmash of several languages strewn together. It could be some secret coded military language so as to keep us all from knowing who they are and where they came from. They certainly don't wear any flag on their sleeve.

I do imagine Ken is correct, that it's not the Russian's. At least they don't sound Russian. I guess China could be funding it, but they're certainly not Chinese troops. It can't be us. The UN, perhaps? Regardless of who they are, they're here, and they're not here to play nicely.

The men continue to blabber about, but still, all anyone knows is that what was once bachelorette party wonderland has quickly become a living breathing nightmare. Death and disease lay at every corner. The smell of rotting flesh fills the air.

All I can do is think of her. Where is she? Is she okay? Did she make it home, or is she stuck in a camp? Is she really alive? I have to know. I have to find her. No invader alive can stop me. Whatever it takes, I will get her back. She will be mine again.

At the first glimmer of a chance I get, I'm crossing the Cumberland to find and forever hold my love. Then together, we will escape this dread-filled city.

I worry about my parents and friends, but I know my folks are much safer in their little town than anyone stuck in the cities. My love is trapped over there, with the invaders. Whatever it will take, I'm coming for her. I will hold her again. We will start our life, our family. We had been putting off marriage until we were more financially secure, but now, now all I can do is spend the rest of my life with her. I have to get her back. If not now, then the next day. If not then, then the next, then the next, then the next. I will never give up. If I must, I will fight until there isn't a gram of fight left in me. I will find her.

The invaders are on the wrong side of this war. They will know that soon enough, I swear it. I will tear them apart limb by limb, for they have taken her away from me. They split my entire world in two. And no force in the entire universe is going to keep her from me, nothing.

War will prove a man's worth. War will separate the cowards from the men. They brought this war to me. If it wasn't for her, perhaps I would choose the other path. But with her stuck over there, never. I will find her, and we will go somewhere that no bastard can ever find us.

I stand to the best of my ability and wobble my way towards the door.

I feel my breath slipping. Every inhale, a suffocating pain. Pins and needles sting my aching legs, where the shards of metal had been removed from my shin bones and calf muscles. My back torments me with a nerve-pinching rush with every move of my neck. I will fight through it. Besides that, I'm fine.

"You're not going anywhere," Ken says as he lays me back down and shoots me with what must be morphine trucked in from Vanderbilt.

"That's better," I think to myself as all of my worries and pains drift away with a warm wave lifting me gently upward into the clouds.

5. The Next Day

SWEATING HEAVILY WITH a piercing pain shooting through my head, I awaken. At first, it's completely unfamiliar. I'm next to nearly a dozen other men and women. How long have I been out? What day is this? Have I forgotten many days? My legs are freshly bandaged. So is my head.

I'm still in this dreadful basement with a few coworkers, office neighbors, and strangers. Over half of the people seem to have left. Perhaps they've gone south in search of loved ones or any way out of town.

Thoughts of crossing the river and finding her fill my mind. But that's not possible. The sound of war rages outside. So, I wait. But I'm sick of waiting.

Everyone sits calmly, drinking wine and quietly sharing stories in the dim candlelight, fearing things may never be the same.

It's night, and it's dark out, except for the fires, which cast an almost darker shadow over the city. I stand and walk to the door. The firelight peaks through the smokey air as I look out the small window above the door.

Through the window, a black-gloved hand appears in silhouette holding a pistol. I lean back against the wall and shush the others. They quietly blow out the candles then freeze, hoping they just pass us by.

This is the first we've seen of the invaders on this side of the Cumberland. And if they're here, they're coming for all of us.

The black-clad invader appears to have gone. I look right, and just as I do, a face peaks through the window. Not just any face, a face I will never forget, yet a face on which I can't see any features. He covers the light with his cupped hands and looks harder until we lock eyes in the fierce darkness. It's the eyes of a demon.

This bastard smashes the window, unlocks the door, then he and five other invaders with the same exact dead eyes and odor storm into the room yelling and spouting gibberish word, after gibberish phrase, after gibberish paragraph. These invader fucks talk fast.

The six heavily armed soldiers force us outside and drag us into the alley next door. They pull the women aside, with one black-clad bastard guarding them at machine-gun point. The women scream and cry, the men beg and protest, but to zero avail. The other five soldiers stand us men, face-first against an old brick wall. The smell of the old brick and mortar brings me back to childhood as I close my eyes, where I'm playing with the other kids on the—

"Pop!" I hear with my closed eyes. A warm thick liquid splatters against my face, tasting of iron and pennies.

The women's screams are quickly quieted by gibberish threats, with the barrel-of-the-gun looking them square in the eye.

Perhaps Carl was right? Perhaps we should have fled south already? At least he should have.

I wipe Carl's blood from my face. Lord knows I'm not leaving, not without her. I think to myself.

I look to my right, and there's Carl, still standing as another man's body falls beside him. By the looks of it, Carl's next.

Sam screams, and the bastard guarding the women slaps her face bloody with his heavy steel pistol.

The secretary, Trish, stands up to the rat bastard. He shoots her dead without a second thought.

"Fuck," the pepper-haired man screams. "You fucking commie fucks! Fuck you!"

I turn my head, and "Pop!"

The pepper-haired man drops after his brain splatters the brick wall.

The three men to my left take off sprinting and get mowed down from behind.

These sick invader fucks laugh together at our doom.

Carl cries and begs until his cries are muted when his body hits the pavement.

Another invader bastard presses my head against the wall, then backs away. I guess I'm next. I can't move, and I don't. I freeze, flinching. Adrenaline pumps through my veins.

I hear the metal of the slide cock against the frame, then "Pop!"

The gun fires. Time pauses. My heart pounds slowly.

Nothing happens.

"Pop! Pop! Pop!"

I hear several plunks, then turn around nervously to find four of the six invaders bleeding out on the ground. The other two cower in fear, returning scarce fire to the westward wall.

"Gibberish, gibberish, gibberish," the demon-eyed invaders shout at Evelyn. One of them turns his pistol on her with a stare of betrayal.

"Please. I'm sorry. I didn't know, I'm sorry," Evelyn begs the terrified rat.

He shoves her in our direction, then "Pop!"

Evelyn falls ungracefully to the pavement as her blood showers the earth.

Ken and I dive to avoid the invader's erratic firing. One bastard runs out and drops his empty pistol. He begs for his life in gibberish speak.

Two shadowy figures walk up from the blackness. The other invader follows suit, dropping his gun, almost apologizing with his movements. It's too late for that.

"Oh, my fuck," Ken stammers, shaking with adrenaline, then stammers some more. "Thank you. Thank you. Thank you."

"Oh my God," Sam says, shaking and breathing heavily. "Oh my God."

One shadowy figure raises his gun, ready to fire. He pauses.

"Harry?" a familiar voice exclaims.

"Yeah?" I ask. "Who's—wait... Deon? Deon Hardaway? Is that you?"

I had worked with Deon years and years ago before he went off to join the Army. Once he stepped into the fiery light, I knew it was him. What's he doing here?

"Yeah, brother," Deon responds. "What are y'all doing out here?"

"What's it look like?" I ask Deon. "What are you doing out here?"

"We smelled these commie bastards coming from four miles away. You can always smell a commie bastard, man. Isn't that right, you commie bitch?" Deon aims his rifle between the eyes of this poor sweaty rat.

"Gibberish, gibberish, gibberish," the confirmed commie spats. But that's not enough to convince Deon, who pops the bastard right between the eyes. His arms splay wildly as he flails backwards.

The last invader standing backs away, crawling, holding his hands in front of his ghostly face to block the 3500 mile-per-hour bullet from piercing it. Neither hand stops either round.

"Follow me," Deon says as he leads Ken, the girls, and I towards the darkness with a mysterious young woman, whom Ken has obvious eyes for. It appears she's flirting with the idea. "This is Vanessa."

"Here," Vanessa says in a quiet fierce confidence, consoling the women. "Come with us."

As the women walk along with the others, I turn east and begin walking off. Deon and Vanessa run to stop me. I try my damnedest to go and swim across the Cumberland, but they hold me back.

"I have to go," I tell them. "She's over there."

The adrenaline pumps like lava through my veins.

"What?" Deon questions. "You can't go now. You have to let the fighting die down."

"I have to find her," I say. "Jasmine. She's stuck in East Nashville."

"We'll help you," Vanessa, the mysterious young woman says. "But not yet."

"You'll help?" I ask.

"Yeah. But right now we gotta go," Deon hurries us along.

"I don't even know if she's okay," I say, trying to push through. "I have to know."

"What if we can get a letter to her?" Deon asks. "And return one from her?"

"How?" I ask. "If I can't cross, how are you going to get a letter across?"

"We'll get it to her," Vanessa says, trying to comfort me by putting her hand on my shoulder. "We'll make sure she's okay."

"Just follow us," Deon leads the way, followed by Vanessa, who shoves me on.

Our group follows Deon through the alleys, into and through this basement, then that one, and onto the next. Deon sure seems to still know his way around town. That's one thing working for the city will do for you. We weave in between the buildings and the shadows, onward and ahead.

Does he even know where he's going?

6. The First

AS WE WALK ALONG, I hear a sound, not innocent sounds, violating sounds, the sound of something ungodly. I disappear from the group into the darkness of the smokey night. The group continues up ahead without noticing. This is something I must do alone. I can feel it.

I was always fairly gentle and kind, but they took that from me. They took my everything. There is no turning back now. I can't just stand by and let what I hear happen.

I step quietly into the small parking lot where one bastard has a young woman pinned up against a brick wall while the second creep holds her arms and throat. They're oblivious to anything besides this poor beautiful woman, caught in the hell that is war. Tears pour from her closed eyes, puddling beneath her.

I pick it up a loose brick and tip-toe my way up behind the black-clad bastard holding the woman. He spins around and shouts gibberish. He falls flat after I whack him upside the temple with the red brick.

His buddy turns and reaches for his pistol, but it's not there. It's in his dropped pants, which I already grabbed. I aim the pistol at him and pull the trigger.

Nothing happens.

I lock eyes with the dead-eyed commie.

He lunges for the gun and grabs it. I fight him and try to pry his fingers off.

The woman grabs the man by the throat and wraps her legs around his chest. He tries to swing her off, but she's got a bear grip of rage. She squeezes and scratches at his eyes.

"Safety," the girl yells at me.

"What?" I ask.

"Safety! Turn off the safety," she commands.

I flick the safety to "fire."

He throws her off and spouts, "I fucking dare you," in total gibberish, which at this moment I can understand.

I shoot the commie bastard right through the chest with his own forty-five, then once again while he's gasping for life from the sinking pavement. I stand above him while the world disappears from his view and gets overtaken by a sweet, sweet hell, forever sinking. Smoke puffs gently from the barrel of the gun.

Deon, Ken, Vanessa, and the others run my way, ready for a fight.

"Thank you, thank you, thank you," the young woman latches onto me.

"What happened?" Ken asks.

"I had to," I respond. "I had no choice."

"Are you okay?" Ken asks.

The woman shakes "yes" with heavy breaths.

"Come with us," Ken says to the young woman. "I'm Ken. That's Harry, Vanessa, Deon, Sam, and Josie. What's your name?"

"Heather," she responds, then follows Ken and the others.

"Let's go," Deon commands, then leads us on, deeper into the city.

And again, we're sneaking our way through alleyways and basements. I can't help but feel Heather's gaze upon me as we move through the shadows, ducking just in time to avoid any of the commie patrols prancing around the streets. We make our way through a familiar getaway down Printer's Alley, where rebels line the streets, as well as booze and women. It looks more like Mardi Graz than a war zone. It's the first sign of life we've seen. And for once, we feel almost safe. We're not completely alone anymore.

This is where Nashville resisted prohibition. Will it also be the place where Nashville resists World War III? One can hope. Perhaps that's all we can do. At least here, there is some vague hope. Here, I feel like my search for her might not be in complete vain.

There are others here who plan to raid the Eastside and free the people. We hear them roaring with booze.

Finally, I'm not alone.

But still, I am. Totally.

Without her, I will always be alone. Only with her, will I have wholeness. Life will have no meaning from here on out until I find her. But here, I feel like I actually have a chance. Before now, it felt hopeless. I didn't know there were others.

If I just walk over and cross, I'll be shot dead. But if we go in the middle of the night, many of us, before the sun creeps up, then perhaps we'll have a chance. We can't risk it during the day. But I will get to her.

Unfortunately, Deon and Vanessa lead us out of Printer's Alley towards a place I've never been too fond of.

There it is, the Library. Books, books, books. While boring, they may offer extra protection against any incoming rounds; until the fires are started, of course.

Who's idea was it to hide in the Library? Yeah, there's cheap parking, but that doesn't really matter anymore. The location? Sure, it's fairly safe, considering. But I sure felt better among the militia-men in Printer's Alley, though we could use the rest.

A room at one of the swanky new hotels would be nice. But we are basement dwellers from here on out.

The darkness of both day and night seems to be having an unusually awakening impact. Yes, I feel delirious much of the time, but I'm oddly energized. And I'm not sleeping anytime soon.

While walking up to the library, a sweet sound starts to rise.

Ken, myself and the ladies follow Deon and Vanessa into the library. The hall is filled with music and at least forty or fifty men, as well as a few traumatized women and children.

Banjos, guitars, horns, and a harmonica ring out. It seems many musicians have stayed behind; not that they had much of a choice, but it is refreshing to hear. They are keeping Music City alive. They were always its heart. Now they are its very soul.

The musicians not only keep the spirits lifted with a mixture of blues, jazz, country, and freedom songs, but they're prepared to take up arms. Their rifles sit right beside them. Their music may be the only thing that will give any of us a hint of sanity over the coming days.

Sammy plays his trumpet, we're told. John picks his banjo. Bo strums the guitar. And Betty's voice is all but saving hundreds of souls this very evening. If we're not destroyed here tonight, her voice will continue to bring a slice of heaven into this hell on earth. Her dark skin shines in the candlelight. Everyone's skin does. We have no running water, only bottles. And what seems like an abundance now could quickly dwindle into scarcity.

After a few quick pleasantries, Deon leads us through the corridors to a hall where we can rest.

7. Rat Bastards

HOW DO WE KNOW THE INVADERS are commies? How do I now personally know they're commies? Not only is it the word around the coffee pot, or drug bin, if you'd rather, but we all know it. They're more machine than man. They move like commies.

All fucking commie rat fuck's eyes look alike, no matter their skin color. Tom, the pepper-haired man was right. You can see it in their cold lifeless eyes. Their cold machine-like stare could rot through metal. It's as if Trotsky himself trained these fucks. And they all smell alike, just like fucking commies. I'll never forget the rat fuck stench in all my life, however short it may be.

Plus, if Deon says they're commies, they're definitely fucking commies. He had spent nearly two decades in the service. He was only in town because he was on leave. He said that the majority of the Army, Marines and Air Force were on leave when this all broke out. How convenient.

Regardless of religion, skin color, or viewpoint, we all now share in one thing, our hatred of these commie rat bastards. Even the most left of the left is aghast at the commie smell, folks like Carl, R.I.P., and even Ken.

America's left is soft. They're humanists. Deep down, they want people to be freer. They just didn't know how to get there. Seeing the extremes of their viewpoint in action, the totalitarian side, they've all quickly turned into American loyalists. They want a fairer playing field for everyone, that's all. They never wanted this.

One may think that Antifa would have had something to do with this, but once war broke out, they ran for the hills. At first, some of the little punks thought they'd be welcomed with open arms by their comrade invaders but quickly found out otherwise when they tried to join up in arms against their fellow Americans and were promptly mowed down. After that, the majority went back to their small hometowns to hide behind their gun-toting relatives.

All they want now is a return to normality. We all do. They were simply people who were unhappy with the system, just like everyone else. You can't blame them one bit. But they were led to fight against the people rather than against those they should have been fighting. They were simply herded like cattle in the elite's game of divide and conquer, as is nearly always the case with cultural revolutions.

For all we know, some of the invaders are Americans. We still have no clue where these commies came from. No flags, just commies in black. That's how they want it, the whole fucking thing, some New Commie World Order Army. We should have seen it coming from miles away. Some did, but their warnings were always unheeded and mocked.

They want to end the nation-state so that they can control the whole thing. Now, these dead-eyed nationless commie bastards come storming in? Coincidence? I think not. They're here to conquer the West once and for all. They had been draining us from the inside out for well over a century with their banking cartel. But we were too strong, even when divided. And now, they've brought us back together. They shouldn't have done that. They've brought liberal, conservative, libertarian, farmer, engineer, server, marketer, artist, hobo, and everyone together.

But the commies will do anything to install their world government. They'd all but nuke the entire world just to get their perfect control system installed, where people are used like cattle and machines, lacking anything resembling humanity.

There are no more Ron or Rand Paul's to stop it. The media wouldn't allow it, nor the fraudsters running the polls or the elections themselves. Both sides brought this on. It's not even the fucking commie's fault. It's our own government's fault. They've been begging for war for decades. They've been sucking the God of War's cock, the central bankers, for far too long.

No empire survives without endless war, nor can it stand. American imperialism had to end one day. I just wish it wasn't fucking today. Give us a fucking warning so we can be prepared. The signs were there, but I would never have expected it to be so sudden.

Communism had engulfed the planet in the past decade, but the people destroyed the elite's chance to fulfill their "Great Reset." The world was once again turning towards freedom, swiftly removing their virus from governments and institutions worldwide.

They were never going to allow us to get away with it that easily. It just made them bolder. These plans have been laid out for more than a century. But we will never let them get away with it.

They had been plotting for years to fully take over this country. They thought they had it, but we pulled the rug right out from under them. That's why they've sent in the clowns, these fucking commie rat-bastards. This isn't nation against nation. This is freedom-loving people against the commie wretches, all the world through. At least there are no nukes. Not yet anyway. As far as we know.

The commies have already turned a quarter of downtown Nashville to ash and have murdered tens of thousands of civilians in cold blood with their cold-dead hearts.

Through the grapevine, we've heard that the commies led raid after raid down in Brentwood and that the entire town of Franklin has been razed, one of the most well-to-do areas in the entire country. Neighborhoods were lit ablaze, and their cute little downtown is completely demolished. Most of the citizens were able to flee in time since this was after the fall of East Nashville, but I doubt everyone made it out.

Stories have been told of the commies dragging the women and children away while executing the majority of the men. Many women are said to have been sent to commie birthing camps, where they are used as cattle to produce little commie bastard children. The commie state will then indoctrinate the children once mother's milk is no longer needed, and the state can raise them to be good cold little machines.

The men that survive will be forced to raise the little bastards in line with state edicts until the children turn twelve and are full-on enthusiastic commie sympathizers. The children's first mission will be to turn their guns against their "fathers." That's the commie's big plan, or so it's been told.

The commies can't get the women they want, so they have to steal them. They can't change enough minds to enslave the world, so the commies must destroy it and manipulate the children to continue their nonsense.

China couldn't have thought of a more commie rat bastard plan. And China has enough problems of its own to be any real part of this as their people rise up against their fledgling regime. Perhaps they tossed some money at it? But that's about it. China's communist party has been crumbling ever since the death of Xi in 2025. The globalist bankers surely funded the lot of it, as they always do.

Now the elite can't even be saved. Their mansions were the first thing the commie bastards raided. Well, that's not entirely true, as the true elite have their vacation mansions down in the places where no war will ever touch, plus their supposed massive underground bunkers.

Some were arrested in the years prior, with Pedogate and the other scandals following the election disasters of 2020, 2022, and beyond. But they were mostly just the bag men and women. The real controllers who sit up top, turning cash into conflict, are still very much at large.

Perhaps once the ash of war finally settles, we will never again let the ruling elite back into any place of power, though power has a way of corrupting even the noblest of men. Perhaps we can level off the playing field.

If once their day of reckoning comes, we will dance in the streets of the rubble. We will rebuild the world in harmony with nature, man, and God. The true perpetrators of this war, and their unholy alliance of evil, have been inflicting dread upon humanity for decades, if not centuries. We will end them. Those doing their bidding will have to pay first. Soon, their commie blood will soil the city—so we hope.

However horrid things are, humanity will survive. However cold the commies are, they can't kill humanity's hope, no matter how hard they try. Humanity is good. In fact, it's great, godly even.

One day soon, Jasmine and I will be far away from all of this, from the cities. We will live on the outskirts, third-class citizens if we must, but free.

But no, that world will never come. The people will not allow it. I've seen the fear in the commie's eyes. There's still a smidgen of humanity in there. One day soon, it will bleed out again, on its own accord, or through our vengeance. The commies will never prevail. The people value their freedom too strongly for that. I hope.

8. Making Friends

DEON OPENS A LARGE wooden container filled with rifles and handguns. A second ammo-filled crate sits next to it.

"Take your pick," Deon says.

"Shit, really?" Ken asks. "Where'd you get all of this, anyway?"

"The Guard, local shops, the ranges," Deon says. "They all support our cause. And of course, the police station."

I look over the weapons, eyeing my perfect fit.

"You're going to need to learn how to use at least one of these," Deon assures us.

"We need to leave," Ken says. "What are we doing?"

"You could have already left," I say. "You know I can't."

"Yeah," a rebel shouts to a rabble-roar behind us. "It's our city!"

"Yeah," everyone in the hall howls in agreement.

"I only have one mission," I comment. "And after that, I'm leaving."

"You're just going to let our city burn?" asks a young brave, but fearful man.

"Nashville's dead, haven't you heard?" I holster a pistol into my waistband.

The young brave, but fearful man stands and gets in my face. "What did you say?"

"Look around," I say direly. "It's over."

"Hey, fuck you, man. This is my city," the young, fearful man says, then takes a swing at me.

I block his arm with my left forearm and fling my closed fist directly into the corner of his jaw. His knees crinkle, and he falls limp to the floor.

Several men jump to attention. They shove and grab at me.

Deon stands between us, holding them back.

"Stop it," Deon commands. "He's one of us."

"No, he's not," another rebel exclaims.

"Are we not all missing something?" Deon asks the rebels. "Has this war not taken something from you?"

"Yeah," a voice from the crowd exclaims. "My city!"

"Yeah!" the men rally.

The fearful young man stands with the help of his confidants, then says, "We don't share with commie sympathizers."

A rage boils inside of me, but I hold back.

He spits blood onto the ground in my direction and says, "Your bitch is probably dead anyway."

I aim the scoped rifle directly at the young, fearful man and pull the trigger. He flinches. The room freezes in disbelief.

"Show me how to use it," I ask of Deon.

"Yeah... Come on, man," Deon hurries me away from the growing mass of men who want my guts torn from me.

The rebels rant and rave as Ken, and I walk down the hall with Deon and Vanessa, rifles in hand. Sam and Heather follow closely behind.

"Fuck you, you fucking lunatic," the young, fearful rebel shouts in distress as he searches for his fleeting breath, but the air seems to lack even a semblance of oxygen.

"Are you fucking crazy?" Ken whispers.

Ken shuts up the moment we lock eyes. He knows something has taken over me. He sees that I'm a man on a mission and that trying to stand in my way or question my motives is not in his best interest.

We follow Deon and Vanessa down another hall into a long room filled with thousands of hardcover books of famous novels and manuscripts from over the past three centuries. Candlelight bounces off them playfully. The door swings to shut but swings right back open.

A young needle-esque teenager enters in a hurry and hands Deon an envelope.

"Deon, I'm here," the teenager says. "I made it. I'm here."

"Hey, Tommy," Deon says. "This is him, Harry. He'll take your letter?"

"You will?" I ask the skinny out-of-breath teen.

"Yes, sir," he states in his ROTC fatigues.

I quickly scrawl out a letter while Deon goes over rifling basics with Ken and the girls.

"My love, Jasmine. I have to see you. You are my everything. How I pray you are safe and secure. I can't live without you. My heart aches to hold you again. And soon, I will. We'll go away together. Just let me know you're safe, and we'll plan for our escape. Your love for all time, Harry."

"You'll get it to her? You swear it?" I ask in disbelief as I write the address on the envelope, stuff the quickly written letter in, and hand it to the young teen.

"Yes," the teen says. "If I can find her."

"Just get it to her," I say. "Please. I beg of you."

"Whatever it takes," Deon confirms. "You know where to find us."

"Okay. Yes, sir. Okay. I'll get it to her."

The young man runs out of the room and shuts the large doors.

A tinge of hope suddenly fills my heavy longing heart.

"Go on then," Deon says. "Shoot."

"In here?" Ken asks.

"Yeah. Put these on," Deon says, then hands everyone ear protection. "Ken?"

"No," Ken responds, backing away. "Someone else go."

Deon cocks my newly owned AR-10 for me and welcomes me to the podium.

"That's it?" I ask.

"That's it," Deon confirms. "Go for it."

Several targets made of books, graffitied with commie garb, stand at the far side of the lengthening room, mocking me.

"Safety," Deon informs me.

I flick the safety to fire and aim downrange.

"Put your cheek on it," Vanessa tells me.

"My cheek?" I ask.

"Trust me," Vanessa assures me.

I rest my cheek, put my eye near the metal scope, look downrange, and the room shrinks. Vanessa's right.

Here I am, right in front of my target. I don't even have to stand face to face with these commie fucks. This isn't even a commie. It's just a target made of books. But still, I smell the commie on the bastard. Still, I rage as I fire round after round through the paper hearts of these commie fucking rag dolls.

Soon they will be real commies, and their blood will fly and splatter about as they dance to the beat of the metal rounds slashing and bursting into and through their soon-to-be lifeless flesh, just like these books are dancing now as they shred, whispering down like raining feathers.

The candlelight shakes relentlessly to reverberations of the bullets piercing the air. The warm jackets float down upon us as I become one with the weapon. I know I made the right choice with this rifle. Soon they will all know.

"Anybody else?" Deon asks gnawingly.

I turn around with the eyes of a beast until I release my rage with a deep breath. These aren't commies. These are my friends, acquaintances, anyway.

I step away from the shooting platform to let Ken have a turn. He steps up with a suspicious eye.

I'm no fucking commie sympathizer, that's for damn sure. If so, I am a commie cannibal, as seeing commie blood spill has been the first warm feeling I've had since we were separated—knowing that I did it. Until I hold her again, that's the only warmth I'll need.

Ken blasts the target, one shot after the other. The booms beat life into my dying heart. The gunshots and mortars are now the only thing pumping blood through my stiffening veins, that, and the thought of her.

My heart will never stop beating for her. No commie will stop it. No bullet. They can't fathom the depths of it. The commie mind would blow. The commie would die or be born again, non-commie. Death will be their only release, their bitterly sweet, sweet release.

Deon knows that one taste of commie blood was all I needed. He can see a change. So can Ken. It shows in their eyes. Deon understands it. Ken's afraid. He saw something he didn't like. I know he hopes he'll never feel this way.

Ken just wants to leave. But where to go? We've lost connection with the outside world. Where is safe? Are commie invaders everywhere? Surrounding us? No one knows the answers. There are a lot of opinions but no truths. Not that anyone would know myth from reality. That's how myths are made. Will they live on? Or will they die with the city?

9. A Sweet Release

SLEEP HAS BEEN BUT A SWEET, sweet dream the last couple of days, especially tonight, all two and a half hours of it. When suddenly, we are awakened to a commie raid outside. Just like a fucking rat, always around when you're not looking. But you try to find it, you search for that rat and you'll never find it.

Several knocks bang loudly on the front door. We join the rebels in the front room.

More knocks sound. No one moves a muscle other than to aim our three dozen or so weapons at the door.

"Gibberish, gibberish, gibberish," we hear, ready to slaughter the bastards.

A few light booms off in the distance, plus several little pops, and these commie rats scatter to the wind. The gibberish fades as they scramble off into the distance. Everyone drops their aim, but me. I wanted them to enter. I'm ready to fight. I mime-shoot the door three times before I drop my aim.

Ken gives me that uneasy look he's getting quite accustomed to.

I lock eyes with the brave but fearful young man as he dances gingerly out of the room. He's afraid. Maybe he should be. Something's been unleashed inside of me. I don't know how to control it. I don't know if I want to.

Deon and Vanessa understand it, but they're watchful of my somewhat erratic behavior. They are good at removing me from situations of tension between me and the other rebels, which have become more frequent over the last forty-eight hours. They take me for more training when necessary, which I happily oblige. They usually do so right before I would have had to knock someone's headlights out of their silly little noggins.

"Don't fuck with me" has basically been my demeanor for the entire time in this place and may continue to be until I reach her. How can I turn this rage off? Why would I want to? The commies deserve what's coming to them.

Perhaps I can sneak eastward, unseen, find her, and escape someplace they will never find us. But no, that would never work. Their patrols are too thick, their curfew too early. There will have to be blood.

I wish I could just walk across that bridge and hold her, but the reality is that it's going to take some work. So, over these last two days, I've trained, trained more, trained harder, and I continue to train. Everyone is pissed, no one can sleep, but I can't help it. I must become one with my weapons if I have any shot at freeing her from the prison that East Nashville is said to have become.

There is a fire raging inside me, regardless of if I want it to be raging or not. The only way to put it out is to use it all up, though it feels endless. It feels as if it's pouring directly from the great beyond, infinite lava flowing forth from creation itself. May it flow out and devour this commie filth. It must. Then it will create life anew. We will build upon the rubble and upon the commie blood and flesh. The ash and lava will turn to rocks and soil, which will feed free generation after generation.

For now, all I can do is shoot, and stab, toss grenades—

"Holy fucking shit, man," Ken storms in shouting. "Grenades? Are you fucking crazy?"

I shake my head and toss another grenade at the already shredded commie paper dolls, then pull Ken down with me below the rifling platform.

"It's okay," I say as I shake Ken, trying to convince him with my lying eyes. The blow doesn't move me in the slightest, but Ken flinches wildly to the boom.

"You're nuts, man. You're nuts," Ken says as he backs away. "I love you, but you're fucking nuts, man."

"Okay, okay," Deon enters and asks. "How about some whiskey?" He takes my shoulders and leads me out of the smoke and shredded-paper-filled room. Once free of the paper-storm, he hands me a bottle of Tennessee's finest.

Behind us, Vanessa takes a fire extinguisher to the "minuscule" grenade-caused flames.

"That was fun," I say before sipping the apparent elixir of life, which dances on my tongue in heavenly satisfaction. Its vapors fill my sinuses and cleanse the stink out.

"I bet, brother," Deon responds. "But I don't think we want to call that much attention to ourselves."

Ken just walks behind us, shaking his head to himself, or so I assume.

Ken doesn't want to walk right into the hornet's nest like I plan to, but he had his chance to leave when the others left. I can't speak for everyone here, but we're not fucking leaving. As we enter the common area, a man steps to us and says, "Y'all can't be here anymore. He's calling too much attention to us."

"Yeah, he's gonna get us killed," another rebel shouts.

"You want to say that to my face," I approach the cowering pale-faced man. I don't much like these bastards.

"Harry," Deon holds me back. "Harry, come on, buddy."

"Get him out of here," a man exclaims.

"Take your platoon," the cowering pale-faced man says.

"I'm not going with them," the young wide-eyed, brave, but fearful man says, trembling.

"You've got your orders, son," says the pale-faced man.

"He's fucking insane," the fearful young man says.

"You'll go with him, both of you," the pale-faced man commands of the fearful young man and his confidant. "Take them with you."

"Fine," Deon says. "We'll be gone in the morning."

"We don't want you here," a man says from the background.

"Fuck this library anyway," I spout. "And these homos. Let's go."

The mood intensifies.

"In the morning," Deon commands. "We sleep here."

"Fine. But I don't think there's going to be much sleeping," I say, laughing menacingly. "Not for me. And especially not for you."

I point to the pale-faced man, then to his friend with my finger-gun.

"Shit, Harry," Ken says. "These are our allies."

"Allies?" I question. "I don't need allies."

"What about us?" Ken asks.

"I don't need anyone but her," I say as impolitely as possible—not purposefully—it's just the way it is. "Until she and I are together again, this whole fucking world can suck it. Including you, Ken."

"I love you, but fuck you, Harry," Ken says.

An actual smile pops on my face for the first time since the morning we were parted. This isn't my normal sense of humor, but war does odd things to a man. And sometimes, the light can shine through the darkest of places. The smile seems to calm Ken ever so slightly, once again witnessing my humanity, however momentary.

Enough of that. I grab my weapons, a duffle bag full of ammo and grenades, and simply walk towards the front.

"Come on," I command my unit. Not that we're a unit, but they know who they are.

Deon, Vanessa, and Ken rush to gather their things, as well as the reluctant Greg and young, fearful Bobby.

I wait at the front door until the platoon enters the room. They're followed by dozens of rebels, making damn sure we leave.

"What about us?" asks Heather.

"Stay here," I answer. "You'll be safer. Then get out of the city whenever you get the chance."

"Okay," she responds softly as she watches me walk away into the distance.

"It will be better if you stay here," Deon states, then tells the rebels to "protect them."

Heather, Sam, the barista, and their friend Josie stay behind with the fifty-plus rebels and less than a handful of other women.

Vanessa and the men, including the fearful Bobby and his bud Greg, follow me unconvincingly into the darkness of night, knowing there will be at least a few commies in the street, patrolling the sewers like the filthy rats they are.

The difference being is that now we're prepared. And the darkness feels good. I'm comfortable here. I'm no longer breathing heavily. I can see everything and hear everything. I can sense the slightest disturbance. My every sense, fully alert.

Wait, I look up. Could it be? I see her running my way from under that small little red brick bridge in a white flowing lacy gown. My heart melts. It's my Jasmine.

I drop my rifle and open my arms as she leaps towards me. The light dazzles all around her. I can almost smell her until my senses come to, when, "Pop! Pop! Pop!"

My love disappears and crumbles in my arms as three commie bastards fall to the ground twenty feet in front of me.

"Goddammit, man," Deon says. "Get ahold of yourself, Harry."

"I'm fine," I say as I pick up my rifle and continue on my way, a tear welling in the corner of my left eye as I step foot after foot back into this cold yet hot and humid reality we find ourselves. "Maybe I could use some sleep."

"I know a place," Deon shares.

We follow Deon along in the darkness. After what feels like an hour, he stops in front of an old green wooden door in some back alley I've never seen. I'm not even sure what street we came from or if we're even downtown anymore.

"We better be," I think aloud.

"What?" Vanessa asks.

"Nothing," I answer.

I can sense that Bobby doesn't much like me or anything about me. I guess he has his reasons. I did stare him down the barrel of my rifle and pull the trigger.

"It's locked," Ken states.

"It was," I say, shoot the lock, then state. "Not anymore."

Deon puts my gun down, "Keep it down, and hurry."

We enter this dark and strange basement. Deon shines his flashlight around, and lucky for us, this place appears to be a bar with all the beer and booze anyone's heart could desire.

Vanessa quickly finds and lights a candle.

There doesn't appear to be any food. But who needs food in a time like this, anyway? Perhaps my body does. But the bottle of JD I spot will do the trick for now. He's been working so far, ever since Deon got me hooked on its burning goodness. Some chips would be good.

I reach behind the counter for the bottle of nectar that lights up as if speaking to me, saying, "For the love of God, man. Drink me."

I grab it, but the bottle resists my effort to lift it.

"What is this?" I question silently.

Again it resists.

"What is this sorcery?" I question.

"What? Who's there? Who is it? I'll shoot, I will, I'm telling you. I'll do it," a drunken voice stammers awake from behind the bar, fighting me for the bottle of golden nectar.

I jump back in startled defeat and raise my pistol.

"Easy. Easy," Deon says. "Put it down, Harry. Jasper? Is that you?"

"Deon?" the old drunkard questions. "What the heck are you doing here? Well, I'll be a monkey's vagina."

"Sorry to barge in on you," Deon says. "I just knew this would be a safe place. I figured you left town."

"I'm stuck here like the rest of you," old man Jasper says. "Have at it, all of it, I'm done for, there is no way out. The commie bastards have taken everything from me."

"I know how you feel," I say.

"You don't know jack shit. You didn't fight these commie bastards in Nam."

"I don't think those were the same commies," I think aloud.

"All commies are the same, you stupid fucker," the old white-haired man stares with authority. "Senator McCarthy was right. The only way to end the commie strain is to rip every single strand of virus from the host, or the host, i.e., us, will be destroyed. And it's too fucking late. The virus is eating the host alive as we speak."

Perhaps the man's right. There sure are a lot of commie rat bastards around. But that's where he's wrong. These commie invaders will burn for their sins. If not now, soon— very soon.

Once again, artillery shells begin to vibrate the city. I'm beginning to like the shaking. It has become comforting. I haven't been standing on steady ground since they arrived. Why should I start now?

I won't know solid earth until I hold her again. My world lays in shattered pieces, strewn out like a lost ancient land of islands and mountains sunken beneath the sea.

She will be mine again. I will hold her. We will again make love all night and day after we disappear from this empty modern life. We will no longer waste our lives working meaningless jobs. We will spend our time together in ecstasy, in this seemingly endless yet extremely brief life we share.

The crew gathers together around the bar with Jasper. I take the bottle and sit against the wall nearest the green door.

"So, what's the plan now?" Ken asks. "What are we doing here?"

"Tomorrow, I'm going over there," I say, interrupting Deon before he begins. "I can't wait around here any longer."

"We're not going through the commie lines to rescue one person," Greg slams.

"I didn't ask you to."

"You'll never make it across the river," Bobby says.

"I'm going to find her," I tell them. "And we're going to escape, with or without any of you."

I grab the bottle and disappear into the corner, away from the others, who drink with this old, rotten man, who continues spattering his nonsense to the unreasonably interested crowd.

I sip the bottle until the darkness finally sinks through my eyes and into my bleeding soul, and I finally fall. I don't know for how long it will be, but here I rest, too tired to even dream. My dreams are only of dreamless thoughts of dreaming. The sleep feels long, but it's already too quick. It will never be long enough.

10. Hunger

IT'S DARK. THE SMELL IS FRESH, always so upon first awakening. It's a mix of burning stink, molten steel, concrete, rotting bodies, and the ever so pleasant aroma of melting tires line the air, tires that melt for days on end, never truly burning out, so it seems. If I don't die from the war, the burning rubble fumes will surely get me in the years ahead.

My vision is blurring from the mixture of booze and lack of food. The concussion may not be helping matters. Perhaps I can eat something today. My body's drying up. Water might also be good.

Jasper continues sharing stories of the time they fought against the commies in Vietnam, "You could smell 'em from 15 miles away. But these bastards started covering themselves in mounds of mud, and these monkey cunts started popping up out of the woodwork, right beside you, behind you, all around. These monkey fucks would pop up from out of nowhere."

"And don't expect these commies to be any different," Jasper continues. "I wouldn't be surprised if one popped in through that door this very second."

Jasper slams his fists down on the bar to the crowd's engaged fright.

I get up and approach the platoon by the bar. The dim candlelight is just bright enough to make out young Bobby and old dirty Jasper's unwashed faces.

"Shut your mouth, old man," I interject. "Food. We need food. Don't you have any food in the back?"

"We ain't have no more food, just the good stuff," Jasper states.

"Then let's go," I say.

"I agree. We need food," Deon states. "But we need to wait till darkness falls."

I walk over, pick up my AR-10, and exit.

"Dammit, Harry," Deon sounds.

Before you know it, they're out the door trying to keep up, everyone but Jasper.

Off we go, out in the open streets, into the dirty, thick, putrid air. Our nostrils twist and flair in un-winnable defense. Most of the dust has settled, but still, a smokey fog hangs over us.

Deon, Vanessa, and I walk up front as Ken and Greg follow. Bobby trails behind, clutching his rifle. They didn't have to join.

Things are eerily quiet. Our footsteps, the only sound. No more cries. The artillery hammering has stopped. No gunshots. It's actually quite peaceful. Maybe they're leaving the city to go elsewhere, and I can soon cross the river to find her.

Just as this thought gives me a glimmer of optimism, dark clouds pass over the sun, and the fog thickens, leaving only a dark smokey haze.

And there it is, the familiar sounds of enemy planes begin to pass overhead. At any moment, they could bomb us into oblivion.

We walk carefully onwards until all of a sudden—a whooshing sound roars by, then a double thump—then another, and another. "Whoosh. Th-thump. Whoosh. Th-thump."

A gunshot rings out, reflecting off every wall. We turn to attention, but it's impossible to pinpoint where it came from.

Another gunshot sounds. We're right out in the middle of the street.

Smoke shoots out of the thumping grenades, filling the molten air with dark and light gray smoke, turning the smokey haze into total blindness.

Black-clad soldiers begin to fall from the sky all around us and beside us. We hear their parachutes and feet landing more than we see them.

Bobby and Greg take out two or three commie troopers before I even see one.

We got low, under cover of the newly smoke-filled air. They can't see us any more than we can see them.

Deon and Vanessa circle back to back in a low stance. As the thick smokey fog washes over one commie rat-toothed fuck's face, Deon shoots him dead.

Down on one knee, I hear a trooper land. I don't see anything, but I shoot.

"Ugh," the rat moans.

"Pop! Pop! Pop!" I fire away. The moans stop.

Vanessa and Deon lay under the fog. I get lower and see them take out several more commie-rat legs, then finish them off after the inevitable fall.

I look over to see Ken taking cover behind a trash bin. An invader sneaks up behind him. As he raises his gun, I fire, hitting him in the arm. He falls, rolls, then grabs for his handgun.

Ken shoots him twice in the chest, then immediately hides behind the trashcan with his back against it, gasping for air, breathing mostly smoke.

Greg and Bobby watch each other's backs as they make their way towards us. I lay cover-fire, but Greg falls.

"Greg," Bobby shouts, then shoots erratically. He doesn't stop until his clip is empty.

Gunfire continues unabated. Vanessa and Deon are relentless, almost dancing ballet as they take out Greg's shooter with machine-gun fire.

The gunfire stops. Everyone seems to be okay, except for Greg. But he's fine. Everyone is fine.

A buzzing–bee sound slowly starts to descend down our way and circles around, just overhead.

Bobby bends down to check on his bud, when, out of the smoke, a dirty commie paratrooper grabs Bobby by the neck and puts a pistol to his head.

"Gibberish, gibberish, gibberish," the poor terrified last-commie-bastard-standing spats as he jerks Bobby around from side to side, finger on the trigger.

"Put him down," I command. "Let go of him, you commie bitch."

The commie backs up while spouting gibberish, holding the pistol to Bobby's head, his finger shaking the trigger.

"I'll fucking shoot," I state firmly, aiming him down through my rifle's offset iron sight.

"Don't fucking shoot," Bobby begs. "Please don't shoot."

"Gibberish, gibberish, gibberish," the commie yells.

"Please," begs Bobby with all his heart as he feels a bullet whiz an inch and a half away from his left ear, which pops the commie right between the eyes. "Pop–splat."

Bobby, in total shock, falls over, intertwined with his new brain-free commie pal. He checks his own face and ears to make sure he's alive.

Lucky kid. Good thing I spent all that time practicing instead of sleeping. But still, I'm not that good of a shot.

Bobby backs away on all fours with his chest to the sky, crab-walking away from the dead commie's grip and the trail of blood leaking from the back of his rotten skull.

"You're welcome," I say as I turn to notice the bussing drone circling down to capture the action. I fire and miss, but not the second shot. The little spy toy flops to the ground some twenty feet away.

Ken helps Bobby to his feet. He's unable to speak, being somewhat traumatized. I'll just pretend he's grateful. He should be.

Bobby hurries over to Greg and begs for help.

There's the culprit that brought this on, the little toy drone. That's the only way they could have known just where to land. I pick the little bastard up and look it directly in its eye.

"Go fuck yourself," I say to those listening in, then rip the propellers from the drone, smash it to the ground, and pop eight rounds through its motherboard.

Ken helps Bobby pick up Greg and drag him to his feet.

Again, we're off. We make our way through the dense smokey fog, guns out and ready for anything.

Things are once again calm and quiet. My senses will alert me if any commie filth lurks beneath the smoke and rubble. And Greg's fine. He can almost walk all by himself.

Before we know it, we're right in front of some old burnt-out unnameable restaurant. Inside, it's pretty much untouched by the war, though the smell of it permeates the building. Plus, the milk is certainly sour.

Thanks to the freezers, some of the meat and most of the veggies have stayed cold enough to be edible. I quickly gather up a feast which will tide us over for several days, if not two weeks. The others do the same. There's all this terrific food, but all anyone else wants is the canned vegetables. And what kind of restaurant serves grilled Spam? Gross. But I guess they do have a point, canned food surely lasts longer than thawing meat and already old veggies.

If only there were power, we could cook up the meal of a lifetime right here and now. But we'll have to wait until we get back. We should be able to cook on the gas stove since the gas works for some unknown reason, most likely so that the rats can use it to burn down various homes and businesses as easily as they see fit.

With the "feast" bagged up, we exit, each carrying as much food as possible in our duffle bags, backpacks, and to-go sacks.

We make our way back outside into the smokey air and head off towards the green door bar, wherever it may be.

I lead the way, followed by Deon and Vanessa.

"Will y'all hurry up?" I question the slowpokes.

"You got Greg shot," Bobby says.

"We needed food," I ask, holding up my bagged feast. "He's fine."

Greg limps along with a look of, I'm not sure what, on his face. Bobby's face isn't much better.

I scurry along as Ken and Bobby carry Greg's weight between the two of them. Deon and Vanessa keep their eyes peeled for signs of trouble.

11. Contact

BACK IN THE GREEN DOOR basement bar, we
cook up a feast in the back, filling it with the smell of fresh
gas-fired barbecue, the first decent thing I've smelt since the
commie filth turned everything to yuck.

While the feast cooks, the gang patches Greg up as best
they can. He'll live, though Bobby and Ken don't look too
pleased. Greg appears to be almost all fixed up. Plus, the
morphine pumping through his system is making him feel
much better.

Once I receive my nourishment and the darkness of
night falls, I'll be on my way to her. I will make it to her.

I grab six AR-10 mags—strap five grenades to my belt—
two pistols in my shoulder holster—one on my ankle—eleven
pistol mags in my pockets. The lead may try to weigh me
down crossing the river, but nothing will sink me. The life vest
will surely help.

"We'll go with you," Deon says.

"No, you won't," I command. "This is something I have
to do alone."

"Fine. Go. Get killed," Ken says.

"You'll find her," Vanessa says. "Be careful."

"You'll never make it over the river," Bobby states.

"Fuck you. And you," I say to Bobby and Ken.

I take the bottle of life-nectar and head to the back to
check on our feast.

While waiting, I decide to get a little more practice by
shooting beer bottles.

"You fucking idiot," Ken storms in, shouting.

I give him a quick smirk and continue emptying my clip.
He slowly backs away so as not to cause any trouble, though
Deon successfully persuades me to stop.

The nectar purifies my soul as I drift into nothingness, waiting for the night. Soon, I will hold her again. That's all that matters.

A series of loud rhythmic knocks suddenly land on the green door. We each aim the door down with our closest weapon.

"Hello?" a young man's voice sounds. "Are you in there?"

"Who is it?" Deon asks.

"It's me, Tommy," the voice says. "Let me in, hurry."

Deon removes the barricade and opens the door. And there he is, the skinny teenager who was to take my letter to her.

Had he taken it? Did he actually find her? Is she okay? How did he find us here?

I walk towards him slowly and begin to ask with anticipation, "Did you—"

The skinny teen hands me an envelope. I rip it open and pull out a letter. I can smell her on it as soon as I open it.

Thoughts burst through my mind. She must be okay. Is it really from her? Or is it word of her death? She has to be okay. She must. What would I ever do if she isn't?

I hurry the letter to the candlelight and begin to read, *"Oh Harry, my love, how I long for thee. But it's too dangerous now. I can't let anything happen to you. I'm safe, I promise. When all this is over, we'll be together again. Forever. Just know that I'm safe. And promise me you won't do anything stupid. We have a long life ahead of us. Your dearest, Jasmine."*

I'm both relieved and heartbroken. Yes, she's alive. But "I can't see her?" How can I live? She's "safe?" What does that even mean? She didn't even tell me where she is.

"Don't do anything stupid?" I question the heavens. "Stupid would be staying in this fucking broken city."

I quickly scrawl out a response: *"Where are you? I miss you with all my heart. I have to see you. We must escape together. To anywhere. The mountains. Or the middle of nowhere, where the commies will never find us. It has to be me and you. It has to be now. You are my everything. I can't breathe without you. I must get to you. On August 23rd at 1:45AM, meet me under the sycamore tree, and we will make our escape together, and we will be free, and we will never have to live another moment apart, my love. Yours for all of time, Harry."*

I hand the envelope to the teen, trusting him with my very soul.

"Get it to her," I tell him. "Quickly, I beg you."

"Yes, sir," the teen runs off.

"Well… so?" Ken asks.

"So?" I answer as my adrenaline pumps, then take a deep breath. "She's alive and safe."

"That's great, Harry," says Vanessa.

"Well, what now?" Ken asks.

"We wait," Deon answers. "We stay safe. We'll connect with the guard, and we'll fight back."

"Fight back?" Ken questions.

"We have to protect our city," Deon states plainly.

"Look around," I agree with Ken. "The city's dead, Deon. It's gone."

I walk off to the back of the room.

"Yeah," Ken responds. "We don't even know what's out there. We need to—"

"Exactly," Deon states. "We've got to get some word about what's really going on before we make any moves. We hold our ground. We don't even know if there's anywhere to escape to."

"It's ready," I tell the others, who react how any malnourished mammal would. They hop to attention and storm the rear.

Once the feast is finished and we're properly stuffed, I extinguish my consciousness with the bottle and drift off into never-never land.

I awaken pre-dawn and immediately began to drink the time away—from that morning—to the next one—the night after—the one before—all day long for these three long and blurry days.

All I can really remember is Jasper going on and on and on and on. He makes a lot of sense, and I appreciate him letting us hunker down here, but—

"Shut the fuck up already for a damn fucking minute already, old man. Fuck," I think to myself. At least, I don't believe I said it aloud. Who can be sure? My memory's faded. My dear friend, Jackie Boy has given me hope and life anew in this bleak, bleak waiting, but he's taken my memories. An even trade in my book.

The days whisk away, with vague memories of insults—fights being broken up—bloody noses—and looks of visceral fear upon Bobby, Ken, and the nearly healed Greg's faces, and in their eyes. Surely, they know better than to say things to make me react in such a way.

I'm pretty sure Deon's been here most of the time, though he may have disappeared for a moment or two. Vanessa's been around.

But who can really be fully sure about anything in a time like this? Not I, certainly. Not in a time like this, I assure myself.

Just one more day, and I will hold her again.

Part Two

12. The Day Has Come

THE SMELL OF DESTRUCTION invades my senses as the day awakens. I must wait till nightfall, but soon, I will get to her. I will find her and we will flee together, far from the city.

Perhaps we should leave straight from the sycamore? How far north or east can the commie lines be? Or, could we travel by river? At night, it could work.

Or maybe we should come back here? It could be safer to leave with the others. But how long until the invaders overwhelm the Guard completely and blitz downtown?

The wait is long. I have sobered up as best I can. Some of the bread is still partially edible. I pick off the moldy parts and drink the barely chewable dough down with a few bottles of water.

I begin to prepare for my mission. I paint my face, neck, hands, and arms with mud and ash. Then, I load up as many extra mags and grenades as possible, pack my pistols and my AR-10, plus a large buck knife that I won off an unfair bet with Jasper.

"We'll go with you," Ken worries.

"I go alone," I wholeheartedly demand.

"Good luck," Vanessa says.

"Just come back," Deon says as I exit for the unknown without hesitation.

I may get shot before I ever make it across, but I don't give a damn. And that's not happening. I will see my love again in this life.

I walk towards where I assume the river is, northward, I presume, but who can be sure with all of this rubble or the blackened night sky. The fires have finally burnt out, and the moon is new, casting darkness abound. Plus, there's a downpour, the first rain we've had since the invasion. We desperately need it. I need it.

This storm is the perfect cover. No commie bastard will be out in the rain. They're rats—rats don't like rain. It sure doesn't help with the smell of the place though, in fact, the wetness only promulgates the rancid odor more deeply into the city and combines all of the horrors into one musty stink.

I walk along, soaking wet but with the wrath of all that is holy burning inside my veins. And for all that is holy, don't a damn one of you commie fucks stand in my way tonight.

I almost hope a patrol does spot me, for if one crosses my path, I will crush them with the heel of my boot and rip their heads from their little commie rat bodies. Nothing will stand in my way.

I make it to the river and trudge through the thick dark mud as I make my way into the water. The current's quite strong with all of the extra rainwater. That's why I'm starting farther northward. I'm not sure if I'll hit my target, but I will make it across.

I begin to swim with the life vest under me, which helps keeps me near the surface will all of this extra leaded weight. There's no use fighting the current's strength. I use its force to help push me across, but I will be lucky if I even make it to the pedestrian bridge in these rapids.

Suddenly, spotlights begin shinning down on the shoreline in front of my gaze. It shuffles around the water as if trying to spot someone. Now I must go further downriver. From the looks of things, it's just as well.

I pass my designated target, as it's too well "staffed." As it turns out, commies don't like the rain. The majority of them appear to be undercover from the storm, if not all of them.

Further downriver, soaked through and through, and with boots full of mud, I crawl my way to the shoreline and rest, just south of the Korean Vets bridge.

This area appears to be where they're storing the majority of their tanks and gunners—good to know.

This is perhaps the best entry point I could have found. No one appears to be on the roads nearby. I spot one or two patrols off in the distance, but Shelby Avenue is clear, and I won't be on the streets.

After I empty my boots and scrape out the mud, I begin to sneak my way around the homes off Shelby, up through the neighborhoods to the park. The path appears to be clear. Now the only question is, will she really be there? Did she even receive the letter? Will the curfew prevent her?

I arrive at the park and wait in hiding behind the bushes. It seems like all is lost, that she will never show. But just then, time slows. There she is. Her hair flows in the wind and rain as she makes her way towards the sycamore. It's really her. This is no dream. I step slowly out from the bushes, and her eyes lock to mine.

Her face. Her walk. Her eyes. Her everything. My everything. It is truly her. It's been so long that it might as well had been forever. That's how long it felt. My heart races as we approach one another slowly and tremendously.

I can feel everything. The world is at the tip of my finger. The whole universe embraces me. I was numb, but here I am alive once more as she jumps graciously into my arms. It's never felt quite like this before.

"I'm sorry, I'm sorry," Jasmine exclaims as we kiss with a towering passion in the pouring rain.

"There's nothing to be sorry about," I assure her. "We're together now, my love. And forever we will be."

"I'm sorry I said I couldn't meet. That was stupid. I love you so. Let's run away forever and leave this world behind."

"Follow me," I say as I lead her, hand in hand, through the downpour. "We must hurry."

She follows closely behind as I lead her back towards Shelby Avenue, through the neighborhoods, then to the river bank, just south.

Holding hands, I can feel the entirety of creation flowing through. I must lead my love back to safety, where we will escape and live off the land together, somewhere far, far away from this war.

The roads are just as free and clear as before.

We turn the corner past Shelby Avenue. Spotlights blast us as two gunner trucks, and at least a dozen commie fucks rise over the small hill directly in our path.

Gibberish spews at us through a megaphone. Many rats walk our way.

It takes all I have not to pull out my pistol and a grenade and take our chance versus the chance of them taking her away from me again.

I let my rifle fall.

The rats surround me, shove me to the ground, and step on my back and neck as they continue to spout gibberish at me.

Two officers pull Jasmine away by the arms.

"Jasmine! My love! Let her go! Please, God."

"I told you it was too dangerous," Jasmine cries. "Why did you have to do something so stupid? What's going to happen to you now?"

"Goddamn you, you commie fucks!"

"Please," Jasmine begs. "Please don't take him."

"I will find you one day, my love, and we will escape," I yell.

"Enough," a stern foreign voiced officer proclaims. "Take him away. You know what to do with him. I'll take care of the girl."

"No, please," Jasmine pleads as the commie filth drags her away.

After they kick me down and batter me a bit longer, they toss me into a fucking truck—an American fucking truck—the nerve of these commie fucking pricks.

In the backseat of this American pickup truck, these two commie bastards zip-tie my hands behind my back and buckle-lock me in. What these commie bastards don't know is that I'm an amateur yogi, so I manage to get my arms out from under my legs and maneuver my hands out of the seatbelt.

Before either of these two commie cunt fuckers knows it, I'm choking the passenger out with my zip-tied wrists while his comrade driver has his own buck knife sticking through the side of his neck.

I choke this commie bitch out with all my might. I push my legs as hard as I can against his seat. He can't react. He doesn't even know how to. He just struggles for air. It's almost as if he's patting me on the head, telling me, "good job." But I doubt that's it.

As we swerve by the stadium, the gurgling driver tries his best to keep the truck from crashing into a wall. The commie passenger decides to get smart and go for his gun.

"Bad move, commie," I think to myself as I take control of his gun and shoot his driver comrade through the temple.

I maneuver the gun and duck my head, then blast passenger bitch straight through the teeth. Only a smattering of blood splatters onto my back while the majority of his brain drips gingerly off the rear window.

Time slows by one-thousandth as the truck slams through a barricade and off the road, seemingly flying off endlessly into the distance until we crash and begin flipping and flopping about.

I'm belted in pretty well, but still, I know that once this slow-motion majestic shit is over with, that "Oh, man, I'm going to feel this in the morning."

We splat-land passenger side down into the dirty brown water of the Cumberland River. The truck begins to sink instantly. Water storms in through the two bullet holes, which crackle until they burst at the seams, flooding the cab.

I'm stuck, locked in. All this for nothing, to die now? Fuck that.

I reach up as far as I can, fingering at the dead commie bastard driver's sleeve. I reach and reach until finally, I take my last breath before the water overtakes me. I continue reaching until I'm finally able to grab the dead commie's sleeve, pull him in, yank the buck knife from his commie neck, and slice myself free.

Nearly out of oxygen, I grab and stash the passenger's handgun before thinking, "These grenades could sure come in handy."

I grab several grenades and pocket them, then slam the knife at the jagged rear window, opening it just wide enough to crawl out. Once again, I think, "These grenades sure could come in handy."

I swim out of the cab, pull the pin of one grenade, and gently sail it back into the truck. I push off and blast my way to the surface.

Guards have already alerted the river-Stasi to the crash, and my "fireworks" don't quite have the effect I was hoping to achieve. They do with the initial explosion—I just wasn't expecting all of this extra attention.

I was thinking more, "Let me let them think I'm blown up." Not, "Oh, hey guys, I just swam up to the surface to get a little air. Nice to meet you. How you doin'?"

No, that's probably not going to go so well. So, I do the only thing I can. I grab my one breath, and here I am, simply a dead prisoner of war, floating face down on the surface after a fatal car accident. I mean, there is a boat full of at least several commies heading my way, and I'm not Michael fucking Phelps. So, here I float, surrendered to the outcome.

Two dirty commie fucks reach into the water and pull me up into their little commie patrol boat. They spin me around. Gun out, I open my eyes and blast one in the chest, then pop the other in the nose with the butt of the pistol. I shoot the third guard in the head, then bash the second in the nose again, then a third time.

The fourth guard is enraged, but he can't get a shot. So I bash the second guard once more, then hug him in a vice grip as a hostage and fire at the last guard. He manages to get to cover, and I'm out of rounds.

"Hey, these grenades might come in handy," I think to myself for the third time. I toss one right to the rear edge, behind the fourth guard, who runs around the corner, fully loaded. I run directly at him, holding his bloody-nosed buddy.

The grenade drops into the river and explodes. It ruffles the boat's rear a few inches into the air, just enough for the fourth commie bastard to lose balance as I toss his comrade into him. They both flip off the railing and splash awkwardly into the water.

I slam the boat forward, leaving the two love birds behind. I have won this battle—but this is a war. And this war is far from over. At least I got a nice new piece of shit commie patrol boat. This, too, may come in handy.

I'm safe, for now. But what about her? What did he mean when he said he would take care of her? It takes all my might not to turn the fucking boat around and head right back into the rat nest. But Jasmine is smart. She will be fine. If she made it through the initial invasion, she'll make it through whatever horror they have laid out for her, the fucking rats. I just have to come up with a real escape plan and a lot more firepower.

I make my way across the river, just north of downtown, near Germantown and the warehouse district, which is not pure rubble like much of downtown.

At full speed, I drive the boat ashore, slamming my nose against the steering wheel. The boat rides up the shore into some bushes. I hop out with my dripping nose, rip off some small tree branches and bushes, then begin covering the boat. Within seven minutes, the camouflage is complete, and my nose has nearly quit dripping.

Shortly after I walk away, my body sinks into exhaustion. I do all I can to crawl into a water drain to sleep the night away. I sure could use a bottle. The scent of war sneaks its way into the dreams that never seem to come. I lay sleeplessly exhausted in my concrete palace.

13. The Return

THE SUNRISE CREEPS UP BEHIND through the thick clouds on the eastern horizon. Once again, the smell of death and disease is all-pervasive on this exhaustingly humid day. The bodies have not been buried, burnt, or moved from the city. The only sign of life is the buzzards, rats, and stray dogs which roam the streets pecking at the many corpses.

I may have gotten an hour or two of sleep last night— much more than usual. I stand and begin walking back into the heart of the city. Where is that damned ugly green door?

I walk along. Then I walk some more. I continue walking; my feet blistered from the dampness. I could stop at the boot store where I picked these up, but they'll dry out. The damage is already done.

Everything looks the same, just rubbish. Where is it? Had I not spent days in the green door basement alley bar? Had we not gone and come back? Had I not gone back alone?

Feeling rather weak, I need a little hair of the dog. To, if nothing else, lift my sunken spirit out of the murk. "Jackie Boy, where are you, old friend?"

After walking downtown in circles, and since Printer's Alley is deserted, I begin making my way back to the only place I know.

Though graffiti'd to death with words of doom, plus images of the unspeakable, the library stands undamaged. I enter into the vaguely lit hall, no longer to uplifting battle cries, but to chord-less half-strummed hopeless sunken voids of nothingness.

The whole library has become more of an opium den than a militia training facility. The musicians remaining are empty shells of who they were only days ago. Rats run rampant through the books and the filth.

What happened here? The morale is gone. Have they given up all hope? Is this what we're all becoming? Are we really going to let the commie filth do this to us? How I feel, I might as well fucking join them.

I walk through the filth and scum, from one hall to the next, then onward. Every man is downtrodden and totally lost in their own bad opiate trip, trying to force all the pain away through the flame and under the needle. From the looks of things, even the dope isn't doing much good for these hopeless young men.

I come across Sam, the barista, in a hallway. She's just as drugged up just as the men.

"Sam?" I ask. "Sam? Have you seen anyone?"

Sam's unable to even look my way. I shake her, but she just falls back into a filthy blanket she shares with a squirrelly looking "rebel." She's barely conscious.

I hear a faint struggle coming from the only room I ever spent much time in, the gun range hall.

I walk to the oversized doors, reach down and pull the large brass handles back, but it's locked.

The noise stops. I knock.

"What do you want?" an angry voice asks.

"Go away," another voice responds. "You'll get your turn."

"Help," a feminine voice manages to scream through obvious covered or gagged lips.

"Shut the fuck up, you cunt," the first voice insists with a slap.

I grab a sawed-off shotgun from the crate, which still sits outside the room. I blast through the door, directly at the voice to the left. The lock shatters, and I kick the door open.

"You fucking cunt," the first voice yells as he tries to pull splinters and buckshot from his face and eyes.

I recognize that fucking voice. It's the same voice that told me I was no longer welcome here. As it turns out, he's the one that's no longer welcome here—not on this earth.

Heather, who is once again the victim of the unimaginable reality of war, flinches as I blast this excuse for a man off the face of existence. "Huh?" is all the bastard can exclaim beforehand.

I walk for the second man sternly. He backs away while holding a large knife with a twelve-inch blade. Heather puts her jacket on and stands behind me.

The man backs against the twenty-foot-tall bookshelf. I'm closing in. He swings the knife around frantically.

I swing the butt of the shotgun his way, then stop. He flinches. I slam the butt of the shotgun against his mouth. I then slam it into his gut, then his nose. He falls flat, and his head slams against the floor. His knife drops. Blood pours out through his busted front tooth as I continue smashing his gut and kidney's with the shotgun.

A half dozen half-conscious rebels storm the room.

"What the fuck?" this dark-haired, dark-eyed rebel yells at me.

I turn with the shotgun pointed at the man, then pull Heather behind me.

"We're done here," I say to the rebel.

"I don't think so," he responds.

"They got what they deserved, and you will too if you don't back the fuck away—immediately."

"What the fuck are you going to do?" he asks confidently, but not so confident now that I've blasted the side of his thigh, and he's fallen to the ground. His junkie rebel mates aim at me in shaken fear.

"You're fucking crazy, man," the little rebel bitch says.

"We're leaving," I state.

I take Heather's arm and lead her through the crowd of sleazy rebels. They know not to fuck with me—not today— not to-fucking-day.

Heather and I clear the first round of men and make our way out of the target hall.

"Open the chest," I tell Heather.

I keep the shotgun aimed at the men as she and I quickly load a duffle back with extra guns, ammo, and grenades. Also, I grab a new rifle for myself, which has an even more powerful scope.

We make our way down the corridor. The rebels follow closely.

"Sam?" Heather stops and bends down to the junkie. "We have to take her."

"It's too late for her," I state. "Look at her."

"She'll be okay in a few days," Heather demands. "We have to take her from here."

"Fine," I agree.

"I don't think so," the scum-junkie rebel next to her says while pulling out his gun. He shoots at me without delay. He misses widely. Thanks, junkie-vision.

I whip out my new 9mm and shoot him once in the stomach. Now he has a moment to think about what he's done. I walk to the bastard and take his snub-nose revolver. He tries to hold onto it, but he's weak.

Heather and I lift Sam up. We each put our arms under her shoulders and carry her out, her feet dragging.

Dozens of men gather down the hall, but not one of them is man enough to stand in my way—except for one— the guard at the door.

"Put her down," one rebel says. "Leave them."

"If you want them, you're gunna have to shoot me," I demand.

One junkie rebel goes for his gun. I pop him right in the chest without hesitation.

Another dusty-haired rebel draws his gun. The others follow suit.

I aim Dusty down with the revolver. We look eye to eye in a Mexican standoff.

He knows this won't end well for him or anyone else, so he slowly takes his finger off the trigger and lowers his weapon cautiously.

I back away and out the door with Heather and Sam, keeping my aim steady.

"Heather?" the barista asks. "Is that you?"

"Yes, Sam. It's me."

The doors shut as Heather and I carry this dirty junkie down the steps.

Free for now, we wander onward, making our way off under the warming sun, in search of Deon and the platoon. "Where is that damn bar?" I think aloud.

"What bar?" asks Heather.

"I don't know," I answer. "It has green doors, somewhere near Union maybe, but not there. It's underground in some back alley."

"Follow me," Heather says as she leads the way, leaving me to carry the junkie barista in my arms with the sixty-pound duffle bag over my shoulder.

Still, I can't recognize a thing. The rubbish makes everything look strange, like we had been transported back to some foreign land a century ago, somewhere in Europe during World War II, where my great grandfather fought among many other young-hearted and extremely brave men.

"Where is that old bastard's place?" I wonder as we wander in what seems like concentric circles for dozens of miles.

In reality, it's only been a few blocks, maybe a quarter of a mile. Perhaps it seems longer because I'm carrying this dirty, smelly, hot, and wet junkie barista over my shoulders. I'm pretty sure she's pissed on me at least once. And she's not the lightest.

Sam certainly doesn't look overweight, but she's a lot heavier than she appears. Perhaps it's the opiates coursing through her veins weighing her down? Or perhaps it's just the effect of my dehydration and sleep deprivation?

Heather continues onward as I waddle my way behind her, through what's left of downtown, climbing over the rubble with all this extra fucking weight.

After what has seemed like an entire afternoon spent in this swampy summer Tennessee heat, there it is, the ugliest green door I could never be happier to see.

I fall to my knees and nearly blackout. Sam falls to the ground with a quiet moan.

"This is it, right?" Heather asks.

"Yep," I respond as she helps me to my feet with her arm under my shoulder.

We help Sam up and drag her towards the door and bang on it.

"Let us in," I demand.

"Harry? Is that you?" Deon asks.

"Yeah. Open the damn door," I exclaim.

I hear the sound of barricades being ripped from the doorway. Deon and Vanessa swing the large green door open and welcome us.

"Heather," Vanessa exclaims, then asks. "Sam? Is she okay?"

I shake my head, "no."

"She will be," Heather assures.

"Come in, hurry," Vanessa rushes us.

Deon quickly shuts the door behind us, then he and Vanessa re-barricade us in.

Heather helps Sam down onto a mattress then hurries to grab her some water and bread.

"Harry, what happened?" Deon asks. "Did you see her?"

"I did," I respond. "But those bastards took her."

"I'm so sorry," Vanessa says.

"How'd they not get you? Did you escape?" Bobby asks.

"That doesn't matter," I state.

"Well, what are we going to do now?" Ken questions. "Can we go?"

I stare Ken down. I say nothing else. I walk straight for the bar and grab a bottle of sweet, sweet Tennessee nectar. I sit down on the floor against the bar and begin to drown my existence away as the muggy heat forces my body to drip every last drop of water from its pores. Luckily, my friend Jackie here will refill my depleted body with all of the nutrients it will ever need.

But then Heather has to come over and ruin it all, "Here. Drink this."

"What?" I worry as she takes the bottle and hands me a tall glass of water.

"You need it," she says as I shrug it away. "Just drink it."

"Fine," I gulp the glass down, feeling my cells re-enliven from the intense drought of this scorching summer.

Heather watches me contently as I finish the last drop.

"Thanks," I say as she smiles at me, still giving me that damn look.

Heather goes back to Sam's side as I drown my cells once again in the finely distilled brown bottled fountain of youth.

My pain melts into the ethers as the nectar burns its way down my chest. Perhaps this is all those damn junkies are trying to accomplish. I can understand that, but don't turn into beasts. Easier said than done during times such as this, I imagine.

As I close my eyes, the last thing I notice is Deon and Vanessa discussing operations, Heather holding a wet rag to Sam's head, and Bobby just staring at me with the fear in his eyes. I fade into darkness.

I'm startled when Deon and a National Guardsman enter and re-barricade the green door.

"This is Alfred, everyone," Deon informs us. "He's in the Guard. He brings word."

"Welcome," Vanessa says to the man. "Tell us everything you know."

Alfred? I question to myself—what a pussy. But this guy is no pussy. He's here to fight and to recruit us to fight. I'm ready to fight; it's the only thing. And he has a plan. It's a stupid fucking plan, but it's a plan. Anything to take out those damn commie lines.

This is only the war of a millennium, pitting man versus commie bastard. And if we're going down, we're taking as many commie fucks with us as all fucking possible. It's time to end them. Now that most of the flames have gone out and the rubble has stopped smoking, it's time to reignite things.

Ken still only wants to leave. I don't blame him. He should. So should I. But never without her—no fucking way. I should just work on my escape plan with her, but I can't help but fume with a little joy at the thought of sniping commies dead in the eye with my newly acquired AR-10, which is much like my old one, with offset irons to boot.

For every bad thought that I've had or said about Greg, he is ready to fight, freshly healing wound and all. Even Bobby's ready to go. For what a pussy Bobby can be, he has a rage in his heart for the commie bastards. We all do. Even the girls want to fight.

Heather and Sam don't want to leave our side anymore. They're stuck to the platoon at the hip. But there's no way they're coming into this fight. The green door bar is safe and hidden. This war is no place for Heather or Sam, even if Sam was halfway clean.

Vanessa's different. She's a warrior and forever a tomboy. But there is a sadness about her. Maybe I've never noticed it before, but she and Ken seem to have connected over something deep. But fuck if I know what. I can tell Ken always cared for her, but I'm not exactly sure she feels the same. A sadness pervades, but she does spend a lot of time with him,

not that I pay attention to much aside from the golden nectar
or my desire to rip every commie's heart out who stands between Jasmine and myself.

They took her from me again. Now it's time for them to
pay. We're not going to be on the front lines for this. The
Guard is making the offensive. We are to be the defensive
line. Also, we're to snipe across the bank when the shot is
there.

Ken, Bobby, Greg, and I will be in one location, while
Deon, Vanessa, and Alfred will be elsewhere. Our go point
will be the symphony fortress between 3rd and 4th avenue,
just north of Korean Vets Bridge—south of the pedestrian
bridge.

"Here," Alfred hands me a walkie-talkie after he finally
finishes explaining the whole thing. "So we can keep in contact. Don't fire until Deon or I give you the order."

"Huh," I laugh in Alfred's face.

"I'm serious," Alfred states deadpanned, with his silly
French or Norwegian-looking wavy blonde hair, which is covered in dirt and smoke.

"Alright," I respond, somehow convinced by his seriousness, even with that silly hairdo.

"Good," he states.

14. The East Offensive

NOTHING ELSE MATTERS—TODAY is D-day—
Commie Death Day. This is Normandy. The Cumberland
will run red with commie rat blood on this day. Nothing will
be the same after this; boys no more. No one left in this city
will remain a child after this day, for this is the day of days.
Will we be triumphant? Or will we be the ones whose defeat
turns the river red? We're soon to find out.

Ken, Bobby, Greg, and I make our way across Korean Veteran's Boulevard. Deon, Vanessa, and Alfred stay on the downtown side.

The four of us head East towards one of the big new-yet-halved hotels near the bridge. As in, the commies basically took the top off. I don't remember the name of it. The sign is nowhere to be seen, so that doesn't help, but it's to be our sniping post.

Before we make it into the lobby, a bullet plunges between us.

It's Greg. Greg gets shot a second time. Of course, he does. And of course, Bobby's all sad and overreactive about it. He and Ken pick him up. It's in the gut, perhaps right where I knocked his breath from him upon first meeting the guy. Or was that Bobby?

"Fire," Alfred yells through the walkie. "Fire. Fire."

They drag Greg back a few hundred feet, a block or two Westward. I cover them, but most importantly, myself. It appears we're about to be overrun. I believe we're on forth avenue, but I certainly wish we made our way further west or at least back on the other side of Korean Vets.

"This way," I yell out and lead them around the corner.

"We need to cross the street," Bobby stammers.

"There's no time," I tell him. "They're coming."

I peek around the corner of Korean Vet's and shoot one commie. But six or seven more rats are right beside him. We gotta move.

Greg's doing okay. Ken and Bobby drag him along. I don't think he's going to make it, so "why bother?" I ask, once again adding a smidge to the great divide between Bobby and me.

"Retreat. They're crossing the line," we hear through the radio.

"Where do we go?" I ask.

"The symphony," Deon yells through the walkie. "Get to the symphony,"

"We can't cross Korean Vets," I tell him. "They're too close."

"Where are you?" he asks.

"4th or 5th avenue," I answer.

"Hold your ground. We'll back them off and cover you."

We're not in the best location, so we attempt to move further west.

We've barely made it thirty feet, with Bobby trying his damnedest to drag Greg on when a shot rings out, and Greg is ripped from Bobby's arms as the bullet misses me and punctures Greg's chest.

Shot after shot rings out. Bobby and Ken stagger to their feet, aim their rifles, and fire into the thickening smoke-bomb-y air.

I splat two commies down, but too many are heading our way.

"Leave him," I shout at Bobby and Ken.

"Leave him?" Bobby yells back in question.

Ken picks Bobby to his feet and shakes him.

"We've got to go," Ken says. "Come on. He's gone."

Bobby pushes Ken away, stands up, and follows Ken my way. We turn the corner.

We can't see any muzzle fire due to the smoke. Bobby, Ken, and I return fire. The sound reflects from all directions making it difficult to pinpoint, but we aim our fire towards the bridge.

And there goes Bobby running out in the open like a fucking lunatic firing away. I quickly snap him back by a whisker before a bullet practically screams into his dumbass chest.

We fire away then run to what must be an old church. We shatter the glass door and enter, then run up the stairs and to the left.

The commies are coming. You can smell them. That fucking burnt rat-hair stench. Bobby, Ken, and I enter the windowless corner room and pull the sliding door shut.

A small winding stairwell rises in the corner to a plat- form at the top of the old bell tower—a sniper's dream nest —if a troop of commies wasn't following behind us.

We drop a shelf in front of both doors. Bar glasses shat- ter in a tremendous crescendo with the backing of gunfire snares, booming bass drum vibrations, and crash explosives.

Ken and Bobby start climbing the staircase.

"We need to hold them off," I state.

"You hold them off," Ken responds as he fights Bobby to the top like a child.

I hop over the bar in the corner and duck behind it.

They've climbed maybe twenty of the fifty feet to the top when a gaggle of commies storm in. They shoot up at Bobby and Ken. I allow it. They're fine. It's a metal staircase. They're not going to get shot.

I simply want the commies to feel safe and superior for a quick moment. Plus, I figure I'll allow the guys to escape to higher ground before I toss this lovely grenade over the bar into this gaggle of cunts.

Lord, I fucking love grenades.

"Gibberish!" one commie shouts.

Then, "BOOM!"

Commie blood splatters the walls.

"Jesus, Harry?" Ken shouts.

"What?" I respond, then hop over the bar and follow the guys up the staircase now that they've fully ascended.

I wind and wind my way up the cold dark shaky metal staircase.

I find Ken and Bobby leaned back against the old stone walls. I like the view from up here—and it's much easier to see through the smoke clouds.

With the death of his buddy Greg, a fire has ignited in Bobby's heart. I see it in his eyes. His face burns with a vengeance. He knows what this war can take. And that was just his stupid friend. Imagine if it were the love of his life?

I know Jasmine is alive, but I feel further away from her now than I ever have. I held her. But so shortly. Would it be the last? It can't be. There was a fear in her eyes. Had something happened to her? It wasn't like her. Could she sense a change in me? Could she see the blood in my eyes? Will I ever hold her again?

Yes, she is the love of my life, and she will be mine again. I will rescue her. She warned me to wait. She warned me it wasn't safe and to not do anything stupid. But still, I did. And I was almost killed. And who knows where she is or what has happened to her?

She was right. But I have to hold her. Nothing can keep us apart. We will leave this fucking place together.

Now, Bobby understands me. He knows that I almost had her again, and again she was ripped from me. Now he understands how that feels—sort of.

"Fuck," Ken worries anxiously. "We're sitting ducks."

"No, we're not," I tell him. "We have the advantage."

We hear gibberish coming towards the room below. Ken takes what he must believe to be his final breath and pushes his back against the stone wall. Two rats enter. Bobby shoots them dead.

Good. Now I've got some help.

Bobby's vengeance rages, yet his hands do not shake.

He shoots any commie that moves through the doorway. He has the bloodlust now. He piles several more rats on top of the others in the explosively bloody scene below. You can tell the rats are scared to enter now, and by the time they look up, it's far too late.

I breathe a sigh of relief and focus my efforts outwards at the commies coming over the bridge and those who have already crossed. Through the old church's bell tower, I can see right up the bridge at the incoming forces.

The National Guard is getting pushed back by the hundreds of commies crossing into downtown, along with a handful of gunner trucks. They're decimating the Guard line.

Ken peaks up in fear, then quickly ducks back down. He's not much help.

I'm torn between my urge to murder as many commies as possible versus wanting to remain unspotted, therefore having a better shot at survival. But who am I kidding? I begin firing almost immediately at the thought of staying unspotted.

I take shot after shot after shot, unloading my magazine, downing at least fifteen, probably twenty commie bastards with my 30-round extended clip.

They haven't spotted me yet, so I begin emptying a second clip, but then several commies begin to fire our way.

I get down. Ken stays down. The old stone is strong, but we are greatly outnumbered.

"Fuck," Ken worries. "They're going to fucking kill us, Harry."

Bobby's still working the doors. Even more rats are now bleeding out below.

I peak out, then quickly duck as shots fire my way.

"We're fine," I unassuredly assure Ken.

I quickly peak out the second tall window and fire a few rounds before a fifty-cal gunner starts raining hellfire our way.

"Fuck, man," Ken cries out.

"Shut up, Ken," Bobby says. "He's right. It's fine."

The stone's holding—for now—not perfectly.

With one shot to save the day, I hop up, aim fluidly down the scopes at the gunner, and shoot—popping him through the temple—most certainly. I quickly cover below the window.

I could swear I got him, but he must have escaped my wrath as fifty-caliber rounds blast the stone walls around and outside of us.

"Look," Ken shouts. "It's them. They're here to save us. We're saved."

I see Deon, Vanessa, and Alfred across the Boulevard. They're looking to cross towards us, but the commies spot them and begin shooting. Deon pulls the gang back while Vanessa returns fire until the fifty-caliber gunner turns towards them.

I aim right between the eyes of the red-headed commie gunner and fire. It fires high. The rat-gunner turns the 50 cal cannon back towards us. I fire the second round, which hits through his left shoulder, causing his barrel to drop.

A little better, but not quite. I aim a little lower to the left and fire, hitting him directly through the belly. I then shoot his little driver friend right through the heart. Much better.

"Ken," I say. "You've got to cover us. Okay? Can you do that?"

Ken takes a deep breath, gets on one knee, and aims down towards the Korean Vet's bridge. Shot after shot, he fires, giving me time to make the needed adjustments to my scope.

Once finished, I move back to the window and aim across the street between 4th and 1st avenues, covering Deon.

A dozen black-clad commies storm their position.

I pop two of the incoming rats in the back. Alfred looks around the corner and fires, hitting another one or two.

Though the smoke is dissipating slightly, the commie's senses seem to be heightened and confused. Shots fire at them from all around, echoing off every building left standing. Deon and Vanessa help Alfred and myself take out the rest of the small commie gaggle heading their way.

Ken and Bobby swap positions, allowing Bobby to help me clear the streets.

The rats on the front line would be easy prey if there weren't six dozen or more right behind them.

The commie foot soldiers are getting closer, so I sling a grenade out of the window, which lands much nearer to the rats than I expected. It takes out a few dirty commies while knocking seven more to the ground.

It turns out, when you're really in it, war can be rather fun. Maybe fun isn't the right word, but yeah, fun. You forget everything else; your every sense is elevated, pure focus. Your heart beats out of your chest in anticipation.

To see commie blood drain in the street is rather magnificent. I must have taken out at least thirty-three commies already, each at least a liter short on blood, if not a gallon or more. Thirty-three gallons of blood from gaggles and gaggles of commie cunts; I'll take it. And I'll take gallons from gaggles more, Jesus help me.

The Guard, along with the rest of the platoon, have taken out a couple hundred more. The Guard has now stopped retreating and is charging the bridge.

Lucky for the rest of these commie bastards, they begin retreating back across the bridge to safety.

We've stopped them at 2nd Avenue. Now it's time to make our escape to join Deon and the gang across the street. Perhaps we can push forward now with the Guard? We can at least move back to safety.

15. Pillars

ALL OF A FUCKING SUDDEN, a roaring metal beast appears upon the bridge's horizon, causing the foot soldiers to stop and turn back our way. Hundreds of more rats follow behind the beastly tank.

"Go," I command. "Now."

Bobby, Ken, and I make our way down the winding staircase as fast as we can storm. The tower above explodes, and stone rains down, filling the room with rubble just as we're out the door; smoke piles around us.

We hurry down the main stairs and out onto 4th Avenue with no trouble. We want to cross Korean Vets to 3rd, but there's a fucking tank coming down the bridge. However, now might be our only chance.

"I'll cover you," I say. "Go."

"What? Fuck you," Ken says. "You go."

Without hesitation, Bobby takes off like a leopard across the avenue. A few shots nearly destroy him but don't quite graze him. I take out two commies who are firing from behind what's left of one of the big new hotels across the street.

The tank fires a blast, and if Bobby wasn't fast, it may have ripped him in half. But he's made it across.

"Let's go," I demand Ken as I yank him off the wall and drag him up the street, following Bobby, who has made it to Deon's position on 3rd Avenue. I'm not sure where Vanessa and Alfred are.

We make a break for it as commie rats flow onto the street from the bridge. Bobby covers us, along with Deon. I return pistol fire, but I'm mostly only worried about the tank, which appears to turn its long metal beak in our direction menacingly. It locks in and blasts.

I dive and tackle Ken behind a giant marble pillar of the Prestige Hotel. The blast shell shocks us and knocks the column off its axis, but still, it stands. So do we—sort of. I hold still. However, Ken gets up and tries to run. I hold him back and signal him to wait. There's no use in telling him. His hearing's surely just as deafened as mine.

The tank plows west in our direction, crossing 1st Avenue. I look around the pillar as this metal monstrosity turns its big burly beak north, down 3rd Avenue, and fires. I grab Ken's shirt, and we run westward together.

The tank turns its fat metal cock back towards us and shoots a shell, blasting a ten-foot hole in the wall in front of us. We're pushed back by the force. My ears ring fiercely.

I pull Ken up, and we continue onward. Another blast fires but hits the pillar behind us.

We dash as the tank fires another blast, rocking another pillar off its foundation and collapsing the front entrance of the hotel.

Ken and I sprint at full speed, turning north. And, of course, the tank follows us instead of Bobby and Deon. Overall, it's probably for the best. But not for Ken nor I— especially Ken.

We keep running. The street we're going for is up ahead. We're at the Hall Of Fame Museum when a blast takes out an abandoned van next to us, walloping us a few feet to the side. Ken receives the brunt of it, but he's fine—just a little red—not much blood—just crispy.

"Come on," I tell Ken. "We're almost there. You're fine."

I hold off from informing him about the shrapnel I notice in his side. He'll feel that when his shock wears off, or if he reaches down and touches it, or looks down.

"Don't look down," I tell him in my mind.

I drag Ken to his feet and onward as we make our way around the corner of the Museum. The tank follows behind us, but we've got a clear path for the symphony.

We're almost there, maybe 150 feet to go when the tank turns the corner. We're done for, but we continue dashing onward.

Deon appears around the symphony fortress gate with what resembles a rocket launcher.

"Get down," Deon yells, which echoes faintly through my busted eardrums.

Ken and I leap to our bellies as Deon fires a rocket in the tank's direction.

The tank blasts the wall Deon just fired behind. I hope he was able to get to cover. The smokey demolished scene doesn't give great hope.

Then, from atop the fortressed roof, Vanessa, Alfred, Bobby, and dozens of others appear and open fire upon the tank with their auto and semi-auto rifles.

Ken and I make our way to cover behind a truck. Several other abandoned cars stand between the metal beast and us, but the tank keeps trudging its way towards the symphony, climbing over the wreckage. It blasts the symphony just below the roof, barely missing our platoon.

"Let's go," I urge Ken.

But just then, Ken looks down, seeing a metal rod sticking out of the left side of his blood-darkened shirt.

"Fuck, man," Ken fears for his life—falling to his knees.

"You'll be okay," I assure him. "I promise. But we have to go, now. It's coming. Can you make it?"

Ken shakes, "Yes." I stand him up, take his shoulder, and we begin to run together towards the gate. Ken roars in pain but runs onward with me to the best of his ability.

We are directly between the tank and the building, not one hundred feet from each.

The tank lowers its giant metal ant-eater beak towards us when Deon lurks out and shoots another rocket in the tank's direction. Ken and I slide below. It probably wouldn't have hit us, but it was too fucking close for comfort. The dive doesn't help Ken's situation much. He screams in severe terror.

The tank fires, just above us, hitting the fortress wall—this time, knocking Deon backwards.

I see more commies heading towards the fortress from the south. Vanessa, Bobby, Alfred, and the others fire upon them.

I lift Ken to his feet. He all but passes out. I dash with him over my shoulder towards Deon. We get to the corner. I shove Ken behind the wall and dive for cover as the tank fires, blasting stone and shrapnel off the fortress walls. Dust and smoke pummel the air.

I drag Deon to momentary safety as the tank encroaches.

"The launcher," Deon points. "Get the launcher."

Through the dust, I see the rocket launcher snapped in half. Plus, I'm not going back out there. I'm out of grenades. It's a fucking tank.

Then I see them sparkling through the dust clouds, the rockets themselves, piled up and ready. Can I just toss one? Or does it need to be launched to ignite? It's too late for questions.

With the tank not fifty feet away and troops getting ever nearer, I rush to pick up a rocket. I then run to the wall and sling it around the corner as fiercely as possible. The tank fires this exact moment.

The blast sends me backwards, smashing onto the fortress grounds. But much to my surprise, it explodes—the whole damn tank.

"I did it," I shout as I try to move but am mostly unable. "I fucking did it. I took out a fucking tank with my bare hands. Fuck you, tank."

And for all intents and purposes, it was actually Alfred from the rooftop who took out the tank. I know this because he peaks down at us from over the fortress top, with a smoking rocket launcher over his shoulder. And if it hadn't been for him, at the very least, the three of us would have been goners.

I would thank him if my consciousness allowed, but the blast has taken that from me. I drift off into dreamland. And if my imagination is as correct as I imagine it is, then I imagine the hundreds of commies storming our way retreat swiftly now that their beast is obliterated. Though in my hope, I wish their every commie life gets laid waste this day.

16. Boiling

HERE I AM IN MY OWN BED with Jasmine next to me. I hear a window break in the living room, and she awakens. I grab a baseball bat from behind the door.

It's fucking commies. I knew it. Dressed in all black, with black wool hats—and it's fucking summer. Only a commie could wear a wool hat in a Tennessee summer. I keep Jasmine behind me as we stand hidden on the wall behind the cracked door.

The first rat fuck comes in and fires his submachine gun all around, then pauses. He looks right, then looks left—my way. I swing the bat and knock his mouth off his commie fucking face. I slam the door shut. The other two commies pour lead through the wooden barrier.

As they shove the door open, I toss up a round quarts stone that prisms the commie gun-light. I wind up, switch-hitting left-handed, and swing the bat with nearly unrealistic force. The bat cracks the quarts ball right on the money and speeds over 100mph directly into the second commie's chest, relieving him of his life-breath for at least the next few moments.

The last commie puts his gun down and throws his fists up. Fine.

I toss the bat into the air.

He reaches behind his back and pulls out a second pistol.

At this same moment, I kick his shin. He writhes his arms in anguish as I catch the bat and crack his temple in one smooth motion, knocking his head and body loudly against the door frame.

With raging eyes, I finish the three of them off, splattering their skull juice about, while Jasmine watches with disgust from the corner.

I walk towards her, drop the bat, and—

Here we are, at the company picnic. Little Harry and Jackie run around eating cotton candy and riding ponies. Jasmine wears an orange and white sundress with tropical flowers; an orange ribbon in her hair.

Little Harry's in a light blue suit, and Jackie's in a white lacy dress.

The sun sets as I watch the family of my dreams in all its golden glory—

There she is, at the army ball, the most beautiful woman in the room. In her royal blue dress, outshining all the others with a pearl necklace and her big bright brown eyes. It takes so much to get up the nerve to go up and ask her to dance. I'll never forget it.

The year is 1945. We have just come back from victory. Celebrations are everywhere, every night, for we have defeated the enemy, and I'm not going to let this most beautiful creature scurry from my life. She is to be my world from this moment forward.

I walk up to her. She turns towards me. I ask her to
dance. She says yes. Yes. From there forth, we spend the
summers at her grandfather's; swimming in the crystal clear
waters, riding bikes down the sandy trail to the market five
miles away, canoeing the reefs, making love in the meadows,
dancing under the moonlight, laying in the hammock sipping
tiki cocktails—

Suddenly, blackness fills my eyes and my heart.

"There you are," Heather hangs over me. "Are you
okay?"

"What?" I nearly yell. "Where the fuck am I? This isn't
where I am. What's going on?"

Heather tries to console me, "You were dreaming. You
were just dreaming. You're okay."

"Shit, man," Ken says. "I didn't think you were going to
make it."

Ken appears nearly healed already—sort of.

"You alright, Harry?" Bobby asks.

Everyone seems relieved yet worried. Bobby may understand me more, but I still give him the willies.

Heather's looking at me just like she always fucking does.
She doesn't stare. But when she looks, her eyes say everything.
I just don't know what the fuck it is. But they're certainly
speaking.

It appears Sam is over with the worst of her withdrawals,
but she's still out of it.

Jasper comes up from the bottle long enough to croak, "I
thought you were dead?"

"Shut up, old man," I respond while pushing myself up
to sitting, then lean against the wall.

Alfred comes my way and kneels in front of me, "I'm
glad you're up. We could use your help."

"With what?" I respond disdainfully.

"Blowing the bridges," Alfred says. "You up for it?"

"I'm not helping you blow the fucking bridges," I state. "Jasmine's over there."

"Do you want the fucking commies to take over the whole city?" Jasper asks in exactly the way you'd expect from such an old bastard.

"I don't give a fuck about the city," I state clearly. "I need the bridges to get to her."

"You will, man," Deon says. "Just——"

"I know I will," I agree, "And I need the bridges, so we're not fucking touching them."

"Try and stop us," Alfred says, then walks towards the green door.

"Wait," I think to myself as I lob a beer Alfred's way.

The bottle crashes and shatters into at least 74 pieces by Alfred's feet as he dances a jig. He turns my way, "What's your fucking problem?"

Heather and Deon stand in his way to calm him down as I throw my middle fingers up at him out of their view.

I don't quite know what my problem is, food perhaps? I have lost maybe ten pounds since the war broke out. Everyone has. This bottle of nectar will take some of the weight off my shoulders.

I'm not even making sense to myself anymore as I sip from the golden fountain of youth.

"That's better," I think aloud to myself.

"What?" Alfred asks fiercely.

"Blow the bridges?" I ask.

"Yeah, what?" Alfred asks in response.

"Fuck it," I say, "But you're not blowing the pedestrian bridge."

"I know," Alfred says. "You are."

"What? No, I'm f——"

"We have to," Vanessa interrupts, always so annoyingly knowing and convincing. "It's the only way."

"You can still get to her," Bobby says.

"I know I fucking can," I respond bitingly, then turn to Alfred. "When?"

"Tonight," Alfred informs.

"Alright. I'm in," I say, then sip from the fountain of youth, which is giving me new life to take on the gravest enemy ever known to earth. No alien invader could ever be as cold and machine-like as this commie filth.

They want to take everything human away. They've been trying to in culture for years. The money men have been psychologically manipulating the populace for decades, propping up and filtering, allowing only the most soulless art to flourish. Just look at pop music and summer blockbusters, not to mention the divide and conquer inducing hatred on all sides of every spectrum of the CIA mockingbird media complex.

What brings us together? What makes us the same? Our humanity. And that's what these commie fucks want to take away from the entire world. And that's what brings us all together, regardless of politics, religion, skin color, or this or that.

That's what's bringing us all together now. Our love of freedom and hatred of those who want to force us into submission in a new communist world order. Fuck that.

Regardless of whatever I may have said or thought just moments ago, nothing will allow me to let an opportunity to destroy the cold machine-like commies go to waste.

The platoon keeps mumbling bluster back and forth. They are having normal, real, and perhaps very important conversations, but that doesn't matter to me.

"Got it?" Alfred asks. "Got it? Harry? Harry? Got it?"

"Oh. Yeah, yeah. Got it," I state, having not heard a word of the plan.

"Be careful," Heather tells me.

I scrunch my eyebrows at her, trying to understand her nonsense, "I'm fine."

Everyone gathers their goodies, grenades, guns, ammo, and best of all, a backpack full of C-4 explosive packets with super sticky peels and all.

Feeling slightly better about our whole situation thanks to Jackie-Boy here, I peel off the sticky strip and slam a C-4 packet onto Bobby's back.

"Five, four, three, two, one," I say in all seeming seriousness as I shake Bobby. "Boom."

Alfred storms my way and grabs me by the neck, causing my smirk to cease.

I croak out, looking him eye to eye, "I wouldn't do that."

He throws his hands off.

Ken and Deon help Bobby up, then Alfred pries the C-4 off his back.

"That was a good joke," I say as I grab my gear and walk towards and out the big green door.

The platoon exits and follows along.

Heather stands in the doorway with that same look.

"Shut the fucking door," Jasper spouts. "I can smell them coming. You bastards better blow the damn things, or we're all finished."

The National Guard line near every bridge has been pounded and decimated over the last thirty-six hours; since I've been out cold. The gunners are down. The makeshift road barrier and sandbags are all pretty much cleared. It's an eerily quiet scene.

Jasper's right. The smell of invasion is in the air. It all smells very... commie. They do have dozens of tanks. At any moment, they could begin to cross the Cumberland on mass. They are right, this may be the only thing we can do to keep the entire city of Nashville from being completely overthrown and razed by the commie filth. We're not going to let these cunt smugglers anywhere close to that. They're already far too fucking close. They've already taken part of the city, and all of my everything. And they are going to pay. They are all going to fucking pay. It's not our fault they're commies. We just have to do what we have to do.

17. Blow The Bridges

WE'RE OUTNUMBERED. WE ALWAYS are. There must be 30,000 commies housed in Five-Points, along with several thousand staying in the casino along the Cumberland. At least two or three dozen rats are on the lookout at any moment from atop the various hotels and casinos, plus along the rim of the stadium.

We begin to sneak, crawl, and dash towards the spotlighted pedestrian bridge with all the C-4 and detonators our hearts could desire. It's the middle of the night. It must be 3 AM. The plan is set in motion, whatever that plan may be. We only know our part.

My job is simple. Snipe. That's all I know about the plan. I like to snipe. And I've gotten decent at it. It just comes naturally. Perhaps because of however many thousands of hours of first-person shooters I had played in my younger days, or simply because of my near-perfect hand-eye coordination—that's a fact.

Throw anything at me, I'll catch it. Drop something; caught. So aiming down a commie with my blood-lusting eyes and steady hands is indeed quite the joy. It will be the only joy I will know until I hold her again and take her away from all of this madness.

Soon, I will find her. I will dawn some commie garb off a dirty rat I snipe through the temple, so it's nice and clean, and I will get to her. Then we will make our escape. But for now, it's go time.

The plan appears to be for two of Alfred's National Guard buddies to plant the C-4, then he'll blow it with the detonators while the platoon and I snipe from the nearby rubble. Our aim is up the bridge and across the river at the various rooftops.

The two guardsmen make their way up the spotlit bridge, keeping cover along the rails, though they're pretty open. They could get sniped from all angles. And, of course, the commie gunner trucks could rip them to shreds if given the chance. They'd like that.

If I were them, I'd just come out firing. But they're "playing it safe." And so is everyone else. It might be for the best.

What about "shake and bake?" But it is their plan. I've got one in my sights right now, but I must wait. However, I sure am ready for the first shot to be fired.

All remains quiet.

Then, just like that, the two guardsmen drop. Not a sound, just blood splattering from the back of their skulls as if by magic. But we all know better than to believe in magic in a time like this.

"Fuck," I pronounce.

And as if by instinct alone, Ken grabs me by the arm and runs, leading me down the stone rubble towards the pedestrian bridge.

"What are you doing?" I ask, laughing at Ken's sudden call to action.

"We have to blow the fucking bridge," Ken demands, unworried about his recent half-healed shrapnel wound. "Lucky we have smoke grenades," I think aloud to myself.

"We do?" Ken asks.

"Well, no. But we do have real grenades," I state, holding up two of them.

"Cover us," Ken yells back to the crew.

"You're fucking crazy," Deon yells. "Push back. Push back!"

"We've got to blow them," Vanessa says. "We'll cover you."

"Fuck," Deon shouts.

Vanessa, Deon, and Bobby start laying down leaded blanket fire while Ken and I rush to the bridge and begin our ascent.

Dozens of other Guard and rebel snipers line the rubbled cityscape, offering us a bit of extra cover. But still, we are pretty much open targets. We keep as low as possible along the rail and behind the scorched gunner trucks and skeleton tank.

The spotlights make the bridge look like daylight, though they certainly impede our view of any trouble beyond the light.

As Ken and I run along up the left side of the bridge, machine-gun fire begins to dance off the metal railing. We hit the asphalt and crawl towards the laid-out guardsmen as sparks spray around us.

I reach into my pouch, grab a grenade, pull the pin, and toss it towards the bridge's center. It lands, bounces, and blows, creating a light smoke cover. But we need more.

"On three," I tell Ken, then toss a second grenade. "One, two, three."

Ken and I run low but speedy like jackrabbits. We dive to the guardsmen as the grenade explodes.

I hear gibberish coming from behind the blast, just beyond the light. The question is, how many? A few dozen? Hundreds?

I aim down my rifle scope. Through the diminishing smoke, I see several diseased rats walking in our direction. I aim down one and pull the trigger. The second falls on his own. I aim down the third and drop him. But the fourth is clever and ducks away. They don't have scopes, only iron sights, but their buddy's across the river sure do, who continue bouncing shots off the rails right next to us.

"Got em," Ken loudly whispers as he begins to un-peel the tape from the C-4.

"What are you doing?" I ask.

"Setting them."

"Not until we're above the water."

"It's too dangerous."

"You wanted to do this," I remind Ken as I pull him along. "Just keep low. It's cool. Otherwise, what's the point?"

We crawl on our bellies up the bridge towards the crest. Ken's stitches cause him to moan and groan his way forward.

I aim down through my offset iron sights as I crawl, using the sling to hold the rifle up while my left-hand helps pull me along.

Shots ring out from behind us, all around us. But this is Deon and the gang firing at the advancing commies.

I pull out a third grenade and toss it. Ken and I get up and run on impact. We run low until I see a few rat-heads pop up. We hit the ground and take cover behind what's left of the sandbags.

A commie head pops up. I drop him. Ken fires and hits another rat, then begins crawling forward with the C-4.

"Is this good?" Ken asks.

"A little further," I state.

"Fuck," Ken keeps crawling.

Then I hear it, a faint but familiar sound that had been seared into my memory a few days ago when I was lifted off my feet and blasted into the stone symphony fortress by that metal monstrosity.

I grab Ken's boot and tell him, "This is good. This is fucking good. Right here's good."

He looks at me with a fearful remembrance, for he too knows the sound of that big metal commie bastard approaching our horizon as the spotlights shine brightly upon the bridge.

"I'll cover you," I tell Ken.

"Where do I put them, and what do I do?" Ken asks quickly.

"One on that side," I tell him. "Two in the center, and one on this side. Push the green button to arm them. I think. Make sure the light comes on. I don't really know."

"Fuck!" Ken sticks and quickly arms the first block of C-4 near the rail, then crawls like a squirming slinky towards the middle of the bridge.

Shots fire over our heads. I look back to see that Deon and Vanessa have made their way up the bridge aways and are offering cover fire upon the approaching invaders.

"Blow the fucker," Deon shouts.

"Shut the fuck up," I respond in kind. "That's what we're doing."

Ken sets two blocks of C-4 near the center, arms one, then the next.

He turns towards me and shouts, "It won't set."

"Just fucking get to the next one," I yell. "If these fucking blow, that one will fucking blow, surely."

Ken crawls towards the final location on the south side of the bridge when a commie bastard fires upon him. He rolls back to safety. I shoot the rat through the shoulder, then four more times through his torso.

Vanessa and Deon have taken cover on opposite sides, each kneeling behind short cement posts and firing up the bridge above our position.

I toss another grenade and shout at Ken, "Go, you bastard. Only one left. I've got your back."

The sound of the tank is getting more and more prominent amongst the machine-gun and sniper fire. Luckily our shooters are causing enough of a distraction from warranting a full onslaught upon us, but not once that tank crosses the crest of the bridge.

Suddenly just south of us, just before Ken places the final block of C-4, the Korean Veterans bridge blows. It comes tumbling down in a fiery rage, right before we're in the clear. Why couldn't they have fucking waited a fucking second? What happened to the plan, "Blow them all at the same fucking time?"

And so, our seemingly peaceful mission quickly becomes a metal monsoon pouring all around us. They've caught onto our plans. Deon has the wherewithal to take out the commie spotlights, offering us at least a tinge of darkness as the tank rises into our view.

"Run," Deon shouts as he and Vanessa flee down the bridge.

"Oh fuck," I shout. "Set it!"

"Fuck," Ken shouts as he activates the final C-4. He dives and tosses it, landing it just near the bridge's edge. He hops up and runs low back my way.

The thought crosses my mind, "Why the fuck are you running back my way? There's a fucking tank not 100 feet from us, plus gunners and shite. What the fuck are you doing, Ken? Just fucking jump. Or at least run away from the thing." But here he comes.

"Blow it," Ken screams, waving his arms like a madman. "Blow it!"

"What?" I respond in his general direction.

"Blow it," Ken yells maniacally.

"Blow it," Deon shouts down towards Alfred and through the walkie. "Blow it."

"Jump," Ken shouts.

"What?" I wonder. "Why is this guy suddenly telling me what to do? What crawled up his snatch and put a pepper up his ass?"

"Fuck," shouts Ken and I as we sprint towards the ledge while warm asphalt smashes against our shins from the spraying bullets.

A tank blast torpedos right by the two of us as we leap off the edge into the great unknown—

Then, "BOOM!"

The bridge explodes, shoots out, and crumbles in all directions. Fire expands, engulfing the smoldering air. We're blown away from the bridge. Our bodies flip, flap, and spin in all directions from the outward heat and pressure of the blast. We fall heavily towards the darkness below.

I hit the surface forcefully but mostly feet first, shooting twenty feet underwater. Concrete and steel debris crash all around. I swim away from the heart of the debris.

I reach the surface. I can't see Ken.

Spotlights shine all around, so I keep my head low and my movements under the thick brown water of the Cumberland. Where is Ken? He still hasn't surfaced.

Debris continues to crash. Several rats fall into the abyss of the vacant bridge as it crumbles further, surely crushing them. The tank follows quickly behind once the structure below it gives way.

The bridge's center is totally destroyed. Though the structure stands strong, there's no ground left for over twenty-five feet, all the way across.

Still, no Ken. Was he hit with fallen debris? There's no way I can find him in this dark murk-infested water. Was he shot? Did the explosion vaporize him? Did concrete crush him?

After what seems like minutes, Ken shouts, "Harry?"

I look around and see Ken thirty-five feet away, safer from the debris than I.

I take a breath and swim underwater towards Ken and the muddy downtown shoreline.

Oil from the fast-sinking tank alights the river's surface, burning the few living commies alive. They squeal like pigs as their blood begins to sizzle. It's either sizzle or drown. Their gurgling gibberish makes it sound like they're having a hard time deciding.

Ken and I make our way to the edge of the river. Bullets splat the water and mud around us as we crawl our way out. We move behind the trees and bushes.

"We'll cover you," a familiar voice shouts. It's Vanessa.

"Run," Deon commands as he, Vanessa, and Alfred fire upon the roof of the casino commie resort monstrosity.

The all too familiar sound of artillery shells begins to whistle down over our heads once more.

"Fucking commies," Ken screams as he and I run with a fiery intensity and heavy breaths past Vanessa. We continue as debris from the artillery shells bounce off the rubble in front of us.

Deon, Vanessa, Bobby, and Alfred follow suit, hidden in the gray smoke-clouded, spotlight-lined air.

Artillery shells crash the buildings around us, but we make it safely past the symphony fortress—our mission a success.

But what about the other bridges? Were they all blown? Or will the commies be storming us from all sides by the time daylight begins to fall? Only time will tell as the ground shakes beneath us from artillery thunder.

"Keep low, you say?" Ken mocks in a little tantrum. "It's cool. No, it's not fucking cool, man. It's not fucking cool! It's not fucking cool at all!"

"Calm down," I tell him.

"Don't fucking tell me to calm down. I just want to get the fuck out of this place. I don't want to be any part of this anymore."

"We did it. You're okay, Ken. You did it," Vanessa gives him a big hug as she joins us. "You may have just saved the city."

"I mean, I was there too," I ponder mentioning, but leave it be.

"Really?" Ken asks like he's special.

"Yes," Vanessa kisses him deeply.

I huff and walk off upfront, leading the way back to the green door as the little pieces of ourselves catch up to us.

"Does it hurt?" Vanessa asks.

"Only when I laugh," Ken says.

"Well, don't laugh," Vanessa smiles as Ken laughs in joyous pain.

Deon catches up with me and puts his arm around my shoulder. He doesn't say a word. He knows there is no need for words, nor would I appreciate it.

18. Go East

ONLY A DAY HAS GONE BY since the bridges, but I can wait no longer. Now, it's time to reach her, in any way I can, "stupid" or not.

If not tonight, in the morrow, I will be with my love. Under the shooting stars of the Perseid meteor shower, we will escape into the wilderness where we'll never be found. We will protect what's ours, and that will be that.

Wearing commie garb that I took from a smoked bloke, I walk northeast towards the muddy banks. Through calf-deep mud, I trudge, then begin swimming across the Cumberland with my AR-10 strapped to my chest and a rucksack full of goodies keeping me afloat.

I aim to skip Five-Points altogether and land much further north, past the blown-out Jefferson Street bridge. It's looking good so far; no spotlights.

I reach the shore without a peep of danger. I shoulder my rucksack and rifle. I am in commie garb, but I'm dripping wet. And being unable to speak rat-gibberish, I figure it best to hide rather than go up against ten thousand invaders on my own.

Therefore, I sneak along, building to building, avoiding the many guards and patrols who are out and about. Buck knife at the ready, I move stealthily down alleys, along sidewalk edges, around the lights, behind buildings and shrubs, then finally down one particular alleyway off Dickerson Pike.

The rats are out and about, but they haven't spotted me. However, one rat guard happens to follow me into the alley, unbeknownst to himself, as another invader walks down the other side while I duck around a short bend, barely hidden by the building's edge.

Both of the dirty commie rats approach. I don't have much of a choice, so as they're about fifteen feet away in either direction, I step out and play it off nonchalantly, with my knife hidden up my sleeve.

"Gibberish, gibberish, gibberish?" both commies batter me with questions.

I spout back some made-up gibberish, mimicking, and surely mocking them while I gesture my arms to play off my dripping wet uniform. They look at each other for a confused moment, each about three feet away from me now.

The commie to my six yells gibberish, while the one to my front goes for his gun. So naturally, I kick the rat to my rear in the knee, snapping it backwards, then jam my knife like a jewel-encrusted dagger into the gun-grabbing rat's throat. He steps back, desperately trying to stop the blood from flowing outward and filling his airways. He gurgles quietly, dropping his gun.

Now the other commie needs to shut his fucking cunt mouth. As he struggles to reach his gun from aside his bum leg, I take out my silenced 9mm that's packed full of subsonic lead-cheddar and make some cherry lead-belly commie pie.

I turn and grab my knife out of his comrade's throat, stand over him, and shut him up for good.

Luck be a commie tonight, for the bloodlust is strong in me. I pull the two dead and bloody rat cunts into the small nook, then continue up the alley, avoiding every sign of life.

The air is calm as I continue towards home. It's cooler than the nights before. It's warm, but the humidity seems less daunting.

Now that I'm past their perimeter, I'm not as worried, yet I remain deep in the shadows.

The street up ahead might be a bit more difficult crossing than I had previously anticipated. I could go around or wait it out, but that would take longer.

A small gaggle of rats stands around out in the street, not doing much of anything, just being the dirty rats they are.

They lean against their gunner truck, speaking gibberish and smoking cigarettes.

I take cover and aim my rifle down commie-way. There's open shot after open shot, but I wait, finger at the ready.

The commie patrol made up of five rats begins to make its way slowly around the corner, shining a spotlight around, searching for any naughty curfew breakers. Unlucky for these rat-fucks, I'm coming for them like the night itself. I'm glad they're on my path. I need fresh commie blood to flow. It's freeing, almost as if their very soul is thanking me. Before it even happens, their souls are thanking me, for they know that I am about to free them from the depths of Hades.

These poor bastards don't even see it coming. Before they can even react, I pop out of the bushes, slit one of their throats, and pop two down with my silenced pistol.

Now for the fourth, I have a little something extra prepared. The poor bastard is gunless. He must have laid it down in the truck. He was the one working the spotlight, which now lays handless, pointing upward, giving the perfect glimmer of light as I approach this commie bitch with the tire iron I grab from the truck's bed.

As for the fifth commie who's running off, I pop him twice in the back, then waistband my pistol.

I slowly approach the fourth rat. He turns to run. I throw the eleven-pound pipe sidearmed, hard and low, twisting and twirling a good 65mph directly towards the back of his kneecaps. His legs fly out from under him as he flops onto his back.

He stands weakly and picks up the pipe, spouting gibberish. Now he has the power, so he thinks. Though he doesn't appear very confident.

I approach him as he swings the pipe out madly in defenseless defense. The fear rushes through him. The fear is strong with this one. Perhaps that's his humanity trying to return or his soul speaking through him, apologizing for his commie actions.

Soon, his very soul will thank me, for I am to send him directly to God; no passing go, no receiving two hundred dollars. This isn't fucking Monopoly. His heart races. Mine doesn't beat one beat. It won't until I hold her. My heart will remain frozen until that time. And this poor commie bastard is in my way, the exact wrong place to be.

After this poor little rat bitch swings that pipe at me, and I catch it against my ribs, as it tries in vain to crack them, I let him fucking have it.

I kick him down, take the pipe, and whack his legs, then his belly, kidneys, arms, and shoulders. Then I move all the way up, and his movements stop.

Knowing there will be other patrols out looking for their lost comrades, I drop the commie jacket and move swiftly in the cover of darkness. I slide from house to house, hiding behind trees and shrubs, fences, and decks. I don't recognize the street, but I'm heading northeast. I must be getting close.

I continue to her, to our home. Today, the day of days, of days and days, of all the days. Soon I will breathe her again. I will taste her. I will feel her. She and I, forever again. We haven't had enough time. Now we will. I'm sure of it. I've never been so certain of anything.

"I'm coming, my love." This time it's real. This time we will flee, whichever direction feels right. "Only you. Only and forever you."

We will disappear together, away from all the nastiness of this world. We will heal our scars and help bring humanity back into this burning world.

Appearing up ahead, a familiar sight, I've run through this neighborhood many times. It's still green and bright, unravaged by the bloody storm. I'm close. The smell of war is all but left behind.

There. Up ahead. My street. There's the Murphy's old house. Everything seems okay, but seems can quickly become unseemly in times such as these.

I run through this yard and the next, then the next and the next, again and onward.

I run, and I run until my heart and belly float up into the clouds as I see it—our home.

I rush to our doorstep, wiggle and work the handle, bang on the door.

"Jasmine?" I yell in a whisper as hope once again returns to my dried-out veins.

I run around to the back door. I take the bottom of my buck knife's handle, smash the window, unlock the door and enter.

"Jasmine?" I whisper in wondering question. "Jasmine, my love. Are you here?"

Where is she? Could she be hiding?

I hurry to our bedroom. I see no signs of her. Things seem fine and unfettered, but where is she? I check under the bed, in the closest, the bath. I check the other rooms and every closet. She's gone. The neighbors must know something. Someone must. However, it will be light soon, so I must wait to make any more moves.

I scurry to the kitchen, open the liquor cabinet, and grab a bottle, plus a proper glass, for once. I sit down on the floor and lean on the couch to stay low.

I fill my glass halfway and take it down in one gulp, feeling the golden nectar warm my chest and fill my lungs with its sunlike goodness. I inhale its luxurious vapors and dream of our life together once she returns.

I imagine how it will be; where we will go; what it will feel like to kiss you again, to caress you, to put my arm around your hips, to hold your thighs back as we make love as the sunshine pours through your hair from the bay window of the house in the country we'll move to once I find you? We must go south or somehow east to the mountains. The mountains will be best. They'll never find us in the mountains. Why do the others want to go south? Sure, it may be easier. But in the end, will it be any better than this? If Nashville falls completely, of course, the rats will head south soon after. And how long until they break through the Texas lines? If there even truly are any?

I pour another double down my gullet, grasp the bottle, hobble to the bedroom, and float back onto the bed. My glass crashes to the white tile floor. I drift, far, far away; forever far, away and away and away; forever and ever. Yet here I remain. But where is she? Will she return? When?

Once again, the nectar has me—the fountain of youth runneth over—forcing my rest.

Old Jasper, you sly dog, you. Not that Jasper, the other Jasper, the good Jasper, Jack Jasper. Mister Daniel-son. Jackie. Old Jackerino. Jack master Jack. Sleepy, sleepy Jack bastard—

19. The Neighborhood

THE DAY MUST BE NEARING an end, as well as my dreamy sleepless slumber. Outside, the commie curfew bitch patrol are out and about, with sirens and loudspeakers blasting gibberish at overwhelming decibels in all directions.

The patrols will be back soon. I need to wait until darkness fully falls. I need God to shut his eyes so that I can do whatever I must do to find her.

The darkness is slow coming. Although the time is near, the pink sunset is taking its sweet time.

She's close. She has to be. Maybe she's with one of the neighbors. Why would she stay here alone? Of course, she is.

The Simon's? The Murphy's? The Crutchfield's? The Perkins'? She's somewhere near. But where?

All I know is that when she and I see each other, every drop of heaven will return to this world. The sun will shine once again—the stars will dance—the trees will breathe in the wind, flowing with its waves—forever dancing in the Garden of Eden.

Once again, the Garden will return. She is the Garden. She will bring all the world back to life, and it will forever shine once more, onward and onward and forever. I will shine in her light. God's light will shine through her and the entire Earth.

Once I hold her again, I will put away the bottle, and I will live every moment with clarity. But for now, ole Jackie Boy is treating me just fine, mighty swell and fine and righteously, indeed.

Ole Jackie and I spend these next forty-five minutes speaking nonsense to each other as I search for my very soul inside the seven-eighth empty bottle.

I'm already about six feet deep when darkness fully falls. The visions are sneaking in. They want to take me with them, to their lands. But I've got work to do. Not just yet, demons. Not yet.

I take my first shower since the war broke out—since the water still works on this fucking side of town—it's gloriously refreshing.

After I shave my beard off, I don the first pair of fresh socks and clean underpants in what feels like a year. I put on a non-bloodstained t-shirt, jeans, and my favorite faded denim jacket, rugged enough to take on the commie scum, cool enough for the southern summer heat.

My feet can breathe easier after putting on my favorite hiking boots. They pack a punch. The boots I've been wearing are severely waterlogged and simply nowhere near as versatile as my good old hikers. I can't wait to stomp on a few commie faces with them.

But now, now it's time; time to find her, to hold her, to feel the very gift of life as we touch, kiss, and caress. I can feel her light shining upon me now, like the sun. She must be close.

I walk outside into the open and peaceful air. I hurry next door and bang on the backdoor. I look through the windows and smash the door down. It's empty. They're not just hiding. They're gone. Who isn't? Is anyone left here?

Someone must be around. But why? Why would anyone stay here when they've had at least some opportunity to flee north? Perhaps she did? Maybe she left, and she's free. But why wouldn't she leave a letter? She wouldn't leave without letting me know or leaving some sort of sign.

I walk back outside, then I see him—the neighbor child looks at me through the window. His parents pull him out of view.

I fucking knew it. They must know.

I approach the house with a calm, hurried, adrenaline-filled stride. I knock quietly on the door.

"John," I say. "John. Let me in. It's Harry."

"Harry?" neighbor John responds. "What are you doing here? Come in. I thought you were dead."

John opens the door. As always, his hair's up in a man-bun. How East-fucking-Nashville of him. I hurry in.

His 8-year-old kid, Oliver, stands aside, waving like a little idiot. How could he not be, being John's child? Poor bastard. But at least he's no commie, that's for sure. He still has his humanity. I hope it always remains.

"Where is she?" I ask.

"Where's who?" John questions.

"Jasmine. Of course, Jasmine."

"You don't know?" John asks.

"No, I don't know," I respond. "Where is she? What don't I know?"

"She's with the commies," John states, simply.

"Shut your fucking lips—she's with the commies," I stand to John viciously.

"She's at their compound in Five-Points. That's all we know," John says. "They came and got her things a few days ago, and she's been gone ever since. She's a rat."

"She's no fucking rat, you commie bastard."

I knock John's un-smirking jaw off his somehow still smirking face with my boney fist. His wife Janet comes to his aide. Little Oliver cries out and runs to his room.

"Stop it, Harry," Janet screams. "Stop!"

I jam one more fist into John's nose, then throw myself off of him. Janet moves in to hug him.

"What the fuck, man," John says, holding his red-dripping nose.

"You're fucking lucky," I say and point at John.

Oliver runs out with a toy, "This i' for you."

Oliver hands me his stupid fucking little toy truck as tears drop from his face.

"I don't want your fucking toy," I say to the silly child. His parents gasp.

"What is wrong with you?" Janet asks.

Little Oliver pulls an envelope out from his wooden toy truck and hands it to me.

I rip the envelope open and read:

"Dear Harry, know that I love you and I'm doing this all for you. It's the only way. He's protecting me. I'm at the compound in Five-Points. As long as I do what I'm told and don't get out of line, I'll be fine. They respect me here. They really do. It's not all so bad. Just stay safe, Harry, and we'll be together after the war's over and the people lay down their arms and accept what's upon them."

I look over the letter again. How could it be fucking true, I ask myself. Who's protecting her? He? Who the fuck is he? How could she be living there? With the fucking commies? They're the ones who did this to us, to all of us. They turned our heaven on earth into a hell. And she's living amongst them? She is safe. But how? Accept what? The fucking commies? Their cold, heartless way of life? What have they done to my Jasmine?

Jackie Boy's not sitting too well in my belly now. He's churning. I feel sick and lightheaded. I turn to the door and walk slowly, and disoriented.

"See, I told you it was true," John says as he wipes the blood from his nose. "She's a fucking commie."

The rage rises inside me, and I walk fiercely to John, shove him mildly, turn around, and walk out the front door.

I walk with a total lack of purpose across the street to my own home. It sure the fuck doesn't feel like a home, like my home. It feels like total vacancy, a lost soul, an empty promise, a broken dream, shattered glass, an absolute void.

What has become of her? They're fucking commies. It can't be good. If she's there, where? How can I ever get to her now? I can't just sneak into the commie fucking headquarters, even if I do have on rat-garb. I can't speak fucking gibberish. Yet there is nothing that can stop me. I must find out where she is. What hotel? What casino? What room? How many commie rat guards?

That doesn't matter. I will bleed out every last fucking commie between her and me. She and I are destined for each other's arms. I will marry her and spend the rest of my days loving her. Nothing will stop that from happening. No force in the world can keep me from her any longer.

She will be mine again. I will bring the whole fucking world down with me if I have to; not that there's much of a world left after what these commie fucks have done to the place.

I quickly scrawl down a letter:

"I will get to you, Jasmine. This war will not keep us apart. Nothing will. You are the air I breathe and the heaven I long for. I'm so glad you're safe. But who's protecting you, Jasmine? How is he protecting you? Commies have no souls. You should know that. You must get out and we will go so far away from this place. We will disappear together and start a family. Come to the riverbank south of Korean Vets bridge on the morning of August 28th, at 2AM. I'll have a boat. And we will escape. Please be there, my love. You hold my heart in your hands."

I shove the letter into the envelope and walk back across the street. I knock on the door.

"Go away, Harry," Janet insists.

"Let me in," I demand.

"Get the fuck out of here, Harry," John yells.

"Just take this letter and get it to her if she comes by," I say, almost begging. "Please, John."

"Take your own fucking letter," John says. "I'm not giving shit to that commie bitch."

I kick the door loudly, then walk back across the street with the letter clutched.

I enter what was once my home and prepare a bag with my trusty knife, clothes, a fresh bottle of nectar, plus another, some various odds and ends, my toothbrush and paste; plus some tea tree oil, lavender, iodine, and cayenne pepper for my sanity and health.

I'm ready to walk out the door, but I hear a faint quick knock at the back door. Could it be?

I turn around and it's fucking Oliver—that poor dumb little bastard. What the fuck does he want?"

I open the door.

"'I' take i'to 'er," Oliver says.

"What?"

"Te letta," Oliver says dumbly. "I know'er' she-is."

"You do? Where is she?"

Oliver shakes "no" and says, "I take d'letta to 'er."

"Tell me where she is, boy," I demand, lifting the little bastard up by his collar.

"Vand'mor. Vand'mor' casino. In t'e pet-house," Oliver informs me.

"Penthouse?" I question, then set him down and go to storm out, but Oliver grabs me by the legs and holds on.

"Stop it, kid. Let go."

"You can't. You can't," he says. "Day'll shoot you."

"I don't care."

"P'ease, give me d'letta. I' get i'to'er."

"Oliver?" the boy's father yells from across the street. "Oliver?"

"Okay, fine," I state, handing the letter to the little idiot, just so he'll shut his little fucking mouth and I can go rip out every cold dead commie heart between she and I. "Take it."

"I promis' I get i'to'er," Oliver says as he hides the envelope in his trousers and turns to run back across the street. He pauses and hides behind some bushes, not wanting his father to see him.

And then, as I see John on his lawn yelling for his son, a commie patrol turns down the road. John moves quickly to hide, but it's too late. The patrol has spotlighted him.

John heads back inside and locks the door shut.

Oliver tries to run, but I hold him still and his mouth shut.

We see the six commies storm out of the truck and bang on the door. John doesn't open it.

"Gibberish, gibberish, gibberish," the commie filth shouts as they bash the door over and over.

I keep Oliver's mouth shut as the commies shoot the lock.

"Shhh," I whisper, then pull out my rifle and aim it through the front window, when...

"POP," we hear the gun blast. Then another, and another.

I pull the trigger. I pull again and again. Oliver runs out the front door.

Three commies down, three to go. Oliver runs out into the street and crosses it. The commies spot him. One aims their pistol at him. I pull my trigger, and red matter squirts out of the back of his rat skull against the door and his comrade's face.

Oliver doesn't flinch. He just keeps running. I smash through the tall front window and fire shot after shot at the doorway.

"Oliver, stop," I yell fiercely.

Oliver stops. He turns around to look my way with all the sadness of the world filling his little 8-year-old heart. I know that look. I know that feeling. This kid is me, and he, I. And he's just a fucking kid.

A commie peaks his rat-head out of the door. He ducks then looks back out to fire and his body falls lifeless. Like a dead slug, he drips down the wall.

The last rat of the patrol reaches his arm out and fires wildly into the street. I fire into the wall over and over. He slams the door shut.

I storm across the street past Oliver.

"Stay behind me," I demand.

Tears pour down Oliver's face, which has already aged at least twenty years in these last two minutes.

I change clips and continue firing into the door. I walk to the side kitchen window. I look in, then quickly cover Oliver's eyes when I see John and Janet bled out on the living room floor. The coldness of the commie's sets winter in early as ice fills my veins.

I see the last rat-fuck in a glass cabinet's reflection, talking on a walkie, frantically informing his command of what hath just transpired here in total gibberish speak.

I knock on the kitchen window softly. His attention turns to me, looking directly into my eyes through the reflection. I pop three rounds through the kitchen bar into his back. He flops forward. The walkie drops several feet out in front of him as the blood slowly begins to pour out.

"Oliver?" I ask with worry.

By the time I turn around, Oliver is gone. I see him run through the front door. Total dread fills his little heart when he sees his parents lying lifeless, John on top of Janet, trying to protect her in vain from the fucking commie filth. Oliver dives on top of them as if to hug them back to life with all his heart, dreams, and soul.

He's forever broken—a child no longer. From here on out, Oliver will be older than I could ever be. Few have had to witness such a thing. Oliver has just joined an elite group of the youngest of old men. He will never be a child again, that's for certain.

I walk around and enter the front door. I pull Oliver off his parents.

"We have to go," I tell him. "I'm sorry, Oliver."

"No, no," he screams in defiance. "Mommy! Daddy!"

"We have to go, now," I tell him.

Oliver gets that fucking look in his eyes. That look I know all too well. That look that Ken and Bobby fear; the animal. Oliver is too young for that, but there it is. He picks up a commie's gun and shoots the dead rat over and over, emptying the clip into the lifeless—already rotten body.

I put my arms around the crying boy and put the gun down.

"I'm sorry, Oliver," I tell him. "But we have to go now."

"No, no," Oliver screams repeatedly.

I grab one of his stuffed animals, carry him out the front door, toss my bag in the commie-mobile, buckle him into the back, then hop in and hit the road. Rage fills his little eyes. It fills mine just the same.

The only thing I want to do is storm that fucking commie fortress and rip the heart out of every last fucking one of them. But now, I have to take this fucking kid to safety, the little fucking bastard; the brave little cunt—dammit.

"Fuck these goddamn commie fucking rat fuck filthy cunt bastard fucks," I mouth under my breath as I drive along the dark streets, northwest, where we will be safe to swim across the river—too far north for the rats to patrol regularly—though they'll be on the lookout for us.

Almost before we know it, we're out of the truck and swimming across the muddy water. Oliver swims with all his raging energy but quickly wears himself out, so as he begins to sink, I help keep him afloat. The rifle weighs me down, but the rage keeps me going.

We make our way through the dark wetness. The night feels eerily quiet. Upon the riverbank, we wade through the muddy murk and hurry to shelter. Oliver just wants to run and run. But I need a fucking break. We sit down in a concrete gully. I pull out the golden nectar of the gods and drown the evil away.

I offer some nectar to Oliver. He is a man now. He deserves a little hair on his chest, for he will never be the same. In one single instant, the child was killed, along with his parents, and a man born. A bitter, sad, lonely, raging bull of a man. The wildest of animals. This poor little fuck will never know what a normal life could be. Forever at war, he will remain.

Oliver takes a giant gulp of the nectar and immediately coughs his lungs out as the heat pools in his chest. He looks at me like, "What have you done to me?"

I try to take the bottle back from the tiny little man, but he rips it back and takes another swig. He then slams the bottle back into my hand, stands with a cough, and says, "Let's go."

Not only is this little bastard taking me away from my mission to storm the commie compound, now he's giving me orders? Who does this little fucker think he is? Heather and Sam can worry about that. They're the motherly types—Heather at least. It will be good for her to have a child to look out for so she can get the fuck off my back.

Oliver leads the way.

"This way," I tell him.

He tries to continue. I stop and once again say, "This way."

He huffs and begins to follow me as I lead him back to the green door.

Upon return, the platoon welcomes and introduces themselves to the child. And just as I had figured, Heather tries her best to comfort the wild little man. Sam, who's feeling much better, tries to help, but I can tell she's out of her league.

Heather feeds and waters Oliver and attempts to console him, but she can recognize the broken look in his eyes. She looks up at me, as she always does, but with an even greater heaviness in her heart.

Heather takes me aside, "What happened to him? Why is there blood on his shirt?"

"They shot his parents," I inform her.

"Oh, God," her eyes say as they fill instantly with tears. She hugs onto me, squeezing the life out of me.

I let her have her moment but only offer a slight pat on the back in return.

She lets go, looks me in the eye for a moment to gather her strength, then returns to Oliver's side, whom I suspect, she will never let out of her sight again.

She is a protector. She only wants the world to be safe and free again. We all do. But her heart burns for goodness, for godliness. Though she also understands our fight if that fucking look is any indication.

20. Shadow Puppet

"YOU CAN'T JUST GO, HARRY," Deon says.

"Watch me," I respond, clutching my many weapons and a rucksack full of explosives, grenades, and ammo.

"Be careful," Heather says, forever giving me that look.

"Are you sure about this?" asks Vanessa.

"It's a suicide mission," Bobby stammers, still haunted from losing his friend.

"Good," I say, then walk out the door to no more protests.

I walk through the dark night; one mind, one mission, one final stand. They're going to fucking pay. She will be mine. I will sneak through the Vandemore lobby, up the stairwell, floor by floor, bloodletting every fucking bastard who dare stands in my way.

The silencers will be of use, but there's nothing quite like jabbing my freshly sharpened buck knife into their rotten commie throats. It always gives me a glimmer of satisfaction. I don't care for the smell, but I've grown to love nothing more than releasing their treacherous souls from their cold, heartless machine-like bodies.

A couple of blocks away from my river entry point, I notice a shadow following me. I stop; it stops. I walk; it walks.

It's that little fucking bastard, Oliver.

"What are you doing?" I ask the child. "You can't come with me."

Oliver just stands there, unmoving, with his little twenty-two rifle in both hands.

"Go back," I demand.

He shakes, "No."

"Go," I shoo him on.

He stands statuesque. I forcefully turn him around and push him on his way, then walk off. He turns and keeps following me.

"Stop. Just fucking stop, kid. This isn't your fight."

"P'ease," Oliver says. "Lemme take de letta. I can ge'it to'er."

"You're not going, kid," I tell him. "They'll shoot you on sight. Do you want to get shot?"

"No, zey won't."

"Yes, they will because you'll do something stupid. You'll get the rage, and you'll attack them, and they'll have no choice but to shoot you."

I turn and walk on. Then I feel that little bastard's hand reach in my jacket pocket and rip out the plastic bag holding the letter. The little bastard runs off towards the river.

I follow him slowly. He runs and runs and runs. He gets to the water and starts to swim across. I grab him by the back of his jacket and pull him back and toss him onto the muddy riverbank.

"Oliver, look," I take the letter back. "I know you want to help, but you getting caught with my letter won't do anyone any good."

"But I know ware she-is," Oliver says. "I taught you wanta get'er back?"

"I do," I tell him. "It's the only thing in this world I want. I don't care if the entire universe burns to ashes, then dust, then to nothingness, as long as she is mine again."

"Den lemme go," Oliver says. "It's-a only way."

"No," I state. "I'm going. You're staying. That's final."

Oliver aims his rifle at me with tears dripping down his reddened face.

"Really, kid?"

He aims. I standstill.

"Da letta," Oliver demands with a calm authority.

"Fine, you little fucker. Here."

I hand the letter to Oliver. He takes it and turns to the river. I pick him up by the back of his jacket and take his rifle from him. He swings his fists wildly at me while I carry him away.

"Pwease," Oliver screams repeatedly. "P'ease. Pwease."

"You're a fucking kid. You'll do something stupid, and you'll get killed. Look at you."

"No, I won't," Oliver squirms. "Leggo."

"Go back," I say sternly.

I set Oliver down, shove him back where he belongs, and keep walking along.

Then, that little fucking 8-year-old bastard's foot comes up from behind, right between my legs, and bashes me right in my boys. I fall hard, and that little fucker darts to the river with my letter and starts swimming his little fucking heart out.

"You little idiot," I shout.

I try to stand, but that fucker got me good. I crawl a bit on my knees, then give up and roll onto my back, then my side. The pain pulses through my body.

So, I simply let him go. "Maybe he's right," I ponder. "If he drowns in the river, I'll just tell them the commies got him."

"Guess I better not let the little bastard drown," I tell myself as I painfully make my way to the river and begin to swim behind him, just in case his little arms and legs give out from the 100-yard swim. And also to offer him a little cover once across, just in case those commie fucks are even less human than fathomable, which there's a pretty good chance of; them being commies and all.

I catch Oliver halfway across the river as he begins to sink beneath the current after pushing himself far beyond his little body's ability. He tries to kick me off but gives up once he realizes I'm taking him across.

Once we reach land, we walk south, stopping near the cement towers off Jefferson Street. Oliver's ready to go, but I force him to wait until sun up. They would never let him through past curfew. At the very best, they'd put him in a camp and steal the letter.

As we wait in the brush near the river bank, I do my best to keep the little bastard from shivering. Even in the Tennessee heat, after your clothes are soaked, you're still going to be quite chilly. And it is the chilliest night of the summer.

As Oliver sleeps, I snuggle a fresh bottle of nectar to keep my guard up for any rats; or stray dogs turned back to wolves from the war and lack of scraps, plus the artillery-induced madness which plagues every creature in the city.

After the sun has risen well enough into the sky, I'm having a few second thoughts, but I send the kid anyway. It is perhaps my only real chance to reach her again. And that's a chance I can't fucking miss.

"Be fucking careful," I tell Oliver. "Don't let your anger get the best of you. Make it like a game. You have to pretend they're your friends, okay? Then later, you will get your revenge after you've returned safely. Play by the rules of the game, and you'll be safe. Okay?"

Oliver doesn't say a word. He just shakes, "Yes."

"Now Oliver, smile and salute them like this," I tell him, showing him how to be a good little commie bastard.

Oliver repeats it rather perfectly, somehow able to hide the rage that boils inside him. Maybe this little fucker will be alright. But will he be able to keep it up, face to face with the wretched commie filth?

"Now go," I tell Oliver. "And please, for the love of God, don't be a little idiot, okay?"

Oliver shakes, "Yes," then runs off south towards the commie compound.

I scurry to the cement tower closest to the river with my AR-10, along with Oliver's twenty-two. I climb the rounding staircase up to the top, then find the best position I can, looking southeast. I can see Oliver run along as he gets smaller and smaller in the distance.

There seem to be no patrols in the area or atop any nearby towers. I'll take it. I guess they don't fear us crossing the river much anymore, with their tank, gunner, and sniper-filled fortress. With the bridges gone, they're surely not worried about a full-scale assault. Their concerns are with invading, not being invaded.

I lay, looking through my AR scope, zoomed in at the max of 12x. I can't see all the way to Five-Points, but I can see several commie guards, plus the first line of snipers who remain focused downtown. I'm fairly well covered from the south, but from the east, I'm fairly open to one with a keen eye in this smoke-free daylight. I can get lower, but I've got to keep my eye on the kid.

I watch Oliver through the scope as he runs along, nearing the first line of guards.

"Please don't be a fucking idiot, kid," I think aloud and hope. "Even a cold-blooded commie can't just kill a child? At least not one saluting them and pretending to be a good little rat. Don't be a fucking idiot, Oliver."

Oliver approaches the first commie guard line. They stand in front of him. He stops and gives them a big stern salute. They salute him back and step aside laughing. He runs on past.

"Commies can laugh?" I question, to myself, figuring. "I guess when it's commie shite."

Oliver passes more rats and is acting like a good little commie fuck, saluting all the men as he passes, somehow showing them respect while his heart rages with bloodlust.

The commies are getting a kick out of Oliver, laughing together as they mock the maniacal little boy, not knowing that at any moment I could rip lead through their chests, grazing their spines, and if not instantly killing them, paralyzing them indefinitely.

Oliver hurries on, saluting more commie troops, then saluting the next until finally, he's behind a corner and out of my sightline.

I wait patiently with the bottled fountain of golden youth in my left hand, my rifle in my right, checking every few moments; minutes; fifteen; keeping extra-low otherwise.

21. Muddy Waters

AFTER A LONG DAY OF BOOZE and partial slumber, the sun begins to set over downtown. There's still no sign of Oliver.

"That little fuck should be back by now," I figure to myself, still perched atop the cement tower.

Just then, I hear a gun blast and feel the warm heat of sparking metal fibers bouncing off my left arm.

I roll over as I hear another blast. I feel a bullet wiz by my hair. I'm ungrazed but open game for whoever's firing my way. I hustle to the staircase with my bottle and rifle clutched. Oliver's twenty-two hangs on my back.

A third bullet zooms by, shattering my two-thirds-full bottle of golden nectar, reigniting the rage inside me, "Jackie!"

I feel the fury and immediacy of the moment as I dive down seven feet to the staircase below. Nearly overshooting, I slam against the rail.

Where are they shooting from? Is it just one? Or is a whole fucking gaggle headed my way? Has he alerted his commie-rads? I'm sure of it. I gotta get the fuck out of here.

I set my scope to 4x for a wider view and look north, then check the rest of my sightline. It's clear.

I move down several steps and peek my head around the corner. I don't see anyone.

I start making my way down the staircase as it curves west towards the city, where I know I'll be safe. The turn south is what I fear.

It's still too high to jump without shattering both ankles, but I'd be totally open to the south, where the various snipers will be looking my way to see what all the ruckus is about.

After a short pause, I peek my rifle around the south corner. A shot rings out and grazes the staircase. I move back, but I've got to go.

Why don't I have a fucking rope? I've got every other fucking thing I need, but not a fucking rope. Or if there was just a ladder, like there used to be, I could just scale down. But no, everything has to be fucking "safe" now.

I twist my way slowly down the staircase as it winds southwest. I look through my offset iron sights, then peak out gently.

Then I see it, a commie rat fuck's rifle kicks back and rises with the spark of the blast, and before I can react, a bullet rips its way through some part of my right shoulder, my good shoulder.

My rifle falls, hanging on by the sling. I back up a few steps.

"Fuck," I pull back my shirt and jacket to check the wound. "That fucking commie rat fuck."

"This can't be it, can it?" I ask the heavens. "Why did I fucking stay up here, and where the fucking fuck is that little bastard, Oliver?"

Knowing that I don't have much time left in this world, I sling my rifle around my left shoulder, then toss a grenade around the corner and westward with my uninjured arm.

At the instance of the blast, I storm my way around the corner and aim downrange, pulling the trigger again, again and again.

I see one sniper behind a building wall 200 yards away. I shoot his way several times, aiming roughly through my iron sights, causing him to take cover.

Just then, another rat sniper begins to sling lead my way. I fire his way as I rush down the steps. I see a gunner truck heading my way from Jefferson Street to the east. The gunner aims me down.

I fling a grenade in its general direction, then toss Oliver's little rifle and leap off the staircase to the southwest, about twenty feet from the ground, holding my AR-10 low in both hands.

Machine gun fire ravages the tower above me as I fall loudly to the pavement. I do as good of a barrel roll as possible, but it's not great. And my rifle barrel is fucked. It's almost snapped off like the busted scope. My legs are fine, but I'm not so sure about my right ankle nor my bloody and possibly dislocated shoulder.

With certain doom heading my way in a constant stream of lead, I pick up Oliver's twenty-two and dash to the shoreline. The gunner truck quickly approaches as I sprint at full speed despite the numbness of my unsteady ankle. I trip, fall, and tumble as the pavement turns to grass, then to mud.

Unable to see me this low, the gunner sprays 50 caliber rounds into the ground in front of me, progressing ever closer as it moves towards my position.

Snipers fire, but just for intimidation, I'm guessing. Or they're just fucking terrible shots. Perhaps both.

With the gunner closing in, I regain my composure and dash low towards the river bank and what's left of the Jefferson Street Bridge.

I toss a grenade behind me, then burst to the first column of the bridge and dive. Mud splatters me. I can feel the vibrations from the 50 cal rounds smashing the concrete column that my back leans heavily against.

I'm pretty fucked now. I can't run into the river. I can't move south, nor in any direction. I'm stuck behind my only cover.

The gunner appears to have stopped, and it sounds like the men have gotten out. I arm myself with Oliver's little twenty-two but have my sidearm ready for when they get extra close.

I can hear their footsteps in the mud and on the gravelly pavement, closing in, approaching from each side.

I dive low to the east, around the column, shoot one commie twice down, then retake cover. The gunner starts to blast the area again, creating a mud monsoon.

The gunner pauses, I peak right, and a commie rat fuck has me dead to rights. I'm in his sights, and it's too fucking late—

I hear a bullet sound as I blink, and my entire life begins to rush through my eyes. It's Jasmine, only Jasmine, forever and only Jasmine. She's my life, my eternity. And it's all gone. All of this whole fucking thing—for nothing.

If only I had fucking gone last night instead of letting that little fucking bastard go. Why the fuck did I stay on that fucking tower? I didn't need to cover the little fucker. If he made it in, he could have fucking made it out. Why didn't I just fucking wait, dug in along the muddy riverbank? Now it's over.

I open my eyes to see the most beautiful sight I've ever seen as red splatter art bursts out of the commie's head. It's as if Jackson Pollock himself created this spectacular moment.

Did his pistol reverse fire? What fucking luck is this? God really is on my fucking side. Perhaps this is the war we've always heard about for millenniums? The war to end all wars, the end of times, good versus evil. Sometimes good must fight evil. Is this that time? It feels right.

This war has brought God back into my heart. I haven't prayed since I was a child, not much older than Oliver, but here I am speaking to God. I have been since I lost her. And he's been listening. Now I know I will get her back. Before now, it was only hope. Now I know.

That is until I hear the gunner truck start-up and begin moving in my direction.

"I'm fucked. I know it. Oh fuck—"

I peek around the corner, expecting my immediate end, but it's a sight to behold. These gibberish-spouting cunts are backing up with all their might. There are only four now.

The very moment I realize it, a beautiful red burst splatters from a commie's throat onto the truck's windshield like one of Pollock's finest works. Right afterwards, his buddy, the gunner, loses his head.

The other two commies are in panic mode. I fire Oliver's twenty-two relentlessly from my left shoulder, unknowing if their immediate demise is from me or blessings from the Lord himself.

I thank him, and I thank him more, asking for only one more thing; well, two, maybe three: The return of Oliver; the safety of Jasmine, and our reuniting love and escape from this damned city.

We've done enough for Nashville. All of the cities are doomed. It's the countrysides and the hills for us now. We know that. But which direction? Where will the commies not have every fucking route blocked? When will I hold her?

Knowing more rats will be storming, I regain my composure and race to the river. I toss the twenty-two away and swim frog style underwater for as long as possible until I desperately need a breath. The swimming motion, along with the dirty water mixing with my wound makes it feel like it's being pried open with a crowbar.

I rise up, then quickly re-submerge as bullets skid through the water. I can't see them, but I can sure hear them slap through the surface. And then they stop. Here it is once more, God's divine protection.

I come up to the surface for air and swim along in silent peace upon this great, brown flowing treasure, knowing that these bullets pose no threat to me any longer.

I reach the bottom on the downtown side of the Cumberland and wade through the mucky water. Shin deep in sludge, I crawl up to standing upon the glorious river bank.

Shots ring out, but I'm undeterred. I walk, slowly, fully enlightened, up to the road ahead.

Dirt, concrete, and debris dust my ankles as I make my way up to the sidewalk and out into the center of the street.

Then I see them, angels shining God's light upon me from the pointy tower of the courthouse. They shower the commie rats with lead bolts of lighting from their long-winged rifles, ripping apart the commie demon flesh, allowing their dirty souls to escape to freedom, to God.

They're thanking us. That's what the screams of gibberish are. They're crying out, begging God for forgiveness.
Now I know it. It's all so clear now.

"We are the chosen ones," I speak silently with blood
dripping down my arm from my open wound. "All of us, not
just me; we all are. Our mission: save humanity from the evil
commie demon virus for all of the freedom-loving people of
the world. He's here, protecting us. No bullet can harm me."

Yes, I'm shot. But that doesn't matter, for the hand of
God has touched me, and I am healed. The goldenness of it
all surrounds me, eviscerating my fears and freeing me from
bondage. I know right here and now that I will hold her again
and that God's light will shine upon us for all eternity. No
goddamned commie bastard can stand in our way, damn
them. Damn them all.

These commie bastards deserve every bullet-hole, piece
of shrapnel, and slash they get. And until I have my Jasmine,
I won't stop fighting the commie virus. This is our country.
This is our state. This is our city. This is our home. This is
our world. It's not theirs, and it's never going to be. This is
God's country. This is God's Earth.

As if out from the ethers, angels Deon, Vanessa, and Alfred appear by my side and lift me back up into the heavens.

"Let your daggers rain forth, angels," I declare, falling
weightless into their angel arms. They drag me to cover by
the rubble of the blown bridge.

Continuing to fire, the commies soggy lead plops all
around, landing everywhere but in us. The platoon fires back
across the river. Bobby hasn't stopped firing.

The Lord is with us tonight. The commies don't belong
here. They're beginning to learn that too—they will, soon.
Thou cannot fight something which thou cannot see, and
these commie fucks sure can't see us under the cover of the
Lord's nightfall which grows ever darker this night. We are

cougars, leopards, tigers, jaguars, lions in the night—any giant cat.

Just look at angel Deon here, the mighty jaguar. He lays
hidden. Only his eyes and smiling teeth show in the night as
he waits to pounce on his prey. If a commie's lucky enough to
spot him, it's already too late. He will tear you to shreds.

Then the cheetah, angel Vanessa, always on the hunt,
always protecting. Anyone in the cheetah's way and she will
end them with the fury of one thousand claws; master of the
M-16 and "the man-stopper," her mighty Desert Eagle,
which alone has freed the souls of dozens of commie wretches.

Then Alfred, almost a lone wolf, but he too, a large feline. A simple mountain lion? No. Alfred is the rare one, the
always elusive snow leopard. You will never see him coming.
He always has the position, the upper hand, the supplies, the
safe house, the base, the munitions, everything.

Step too close to Alfred, and he will rip you apart with
one paw while you're still breathing. Well, perhaps if Alfred
wasn't so skittish about flesh. Blood, he doesn't mind. But actual flesh and the thought of touching it, he doesn't go for
that. He goes for the jugular. He's a pussy vegetarian, and I
respect him for it. It almost makes sense. But as a cat, I need
to feel the commie flesh melt warmly over my paws as all of
God's blessings reverberate through my being.

Then there's Bobby the bobcat. Though he's no angel,
he's on God's gracious side. Though surely my Judas, I keep
him closest.

Ken—perhaps not a great feline, more of a house cat,
but a good and loyal one—brings comfort to the weary souls
when we return from battle, where he has remained this
evening.

The angels continue to tear open the commie demon
flesh with their leaded daggers until all of the opposing firing

ceases. The fight doesn't last long this night, for the commies know that it would be futile, if not downright suicidal.

22. Awakening From The Darkness

I AWAKEN TO A SHAKING feeling. Then again, I know that feeling. I know that hand. I open my eyes, and I'm back in the green bar. It's Heather smacking my face awake with her open hand, both front and back, over and over, in a fiery rage.

"How could you?" Heather shouts at me. "What is wrong with you? He's just a child. We're all he has now."

"Not anymore," I respond poetically.

"What? What does that mean?" Heather asks, then she shoves herself away from me.

Sam butts her druggie ass in and asks, "What's wrong with you?"

"What?" I respond.

"What happened?" Ken asks worriedly.

"He wanted to go; he went," I say. "That little bastard wouldn't take no for an answer. Believe me. I tried."

Ken throws his fist directly into my lips. It was a good one too. I turn and put my hand to my mouth. There's blood, more than I'd expect.

I'm surprised by him, almost pleasantly. I laugh at him with my bloody teeth showing. The blood tastes nice. Perhaps I'm just thirsty. I walk to the bar to retrieve the golden nectar of the gods.

Ken flips around in a tizzy and steps away with Heather.

Deon, Alfred, and Vanessa stand by, a little uneasy but mostly unphased. They're soldiers; they're used to these little tiffs; at least now they are.

"Good, he died," old Jasper speaks. "He's seen enough death and destruction for one life."

"He's not dead," Heather hopes and prays. "Don't say that."

"As good as dead, at least," Jasper spouts.

Heather ducks into Ken's shoulder as I duck into a corner with my very best friend, Jackie Boy.

Old Jasper hadn't seemed to say much in a while, or I've just gotten good at filtering out his rubbish stories. But he has a point, the boy has seen more than any child should ever witness; but there are those who have, even before this war, even when things were good, and in all the wars past, in the lands we try to forget—bless them all.

Even if letting the child go was perhaps cruel, I couldn't stop the little idiot. It's not that I have become cold. It's that I have moved beyond emotion. I'm enlightened now. God's inside me, living through me, flowing out of me. Perhaps he always has been, and I had just never cared to notice. I'm noticing now.

Through his three angels, God will free this city, then this world with other angels. We will soar freely again and build a newer, better, and fairer civilization upon the destruction of this one. Usury will be ended, and we will invest in each other, not in our overlords.

God will blossom on this earth once again; through the grass, flowers, and trees; through the animals and the clouds, water, and rain; through the rocks, and through us.

God will shine in this new world, and we will be the architects, all of us. We won't lay down vacantly as the monster devours us. We will chew up and swallow the monster down, and God will digest the monster and shit him back into the very depths of hell, never to return to this earth, for this is God's earth once more—it will be.

We all know it. I don't even have to speak it. They know. There will be love again on this earth. Soon, she and I will be together and live off the land. The puffy white clouds will dance with the breeze as the sun prisms through.

But for now, the nectar will suffice as it fuses my bloodied lips and soul back together, along with my newly sown shoulder. The morphine may be helping with that as it pushes me back into a darkened slumber—

My breath fills my lungs fully as my heart expands infinitely. I see her in the darkness, walking my way through the river, which sparkles like diamonds dancing off her skin. The stars shine off the calm Nile as the moon steps up to the top of the great pyramid, ready to dive in.

Lions swarm around, protecting us in this dessert of thieves. Giraffes eat leaves off the trees while zebras gallop about.

She comes to me. I'm stuck, laid back in the sand, but she's close. She reaches out for me as the light flashes.

Here she is, with all of the love shining in her heart and eyes, just as it always has, almost shining as if she were the sun. Her dark hair sparkles in the moonlight. Her eyes shine like jewels.

Closer and closer. I can almost smell her. I can almost feel her. Her scent overtakes my senses. My heart's ready to explode as we touch. Her body grazes upon mine, smooth and supple, a cool breeze dancing off my skin—my hands on her hourglass hips—hers wrapped around me.

She reaches down, from my chest to my belly, my hips, down to my thighs, and back up. I'm melting to her touch.

How has this happened? Did I just awaken from a horrid nightmare? What is this smell creeping in? What's happening to me? I'm beginning to feel distant. But still, here she is, touching my thighs as our lips lock and tongues dance with passion and joy. I sink deeper into the sand.

I slowly squint my eyes open. There's darkness all around. But still, the touch. But she's gone—vamoosed. All I'm left with is a damp darkness. Where has she gone?

I close my eyes and her hand continues making its way slowly up my thigh. I reach down and touch her lovely hand. It's cold. And dry. Hairy. Large. Really hairy.

I jump up, open my eyes, and see nothing but bright white eyes and teeth smiling like a mad child—and a corpse —a dead fucking commie rat bastard which Deon holds up as a prank. And just like that, Jasmine's lovely hand becomes dead rotten demon-rat flesh. They all crack up with immediate laughter.

I punch the dead commie fuck in the mouth, cracking at least three of his rotten teeth with my jagged fist. This really gets their laughter going as I beat the death from this rancid bastard.

At least some can find a hint of joy in this hell on earth. I won't know that again until I have her back in my arms. But I let the gang have their moment. They've gone through enough. We all have.

The devastation has ripped all but our very spirits from us. That's the one thing the commies will never take, no matter how hard they try. They can take our cities, even our bodies, but they'll never take our souls, nor will they ever take our freedom. For as long as our spirits are free, we can never be shackled.

This son of a bitch has the biggest, most dickish smile on his face as he dances the body in front of my face. Okay, the moments up. I shove Deon and the dead commie away.

"Cheer up, mate," Deon says. "Give your old matey a hug, won't ya, mate? Give him a smooch."

Everyone cracks up but shush silent once I pull out my handgun and pop a few hollow points right through the commie's rotting heart.

This shuts them up, minus a few, "I better shut the fuck up before this guy really snaps," chuckles.

"Jesus Christ," Ken exclaims.

"I was just having a laugh," I say in all seriousness.

Deon shakes my shoulders, "Cheer up, will you? It's a good day. We're alive. Doesn't that mean something?"

I grab Deon by the collar, and shove him. He's moved a couple of feet but isn't shaken. He stands up to me and grabs my collar. I grab his. He wraps me in a bear hug and says, "I love you, man. I know you're hurting, but you've got to loosen the fuck up."

"Get the fuck off me," I state while trying to shove him away unsuccessfully.

"We'll get Jasmine back, Harry," Deon tells me. "If it's the last thing we do."

Deon let's go. For some reason, my body loosens. I sit back against the wall and look around. Everyone's feeling my pain. Heather's looking at me how she always fucking does, with a little extra side of sadness. I close my eyes and rest my head against the concrete wall.

I hear four different feet stepping my way. They're each soft and dainty.

"Tip tap," I hear. "Tip tap."

A hand touches my shoulder. I want to shrug it off, but I accept it. Another hand touches me softly yet firmly and warmly. I feel something. I've been forcing everything outward and away. I've been unable to accept anything since it all happened, until this moment.

I relax my head forward before the tears well up in my eyes. The world will never see them. I keep my head buried between my legs as the salty water drips.

These people care about me; that's obvious. We have been through hell together. Maybe they feel just as awful as I do? Maybe they actually do know my pain, and I'm not solely alone in this world? Maybe there is still some humanity left in this world. Maybe God's love truly will shine upon all of us once again. That's what I'm feeling right now with these warm loving hands feeding me with the energy of life itself.

What had I become? I was losing everything. Have I lost my humanity just because I've lost her? I can't let that happen, can I? Or have I already? Is it too late? Is it all gone? Am I?

"Sorry—thank you," I say as I get up and leave the safety of the room and the warm, loving hands of the two women. I can't even be sure whose they were, but I know. I make it outside in the rank darkness, barely able to breathe.

I hear dainty footsteps step out of the door.

"Come back in," a soft, warm voice says.

I look up and see Heather giving me the same look she always does, yet a little softer now.

"Give me a minute," I manage to utter.

"Okay," she responds, reaching out with a glass, "Here's some water. Come in when you're ready."

I take the glass, "Thanks."

Heather returns inside as I sit back against the brick wall. I take a sip of water and try to find my bearings.

Am I coming loose? Is it over? Should we just leave and try to survive out there? I could never do that, but now I have other people I care about. Not as much as her, never. But these people are my family now. We must leave. But I have to get her first. But how? We can't just keep doing this. And where is that little bastard, Oliver? I pray he's okay.

The door opens to a whiny creak of its hinges, and out steps the timid Bobby.

"What the fuck's he doing?" I question internally.

Bobby doesn't say anything. He just sits down against the wall a few feet away. We don't speak a word. We don't need to. Now I know that he's just the same as me. All he wants is to live and love. But now, he knows may never get the chance. He's just another hopeless romantic trapped in the middle of this hell on earth. He knows who the enemy is just as well as I. It's not just the commie rat invaders. It was all around. It had been brewing for decades under the guise of this or that disaster, some upcoming climate apocalypse, terrorism, pandemics, racial division. In reality, that was all media madness, fear-mongering, false flags, divide and conquer. It's almost as if an alien invasion had occurred here. That's what it feels like. The commie scum; alien in nature perhaps, but not origin. It's here, and it's been here for a while. They can make it sound so great in theory, Marx and all. But in reality, always, in reality, it becomes a devouring machine, devoid of any morality, let alone humanity.

First, communism devours its host, then itself—forever starving itself as it starves its people of any nourishment—body, soul, or otherwise. The commie spirit swallows its own tail, always. And it always devours the host in the same cruel self-devouring.

This isn't a country that invaded. It was an idea. The commie invaders look just like us, diverse like us. They just speak differently. It's almost as if they are A.I. clones, an answer to mankind's inefficiencies, but we know that's not it. These are corrupted, brainwashed men. They've lost their humanity. And they've nearly stolen ours, but that's never going to happen. Sitting here with Bobby, I know mine is still intact. It's tired, dirty, sad, and nearly defeated, but my humanity will remain. All of ours will.

The freedom-loving people of this world will rise again and take back what is rightfully ours, this entire world. It's for us, the animals, and all of nature. It's not for the faceless government droids and the elitist of the elite bankers and CEOs. It's for all of us.

Freedom will once again shine in this land. We will never let them take that from us. Our speech will always be free. No more outlawing words or opposing views, even if hate-filled. We're stronger than to let words divide us; or skin color, religion, beliefs, or politics. No matter how much we disagree on this or that, we all must believe in the freedom for the individual, the individual being the most important thing in this world, including you and me.

For without our individuality, we would be nothing. We would be just like them, just like the invaders, just like the cold dead-hearted commies. The pandemic wasn't the virus; they're the virus. We will never succumb to their ideals. We will always remain free.

If we hadn't held firm in keeping our 2nd amendment rights, we would have fallen like the Czar in Russia when the Bolsheviks invaded and took control. Not here. Never here. We will never allow it. Not without one hell of a fight. A fight in which we would never give up.

My fight is to get to her and free her. Nothing will stand between Jasmine and I. She is the one, the light, my everything. I will do whatever it takes, even if I do have to lose all of my humanity to do so. She will pull me back, my Jasmine, just as these people have done tonight. But she, she will make me truly whole again.

23. Into The Night

NOW THAT NIGHT HAS FALLEN, the angels prepare their munitions. Alfred loans me his extra M4 to replace my destroyed one. We are all to be fully armed tonight with the blades of his majesty.

Even if they're all horrifyingly angered at me for letting the apostle Oliver go into the depths of the commie rathole alone, they are with me in this fight. If not, when would they see him again? Never, I can only imagine. I have forced their hand. No, God has.

Jasmine, my love, I'm coming for you.

Deon, Vanessa, Alfred, Bobby, Ken, and I step into the darkness of the fresh night with its waning moon. Our quiet steps, the only sound.

My shoulder is doing surprisingly well. The nectar has surely helped with that.

As we step foot onto 1st Avenue, a stiff breeze sets in, and the clouds begin to dump buckets of their tears upon us.

I turn, and all of God's light shines directly upon me; all of the darkness melts. There she is, in all her radiance.

I drop my rifle and slowly walk in her direction, then leap wholeheartedly into a sprint as time slows to a trickle.

She walks my way with a purpose. I can feel her feel me and I, her. This is it. She is mine again. This isn't a mirage or a dream. This is real.

That little fucker Oliver did more than his mission entailed. He has saved my entire fucking world. That little bastard brought me back from the gates of hell and delivered heaven to my doorstep. Bless the little fucking bastard. Thank you, Lord.

Jasmine and I run into each other's arms, and the world melts around us; we melt. I've never felt this fevered joy, sadness, and bliss. I never knew it existed. The entire world has disappeared, and it's only her; it's only ever been her. She is it. She is everything. The Lord has answered my prayers and has given me life anew, for she is free, here, with me again. I know she feels it too.

There isn't a single cell in our bodies that is not enlivened, lifted, freed, floating, and joyous. No matter what has happened, this is all that matters. Every hair on and atom in my body stands in ecstasy.

The rain pours down on us in near-total darkness, just like her deep soulful eyes, the very essence of God in a woman; her silkened skin alight with God's love. The world is alive again. The water dances around her body, through and off her hair, over her bosom, on down her thighs, all around. We hold each other and spin slowly in the dance of dances, the feminine and masculine colliding. Nothing could be more raw or natural. The sky lights up in a golden glow as fireballs erupt south of us—far south of us. It's glorious. Smoke climbs majestically in the golden glow as we dance together to the vibrations.

"Come on," Deon yells. "Yo, Harry. Harry. We have to go, now."

"Oliver," Ken exclaims. "Glad you made it, buddy. You are one brave little guy."

Oliver doesn't say a word. He just walks along, leading the way back towards the green door in the storm of the summer. Rain falls like a waterfall. Perhaps it's God's tears washing all of the pain and horror away.

Jasmine and I follow the platoon along slowly, hand in hand, arm in arm. They scurry along like wild animals in the night.

She and I, here again; this moment; now; only her, only now. I will never let her go again, not in this life, not in all eternity, infinity; any of it. I have her. She's here, and this is real. Thank you, God. Thank you for shining your light on me through her. We will spend the rest of our moments together in this heavenly world.

God's lightning and thunder strike down all of the evil upon this planet with golden flashes of light. She and I disappear from the platoon as they cross Church Street.

Dripping wet, Jasmine and I make our way up two stories of rubble towards a window that leads into one of the least decimated hotels. Most of the windows are already broken from the war's destruction, but the hotel itself remains standing.

We enter. I climb through a crack in the stone and metal debris, which nearly blocks the hallway. We dip and duck under, over, and around the jolting and jagged edges, pipes, and glass.

Water pours around us like a river as we walk up flights of broken stairs, around six-foot floor-holes, climb one railing up seven feet to the next available stair; until finally—there it is, the perfect room.

At the end of the dark red hall, untouched, perhaps totally dry, sits room number 527. It sits on the north side of the building. We can barely contain ourselves as we walk to the room, and alas, I shoot the door handle open. Jasmine flinches.

I take her by the arm and pull her into the room. We swing and jolt each other back and forth, flowing towards the bed in perfect harmony and rhythm. Pushing, pulling; lips, tongues, hands, arms, feet, legs; all wrapped up, dancing like the greatest ballet of the century—every part of each other.

Joy dances with every touch, flowing outward and inward, into each other, throughout our every fiber and cell. We dance, we play, we touch, we squirm, we breathe, we love. Our clothes litter the room.

I touch her. She touches me. Lower, closer. Not yet, but imminent. We savor the moment, every touch, every breath, a miracle.

Her gorgeous lovely beauty, so brave and so feminine in the darkness, alive in full. I'm overcome by it all. We melt together as she wraps herself around me, and through her, I am born again. All of God's light reawakens my every atom and cell. I am Adam, coming back to the Garden of Eden. She, my Eve. Back in the garden, the Earth is born anew, along with everything, and every piece of every one of us.

Tonight, it's the same, but different than all of the other times. She and I are different now. This war has hardened us both. I can see it. But still, our very beings are enlightened by the presence of the other. Our senses heightened, feeling things before unfathomable.

It's truly electric. Our lips all but spark as the holy war rages outside—only seeing her beauty in the golden flashes through the open window shade—feeling her, always.

On the bed, against the window, on the table, the counter, the chair, the floor, we dance. She screams. She moans. Our hearts beat as one. The entirety of the new world is being conceived here and now—Adam and Eve, reconceiving the world as it could be, where a new garden will be born upon the rubble left behind.

Back on the bed, we melt as one. Inside her, I dissolve completely.

We lay, breathing in the heavens.

I don't know if we're shaking the entire building or if it's God himself, but we are vibrating as if coming undone.

"Shouldn't we get out of here?" Jasmine softly whispers as we lay together in post-coital bliss. "Take me to the others. We need to prepare."

"Not yet," I tell her, then roll her over, and we begin anew as if more than three minutes had gone by. "Tomorrow."

I simply must have more. I am a wild animal for her. Not the animal which Ken and Bobby fear, but a ravenous lover for her and only her for as long as I live, throughout eternity.

Here, we dissolve together as one, into one, into each other. One. Only one. And now, just now. All the universe's love shines down upon us; together, pure love, free, flowing, melting, pouring, raining, dripping, dissolving, coming anew, always, free, freer, flying, floating, vibrating in totality.

24. Love In The Rubble

I AWAKEN TO JASMINE'S PERFECT naked body as the sun rays bounce off her curves through the extra-wide windows.

The day seems to drift along without moving; she and I intertwined. We want to flee, but we're not ready to move from each other for a single moment—I'm not.

There will be nothing getting between our love again. I'll make damn well sure of that. Not a commie, not a rat, not the entire fucking universe itself will keep us apart.

After the long and glorious night and day of passion, and after all the rain has washed away much of the stink of this war-torn city, once the Lord's thunder has calmed, and once the sun finally begins to fall below what's left of the skyline, Jasmine and I set out to return to the others so we can make our escape.

Down the broken staircase, down the railing where the stairs are missing, we wind and sink, down and down, to the lobby. I check the streets and remaining rooftops for commie patrols and scouts. It appears clear, so we crawl out through the broken window.

I keep Jasmine well covered under my arm as we head off to the green door bar. I'm fully alert, but there's naught a commie scent in the air. However, up ahead, we see various rebel militiamen. So, we take a left. But there's more.

"Stay close," I tell Jasmine. "You can't trust them."

"Okay," she says. "I trust you."

I have my pistol at the ready. The rebels encircle us.

"Relax," one rebel says. "Harry, right?"

"What's it to you?" I respond, holding Jasmine behind me with my left arm while my right hand rests ready on my holster.

"Let us help you," he says.

"Help? There's nothing to help with," I respond. "We're leaving, and I suggest you all do the same. There's nothing left here."

"But sir," the rebel asks. "What of our city?"

"Let it burn," I tell the rebels as I lead Jasmine out through the sea of parting rebels. "Come on."

"Anything you need, sir?" the rebel asks. "Anything?"

"Anything?" I question.

Another rebel opens a chest of tools.

A nice gesture, but I can't take my eyes off them or Jasmine. Though I do need a new rifle. And we can surely use ammo for the escape ahead. So, I quickly grab myself a trusty new AR-10, then stock up on ammo, mags, and grenades—a few smoke, but mostly the good old-fashioned kind—plus a couple of extra handguns. I quickly stuff them into a bag that one of the skinnier rebels hands me.

"If you need help with anything. You know where to find us."

"Thanks," I tell the rebel. "But we won't be here for long."

I lead Jasmine away as the sea of rebels parts once more. They gather behind and watch us walk off into the distance. That was a little odd, I'll admit. But I'm thankful they've had a change of tone since last I saw them. We are still on the same side in this.

If there were birds or butterflies here, they're be singing and dancing as Jasmine and I stroll along. The scent of spring almost cuts through the horridness of this wretched summer. But it's just the extra moist dampness in the air, plus the piled-up trash full of composting food rot, still-burning tires, and all of the various fragrant mounds of rubbishing rubble. That's all much worse from the rain, but at least some of the death smell has washed away.

I walk like a king. And she, my awe-inspiring glorious queen, queen Jasmine of Free Nashville, shinning in all her glory. Soon, we will begin life anew in a faraway land, which we will fill with fields of wheat, corn, barley, beans, greens, grapes, hops, and cannabis.

We continue into the shadows. I watch the various rooftops and alleys for any sign of the commie bastards. My nose raised for any whiff of commie rat stink. Besides, God is with us, watching over us. He will help see our escape through, all the way to a new holy land—just like he's keeping us safe now—how he brought her back to me. It won't be the only holy land. No, the whole of the Earth will once again be holy.

The ground you walk on is holy ground, Jesus said, I remember. Or something like that.

Once again, the people of the earth will know and feel it. Even this war itself has brought godliness back to us all. We can feel everything. Every moment of peace, sacred. Even the fighting has been noble and good, even as our tactics have gotten dirtier, even those moments shine of God's glory.

God is here, living with us, in all of us. We are God, and he, us, all of us. God lives even inside the commie but is fully trapped in the machine. God lives freely in and through us.

Only by freeing God from the cold commie machine flesh can God once again shine fully upon this whole world, his creation, upon and within us all, in all his glory, in our own, in freedom and free will itself.

The commies can devour our cities all they want. We will build new ones, where we will live totally free. We will live by the law of no harm, God's law, the golden rule. Do as you please as long as it brings no harm to others. Perhaps that's not what everyone believes to be God's law, but that's it to me—free will.

Even the godless commie sinners will be saved in the end. They may have to burn first, but they will burn and dissolve and melt, and their very being will be born new in the light of God. Something special is happening. With her and I together, the world will part like the Nile for us to make our way freely, everlasting.

25. Bye Bye Green

AND THERE IT, THE GREEN door. I knock the special knock, holding Jasmine. The door opens to the dim candlelit basement bar.

"You made it," Deon welcomes us. "About time."

"Hey everybody," Jasmine says to the group. "How is everybody?"

"We didn't know where the fuck you guys were," Ken says. "If you left or died."

"We're fine," I state in a much friendlier tone than I've taken since that fateful day. "Now, let's prepare."

Heather's still looking at me with that look while little Oliver sits by her side, drawing. He's wearing the same ragged clothes and his stupid little Indian Jones cowboy hat he picked up from the rubble off 2nd Avenue.

Oliver has just begun to draw. And he draws a lot. He draws and draws. It's all he does. And it's rather morbid. He draws little comics mostly. It's probably a healthy release. However, it would be nicer if he could paint rainbows and sunsets. His sunsets are filled with fire and brimstone, just like his broken little mind. His entire being is burning red.

The little man has no hope of relief in this life, like that which he returned to me. Now, I'm whole again. The poor kid will never know that feeling, not after what he saw. You can't come back from that. Not in this life. He will have to have his memory wiped and be born again in a new existence, possibly one far away, even dimensions away, some-where in life's grand beautiful infinince.

"How have you all survived?" Jasmine asks sincerely.

"You can always smell a commie rat," Jasper says, sniffing the musty air he breathes.

"Not all of us have," Ken states grimly to Bobby and Heather's agreement.

"You're all so lucky," Jasmine says. "Thank you all so much for keeping my Harry safe."

"He hasn't needed much help," Vanessa responds with a smirk.

"Only a little," Alfred says while going over escape routes on a large fold-out map of the greater Nashville area.

"God himself is watching over us," I say in all my truth.

Some of the crew look at me like they believe I've gone insane, but Ken understands. I can see this eases his weary mind. Now he knows that I'm on his side, for Ken is a God-fearing man. He could only see the animal in my eyes before. But now, now he can see the truth; and in Jasmine, for she brings all of the good out of me.

"Do you have it?" I ask Alfred.

"Almost," Alfred tells me. "We need to do some recon. We don't know what they captured last night. We leave the night after tomorrow."

"Tonight," I tell him.

"We don't know what's out there," Alfred says.

"Yes, we do," I tell him. "Commies. We leave tonight."

"What?" asks Alfred.

"Tonight," I tell him. "I wasn't sure y'all were coming."

"We have to" Vanessa responds. "Even the National Guard has left the city and regrouped elsewhere, aside from a few stragglers."

"So we need to leave tonight."

"We need intel," Alfred insists.

"I'm all for getting out of here," Ken says. "You know that. But let's be smart about it."

"They've taken the Gulch," Deon says. "Maybe even Germantown. Who knows how long until they take the rest of the city."

"Exactly," I say. "So let's go."

"He's right," Jasmine interrupts calmly. "They're coming."

"They're not coming," Jasper croaks with his old raspy voice. "They're already fucking here. They've always fucking been here. They're just sprouting now. And I'm staying right the fuck here."

"No, you're not, old man," I tell the old bastard. "You're coming too. We leave now."

"He's right," Vanessa agrees, always the most knowing and noble of the angels. "We need to leave tonight. And we're all going. They'll be coming for downtown sooner than later."

Alfred huffs, somehow convinced by Vanessa's always convincing presence, "Okay. But we must be smart about it."

"Northwest to Church," I tell them, having it all figured out. "West towards 21st. Cut through near the Parthenon, then head through the neighborhoods of Belle Meade; only a few miles a day if we have to. Then once we're truly free of the city, we'll commandeer a vehicle. Getting out of the city, now, is the important part."

God has shown us the way out. I can see it. We're done with the bloodshed. We need to wash our hands of it all. Perhaps the rain has. It brought her return; God has. I hold my Jasmine as if she is the jewel of life. She is.

Everyone's bags are packed full with ammo, explosives, toothpaste, packaged food, and anything else they can carry.

Ammo, explosives, and Jasmine are all I need now, no more nectar, for she is my nectar now. Jasmine and I follow the platoon out of the old green door for the last time, her first and final.

That ever so fateful time has arrived. We are truly off. We can finally leave the wreckage of the war, the burnt-up, and collapsed buildings, behind us. Fires again smolder after last night's invasion of the Gulch and bombardment in Germantown.

Will we ever again have to smell the rot of war? Or is it so truly burnt into our senses that we will never forget it? Perhaps we'll move beyond it all, but how? Will it not forever haunt each of us?

Little Oliver won't be able to move beyond it. He may bury it down deep within, but it will always remain with him wherever he goes. Saint or sinner, monk or businessman, it shall remain.

Holding my love as we walk one final time through all of the memories of this once living, breathing, thriving city is almost surreal.

Heather, Oliver, Sam, and Jasper hang in the middle of the group. Jasper's being oddly quiet out in these streets. Sam has also been quiet, but Heather was right. She's pretty much well from her newfound addiction. I'm surprised she made it.

Jasmine's just in front of them, right behind myself, Deon, Alfred, and Vanessa. Bobby and Ken watch the rear.

Dark and quiet, the night sits heavy. Moisture hangs at neck level. You can feel the fog forming. It will be thick this night; it's already becoming so.

The fog may be good or bad for us. For we can sneak beneath it or be gunned down by a patrol we walk right up to. But no, we are protected. We move like cats through the night. I protect Jasmine with my every instinct, shielding her from any unrestrained fire. Touching but not holding my rifle,

I'm ready for any commie movement or stink. My shoulder pains me, but it's beginning to heal.

We walk against the wall, making our way north towards Church Street, where we will head west towards Centennial Park.

26. Leaving The City

WE REST IN THE FOGGY night air while Alfred, Deon, and Vanessa do a little scouting. I sit back against a large oak tree, holding my Jasmine in against me. I caress her beneath the fog-line, our fruitful escape nearing completion.

"How are you, my love?" I ask of Jasmine. "We'll have to move again soon."

"I'm okay, Harry," Jasmine says. "What's going to happen to you? There's nowhere to run. What's all this really for?"

"What do you mean? We're going to start over, free in the countryside."

"That's crazy," Jasmine says. "They'll never allow that."

"Allow? They don't allow or disallow anything. What are you talking about? That's why we're leaving. We're starting over."

"Well, I just don't understand how you can be so foolish and how you think you can just start the entire western world all over again?"

"The free world will rise from the ashes. You and I, all of us, will live freely in the new land, living by God's law."

"Harry.. Stop," Jasmine says. "Just stop. You need to really think about this."

"What are you talking about?" I ask.

"We need to move," Deon interrupts and informs us.

"Let's move," Bobby says, ready to get the fuck out of Charlie.

Ken is certainly ready to leave this wretched place, yet he seems anxious, but I guess he always is when we're out in the streets.

I help Jasmine up. She follows closely as we walk south towards Midtown. Alfred and Vanessa lead the way. As soon as we step foot onto Division Street, a shot rings out, and old Jasper drops dead in his tracks. Bobby and Ken pull him back onto 19th Avenue. The rest of us cover fire.

I pull Jasmine back behind an alley wall. If only we'd gone through the fucking park like I said.

Bobby and Ken pull Jasper's body into the alley, out of firing range, but he's done for.

"Fuck," Ken says. "Jasper. Come on, buddy. Wake up, Jasper."

"He's gone," Bobby says, then takes his rifle, steps out, and lays down a wall of fire.

Sam hurries to enter the alley but stops and looks back.

"Sam," Heather says, holding out her hand.

As Sam turns to us and reaches out for Heather, a bullet bursts out the front of her heart. She falls motionless.

"Sam?" Heather screams as she pulls Oliver into the alley and grabs her handgun.

I take Jasmine by the hands, "I'll protect you, my love. We'll get out of here."

Jasmine kisses me with a quick adrenaline-fueled passion and whispers softly, "I love you."

Deon rushes back into the alley to reload.

"Let's get the fuck out of here," I tell him.

"Okay," Deon says. "We'll have to clear a path for the others."

"Okay," I respond, then turn to Jasmine. "Stay here. You'll be safe."

"I'll always love you," Jasmine tells me.

"I'll be back soon, my love. I promise," I say, holding her close. "I'll never let anything happen to you."

"Okay," Jasmine says. "Just go, get us out of here."

"I will, my love," I kiss her, then move in to huddle with Ken. "Stay with her. Protect her."

"Okay," Ken tells me. "I will. Of course, I will. I see it now, Harry. You were missing a piece of yourself. And now you're back because she's back. And tomorrow, we'll all be free of all of this."

"Thank you, brother," I hug Ken, then look him in the eyes, trusting him with the very lifeblood of my soul.

Heather's still giving me that fucking look like she's afraid, but as if by looking at me, she's not afraid, yet even more afraid. She holds little Oliver back from the fight. He's ready with his little rifle and stupid Indiana-looking cowboy hat, but she grips him tightly.

I take my Jasmine's hand, "I'll see you soon, my love. Just stay here. I'll be right back."

Jasmine kisses me goodbye, then stands back with her deep dark eyes in near-total darkness. I take my rifle to join Deon, Vanessa, Alfred, and Bobby to part the very seas we're soon to cross.

Our lead will spray the commie rats and suffocate their bloody lungs, and we will walk through the sand to freedom like kings and champions.

But here comes stupid little Oliver running up beside us, aiming his new twenty-two downrange at the commies. Heather runs out after him. I begin firing, but the night is dark and fog heavy.

These are not ordinary commies. These are their more "elite" rats. They're preparing something. They're surrounding the city. If we had waited any longer, we'd be finished. God brought her back to me just when we needed to flee this doomed place and flee we will. Too bad ole Jasper won't be around to see it.

And right then, when I finally have this commie in my sights as the fog washes over his soon-to-be bloody lifeless body, a gun fires twice, but it wasn't me. Nor was it little Oliver next to me. It was behind me.

I turn and run back into the alley, and it's her. We lock eyes, unmoving, un-breathing.

My heart drops out of my chest, my stomach rollercoasters, my senses deaden. I can't move. It's impossible.

Could it be true? Could she really be?

Jasmine drops her snub nose forty-five slowly as a warm flowing cloud of smoke pours out of the barrel. It falls heavy on the asphalt.

After a brief moment shared, Jasmine turns and runs through the alley, hops into a truck bed, and off she goes. Ken lays bleeding at my feet. I stand heartless, dead, completely lifeless. I'm unable to even fall to the ground. I'm already six feet below.

Heather runs into the alley to find Ken, dead on the ground at my feet, and asks, "What happened?"

"I don't know," I whimper out, barely audible.

"Ken," Heather cries out, then looks at me. "Where is she?"

"She's gone," I say in a true monotone. "She's gone."

"What happened?" Deon runs in.

Little Oliver pokes at Ken's corpse with his rifle, then checks his pulse, looks up, and says, "Dead." He then shuts Ken's eyes.

Lord, please let this be a bad dream. Everything holy is desecrated. Is she gone for good? Have you gone with her, Lord? I'm gone. I am no longer here. My heart is gone, dropped, sayonara, goodbye, see you next life—never. I'm fully shattered, non-breathing.

"Retreat!" Alfred runs up, yelling. "Retreat!"

Vanessa follows, "We've got to go. Move."

Then she sees Ken lying dead on the hard ground. She falls to him, "Ken?"

"He's gone," Deon says. "Let's go."

"Where is?" Vanessa asks, pausing as she sees me in stunned silence.

Deon almost asks, but looking at me, he doesn't even want to know.

Everyone scurries off down the alley, northeast, back into the fucking rotten, putrid city, the deep dark never-ending dampness; our numbers dwindling. I follow them slowly in our retreat, moving vacantly.

Deon runs back to me and pulls me faster as bullets spray non-uniformly, "Let's go."

The rest is just a blur as we trot along in the rancid darkness.

Before I know it, here we are, back at the ugliest fucking site I've ever seen, that green fucking door. But behind that stupid fucking green door, layeth at least a few bottles of golden reviving potion, which is all I will ever need again. What else can keep me going in this lost, godless world?

The others enter and regroup. I only do so to grab a bottle, then quickly exit to grabs, tugs, and pleads, which do nothing to keep me.

I prow the streets with a handle glued to my hand. I try desperately, but no howling will come. My voice is gone. I can hardly breathe. I pour the potion down the back of my tightening throat, which burns its way down into my chest.

All I want is to howl at the moon. But I am no wolf. I am a lion. And I will save my rage to devoir the commie filth from the depth of the silent shadows or lay here burning as the world burns beneath my feet.

27. The Boom Boom Room

UPON AWAKENING IN SOME alley ditch to the sunlight burning through my eyelids, I grab what's left of my nectar and stumble back out onto the street.

Things feel real, for perhaps the first time. Heavy. Real fucking thick and heavy. Where you feel, breathe, hear and smell everything. And it's all thick and terrible, revolting and dead. Death abounds, yet the rats flourish. Their population has grown one-hundred-thousand fold, at the very least, since this all began.

God is gone. That's why things feel real here because God has left. No more magic. We're swimming in the godless murk and grime, the gutters, the sewers, the filth, and scum.

The air is thick with all things horrid. That's why it feels real. It's rotting, all of it. You can smell the wood rot, the garbage, the flesh rot. We're the lost souls forever in the void of nothingness, devoid of anything good. Dark, damp, and ever lonely.

God has left this place, perhaps this entire world. I'm left with nothing. God vanished and stole everything good with him. Only the devil is left here as this world burns. Perhaps it needs to burn? Perhaps I do? Perhaps we all do?

Just think of poor little Oliver. Just look at him. How could there be a God here? We're not fucking chosen.

With the seven-eighth empty bottle, I stumble back into the dark and dirty green door bar, where we remain safe for the time being. Alone, but safe.

The day is long and heavy.

It washes away as quickly as it came.

Now that night has fallen, Bobby is on the lookout atop one of the nearby buildings. We know they'll be moving into downtown imminently, so we must keep a watchful eye.

The nectar moves time swiftly in this broken world.

The green door swings open, and Bobby rushes in.

"They're coming," Bobby panics. "Now. Let's go. They're coming. From the south."

"We'll take them," I say.

"There's too many—dozens—at least," Bobby stammers.

"Hurry," Heather says, leading Oliver to the door with his small go-bag.

Alfred, Vanessa, and Deon gear up and join at the door.

I slowly grab a stash of nectar and my weaponry. And while doing so, my mind begins to veer into avenues it has never drifted before. It's thinking more, planning, processing, adapting, brainstorming. And there it is.

I reach into a bag we have stashed away in the back to find all the makings for a booze-inspired tripwire which will ignite the C-4 and the 151 and fry the bastards.

My brain is working in ways I can't explain, and with only one goal: to do what Jasper had said, to rip every last thread of commie virus from this universe.

I tell the others to go ahead while I set the tripwire trap. They're not happy about it, but they go on without me.

I set the trap back by the bar so that we don't just get the first few. Once set, I turn on Jasper's little windup radio. It won't play anything, for there is nothing for it to play, but they will hear the white noise, the white noise of their impending doom.

I sidestep the tripwire and quickly make my way out into the alley to join the others. We disappear into the darkness just as the commie patrols spotlight the alley. Dozens of young commie rats run towards the green door.

The platoon runs on, but I have to watch. Which means, so do they as they stop to fetch me—when, "BOOM!"

"Commie-go-boom, Commie-bang-o, the boom-boom-commie-room," I almost laugh as my dead heart pumps several pumps of fresh blood once more.

Smoke fills the alleyway, while gibberish screams and shouts cower away. Deon and Alfred pull me off the corner and drag me along.

We move north towards Church Street. Vanessa and Bobby run on ahead with Heather and the child.

I follow the six ragged bastards down the sidewalks in the night as my mind disappears into the murk and grime, between and into the cracks and crevices, and rot, and grime, and death.

I stop once again, for I know, I know it was her. That's why they came for us. She has lost all of her humanity. She's just like them now. Her poor sad spirit locked inside a cold dead commie-hearted machine. My heart stops once more. I can never tell the others. I couldn't. I couldn't look at them. I can't. I continue onward, trailing behind.

That's why she was asking all those fucking questions; about our supply and ammo and fucking everything, that commie bitch. How did they turn even her commie? How did they infect my pure Jasmine? Just yesterday, I felt love in her. It may have been a colder love, but love nonetheless. I thought it was the war, not this. There's still love in her, so she can't be full commie. The godless commie can only do machine tasks as their souls rot in the commie prison body-mind. There's still time.

"We need to go, Harry," Heather says, tugging on my resown denim jacket with that stupid fucking look on her face.

I know it's not her fault. And perhaps she's the only sane one of us left, the only speck of God left in this forgotten land; at least the only speck of humanity. The others aren't bad, but she is truly good. Just if she would get that stupid fucking looking off of her face.

"Fine," I almost yell at her. "Let's go."

She's right. We need to move quickly. You can smell the commie tonight, and not just their burning flesh from the C-4/151 tripwire blast.

Of course, I'm ready to disappear for good into this dark night, but what chance would I have of ever seeing her again if I were to? Why do I still want to? Could I even reach her if I were right in front of her? Or is Jasmine already too dead inside?

Heather, Oliver, and I catch back up with Deon, Vanessa, Bobby, and Alfred. They walk along carrying what's left of our goods and munitions, always keeping a cautious eye with nose lifted for any scent of the commie stench up ahead.

"Here," Deon hands me my bag of weapons and ammo. "Carry your own load."

Then Bobby hands me my sweet sweet nectar. Perhaps God hasn't fully left this place, as even this small moment seems to touch my very core. But without her, here I stand alone; again alone; forever alone; here alone, always.

They're here with me, yes. And perhaps I do care about them and their safety, but I had her, and now she's gone. You can never know how that feels, when the love of your life is here, then gone the very next moment, into the commie darkness, turned into all that you hate; when all the light in this world was shining upon you, then it just goes dark, all of it. No more love. No more warmth. Just cold, cold heat, burning frozen eternally.

No soul will ever know of her treachery. I couldn't bear it. I can't. It hangs on me like vomit chunks stuck in your throat the morning after an open bar. It just won't go away. It's almost attached to you now. You think sleeping it off might make it go away, but you wake up, and it's worse, and it's where no fluid can get to it, almost like it's under your skin. That's how she feels now. Deep, burying inside, making me wretch.

Her love has turned to black sludge flowing forth from her open mouth and black-blooded eyes. The commie wretched filth fills my nostrils—forever burnt and singed.

28. Quest No. 1

THERE IT IS, IN THE NEAR dark distance, the fucking library, not one hundred yards away.

I follow slowly behind what's left of the platoon, down old Jasper, Sam, and Kenneth McColmes. I never knew Jasper's last name, but the old bastard had grown on me. He understood the commie virus, perhaps better than any of us, and it finally took him. All that time in the shit, and here, in his old age, he gets got by the commie.

Sam would've probably had a better shot staying here with the addicts than going to the green bar, but Heather's heart was in the right place. I guess old Jasper should have stayed put as well.

The rebels make way for the platoon to enter the library.

Instead of following the others in, I set out on my own, walking right past the entrance and on down Church Street. I guess I'm just not in the mood for socializing. I have only one purpose now. I keep low over the railroad tracks as I make my way towards the Gulch. I know the rats will be guarding these positions. I will snuff them out, burn them down, and send them to the river Styx.

I can smell a few rebels following behind. They have a different stink, but I know it's them. They know to stay back. They know this is my fight.

I walk alone into the maddening darkness, sawed-off shotgun in hand, rifle on my back, dual pistols at my sides. I slide, building to building.

I hear them, that same fucking gibberish. Sure, I could blast his brain clean out of his skull with my sawed-off monkey fucker, but that would attract too much attention. And tonight, I don't want attention. Silent, I will be this night.

There it is, the perfect tool.

The men approach without noticing me, "Gibberish, gibberish, gibberish."

These are the leftovers, glorified security guards, not warriors. It's only two of them when it had sounded like seven. Perhaps I feel like a challenge at this moment? Whatever the reason, I pick up a slice of cement and a rock. I toss the rock through a window across the street and watch these two dumb fuck bastards come running by. Stone in hand, I whistle.

The two gibberish-spouting bastards actually think they have a chance. They smile at the thought. They're some pretty big bastards. You can tell these rats only eat swine.

The largest rat pulls out his knife while the other grabs his nightstick. I laugh, then subtly wind up and sidearm this piece of cement straight into the little knife-wielding pussy's rat-nose. The knife drops as hard as he does. That was a mistake. The pain from my shoulder wound once again pulses up and down my arm.

Nightstick bitch walks my way, ready to slap me silly. I toss dirt into his eyes to slow him down. He's angered. He swings, and swings, as do I. I get couple punches in, then he gets me one in the chin with a backswing, and it fucking hurts. But I need to hurt. Because now, it's his turn to hurt. Though I'm not here to hurt him, I'm here to free him.

The pain I inflict on him over these next twenty seconds will last this commie bastard for eternity. And he'll be better off for it. I can only imagine what the rebels following me think I'm doing to these poor wretched commies. Their screams echo off in the distance.

Now, it's his buddy's turn. Granted, knife-bitch can barely even see now, or stand. He spouts gibberish at his buddy, but his buddy has stopped responding. I didn't bring about this war. This war was brought to me. It's not ever this poor bastard's fault that I'm about to cripple him for life and take his scalp. Never a war has been made without the money men being involved: the banks, the councils, the presstitutes, all of them. Clean out these bastard warlord leaders of all these fucking wannabe empires, Lord; every one of them; our own. Send a great flood, God, if you're so great. Yeah, yeah, free will—okay.

This half-blind, puffy-eyed rat starts shooting at me, and just in case he gets lucky, I use his little buddy's corpse here as a shield. Since he's making so much noise, I grab my sawed-off shottie and blast that fuck-dicker's leg in half at the knee with two point-blank buckshots. Now I can understand that fucking gibberish once more. This poor fucking rat bastard is talking to God. I brought God himself to this fucking commie wretch. He should be fucking thanking me; so should God. I'm doing his fucking dirty work, am I not? And what do I fucking get, God?

You can never understand a commie bastard. It's just gibberish until you slit their throat. Then we all speak the same language, the unspoken language of life itself. Death will be this rat bastard's sweet release. I can hear it. He's howling to God, praying I'll release his starving spirit from the bloody, rotten, dirty commie flesh he's trapped within.

"Night, night," I tell the poor bastard before I kick his teeth in with my trusty hiking boots.

"Tell me this is all just a fucking nightmare and wake me the fuck up," I demand, as I continue to beat this commie fucks face into a pulp, screaming out into the night for my Jasmine.

My lovely Jasmine, how hath God taken her from me again and turned her commie? Is this another fucking test? If it is, I will never forgive—no man, no God, nothing. Fuck your tests.

After the reckoning's over for these two rat-fucks, I claim my prize, dawning one prize atop my head. His commie blood drips from his scalp upon my own. Mad? I haven't gone mad. Not yet. Though I probably shouldn't show the others.

I hear footsteps approach quickly to a stop. From kneeling, I stand slowly with my back turned to the man.

"Gibberish, gibberish, gibberish," I say in 'commie' speak to the poor young rat.

I turn around to see him dripping in fear. His gun shakes tremendously. His fear drips heavier than his comrade's blood drips from my lips. He tries to run. But it's no use.

I blast him in the back with my sawed-off. He falls. I walk to him and turn him around. He screams gibberish until I shove the shotgun into his mouth and make him deep throat a buckshot. His wails echo off the quiet brick walls.

I know more will be coming now, so I pull out my trusty new AR-10. I toss off my dripping warm hat, wipe my face, and walk straight towards the commies in the Gulch.

As the road narrows up ahead, I spot an enclave of commies; a true fucking rats nest. Before thinking, I toss a grenade their way and take cover behind a white planter. They pile out. One by one, I pop them down with ease, almost too much ease, particularly with the grenade's help, along with the second one.

It's dark and cold, but the sun is already starting to rise and shine through the smokey haze from the horizon. The commies run for cover but cover they will not find, not on this day. Through the fiery haze, I lay out one rat after another.

I empty three full clips, then begin walking through the street as a dozen commies howl their dying breaths. Some run towards me. Some run away. Whichever direction they run being the wrong choice. I will slay at least three dozen of these commie bastards this moon.

Out of nowhere, a commie appears, ready to pop my head off. Before he has the chance, on pure instinct, I jam my buck knife into his chest. I pull on it, but it's stuck. That's gotta hurt. As another commie-rat runs for me. I take his friend here as cover, and he takes three rounds in the torso. I spring towards the gunman, shove his friend, and shoot him down.

The majority of his comrades run away, except for one huge rat-fuck who is ready to go. He drops his gun and approaches, ready to rip my head clean off my shoulders.

I drop my pistol, but I'm just not in the mood any longer, so I flip my rifle around and pop the big guy three times in the chest. I stand over him and pop him once right between his retracting eyes.

"It's his lucky fucking day," I think warmly to myself. He would have made one wretch of a blind-crippled-speechless commie-rat.

It appears the fleeing commies, instead of fleeing, just went to get their comrades. Dozens more begin to storm my position from up the road. To my luck, several rebels begin to pour lead through their commie flesh. I stand and watch as they drop one by one.

I rip my knife back out from the one rat's chest and retreat back behind the rebels. I've had enough fun for one night. I need my nectar. I'm all out.

All in all, it was a good night.

29. The Library

I WALK, DRIPPING RED, BACK into the library. No one says anything as I enter, but Heather's look says it all. It's the same look, but I'm not so sure the blood's helping—it's not my blood. Little Oliver sits beside her on the floor, eating a sandwich. The rest of the platoon sips wine, gathering themselves in their new abode, trying to remain hopeful in this hopeless city.

The rebels seem to have an odd—I don't know if it's—respect or affliction for us, particularly me. Or is it something more sinister? It's hard to tell their level of suspicion with their cockeyed, slanted, drugged-out faces.

They almost circle us like wolves, keeping a distance but a constant eye. I don't like it. I don't think anyone does. But we're safe here, seemingly. We're on the same side, but I must keep an eye on these sick puppies. I know what many of them are, and it's not good.

I've seen what they were trying to do to the women, to Heather. How they turned Sam into a dope fiend, and who knows what else. If they could do those things, what else could they do? There's certainly no humanity in what I walked into.

I took care of it last time. Would I be so lucky now? Would Heather? Or even Vanessa? We better get out of here soon. That's all I know. But where else is safe? The commies are coming. We know that. All of Alfred's National Guard mates fled. They couldn't stop the commies, so all but a very few have left.

All that remains in the city is this rag-tag group of rebels comprised of unlucky souls, misfits, weirdos, several near-do-wells, plus a few musicians still hanging around for the morphine drip. We're all on a mission together, no matter if we like it or not. We're all here for the same reason: to destroy these invader rats, to smoke them out, to expire them.

There are no politics here, only fight, only joining together against the common enemy, the commie virus that just will not go away. There's no vaccinating the commie virus away.

The only way to defeat the virus in the future; if we ever make it there, world intact; is to never let their kind into positions of power again, to clean them from the schools, to teach our kids about the importance of freedom, and to always be wary of those who aim to take our freedoms away, no matter what righteous cause they claim.

Never again will we give power to those curtailing our rights, our humanity, our souls. They don't want you to be free. It's what they fear most, but freedom has given us everything. Freedom is our birthright.

The commie virus wants to take all of that away from us and make us cold, functional machines. Especially this new strain of tech-commie, the ones who have been systematically curtailing our freedom of speech for decades, along with tracking our every move. Time for commie to go boom— once I get some rest.

After a surprising amount of sleep, I'm ready for more, but the platoon has other plans. With darkness closing in, the others are still intent on escaping south. I'm over escaping. They should know that. This is the last home I will know; this city. We will die here. We all will. I know it.

The platoon continues discussing escape plans, scouting missions, diversions, and this and that. I just sip the bottle with myself, ignoring their questions and discussions.

There is no escaping. We never had a chance; perhaps if we had left after those first couple of days like Ken wanted. Now, there's no chance. It's too late. I doubt there's a place in this world free from this commie hell—not yet—not one we can get to anyway.

"Perhaps we could get a plane," I ponder. "How hard can it be to fly? I'm sure Alfred can."

"But we'd be shot down immediately," I know it. "We're here. We'll always be here, and only here. Just us. Alone. Forever. Until we're sent to God, finally freed from the prison this earth has become, free from all the wars, and death, usury, and deception."

"Harry? Harry? Harry?" Vanessa questions, shaking me.

"What?" I ask with zero care.

"It's time," Alfred says. "Are you coming or not?"

"Why?" I question. "We're not getting out of here. Not alive. No one is. There's no escaping."

"We're scouting our route tonight," Alfred says. "And we're leaving tomorrow."

"And going where?" I respond, almost laughing.

"Southwest," Alfred says. "We go to Dallas. It's pretty much free of the invaders."

"You don't know that," I say. "And getting there?"

"We'll figure it out," Deon says. "It's now or never."

"Then I choose never."

"Come on, Harry," Vanessa all but begs.

And then there's Heather giving me that same fucking look. It's probably that more than anything as to why I agree, just to get out of the damn room.

What does she fucking want? What anyone wants. Peace. Friendship. Family. Love. But that's all gone. We're all alone now. But still, I agree. And it's all her fault.

"Fine," I say. "Let's go. But you do know I'm not leaving."

"Fine," Alfred spits fire my way. "But we are."

Bobby, Vanessa, Deon, and I ready for the door.

Heather holds little Oliver tightly so that he doesn't follow us.

Alfred collapses the map back in upon itself, grabs a long camera bag, spurs for his rifle, then joins us as we exit the library. The five of us head south towards Broadway. It's dark, as usual. It smells, as always. The only difference in tonight is that all of my fucks are gone; none left to give, not a one.

The rat-bastards are everywhere now. It's more likely than ever to get spotted by a commie patrol or sniper rat.

We know the commies have taken parts of the Gulch, and things don't sound good up in Germantown either. So, I guess it is good to know where they'll be coming from when they march on downtown.

There's not a sound in the city tonight. It's dry but overcast, casting a deep darkness over us, blocking out any moon or starlight. That's good for us. We creep through the darkness as we make our way closer to the big art museum and Union Station, much closer to the commies in the Gulch than we would like, but perhaps the best vantage point.

We set out for higher ground and make our way silently to Union Station, which is still mostly untouched by the war. We could have gone directly to higher ground a couple of blocks from the library, but I'm not asking questions tonight.

We climb our way to the top of the tower. The view is almost as wide as the city itself. We can immediately see that they'll have to make their escape further north.

After what feels like an hour, Alfred has his camera set up on the stupidly heavy tripod that he lugged up here. No wonder it took so damn long to get up the stairs. I thought he was just being a massive vagina, but that bitch is heavy. I know because I had to carry it the last few fucking flights as we took turns lugging it up. Good thing my shoulder's feeling better.

Alfred holds the corded button down as we wait. Then, he moves the camera ever so slightly. Then again. We wait. Then again, we wait.

As the rest of us wait, we eye various commies down through our scopes. First wide, then tight, then wide again. We see several rat-men in the Gulch, but only two or three of them pose any threat. We keep our eyes on them just in case they catch a glimpse of us, which is unlikely under this cover of darkness.

With a commie standing right in my view, I'm ready to pull the trigger. He's smoking a cigarette with his thin, twirly fucking dark mustache and commie rat-hat. If I didn't know any better, I'd say he was a twit from the west coast. A lost tourist turned pussy commie but a commie through and through.

I want to see what his blood splatter looks like through my scope, re-sighting him quickly after the ghost kick. But I wait.

Again, Alfred moves the camera slightly and holds down the shutter for a long exposure shot, turning dark to light. Hopefully, he's not fucking it all up, considering it's a film camera. And hopefully, he has the dyes and what-the-fuck-ever-you-need to develop real actual film photos.

They need the photos. I get it. I don't need any fucking photos. I finger the trigger, toying with the action-point, aiming this cig-smoking cock-dicker down in my scopes.

Puff, puff, puff, he sucks away at his ciggy. The smoke twirls out from his hairy nostrils. I play with the trigger, and I play with the trigger.

"Eeny, meeny, miny, moe. I smell a dirty dead commie, and you are not, not, it," I think to myself as I pull the trigger past the breaking point and watch the cigarette drop from the rat's lips.

The rebels sure gave me a properly sighted rifle. Maybe they're not so bad after all.

"Dammit, Harry," Deon whispers loudly.

"We need these pictures," Alfred says.

"Do we, though?" I question. "You were taking a really long time. I told you I was ready to go."

"Let's get out of here," Vanessa says frustratedly.

We quickly grab our things while Alfred tries to bag up his stupid 45-pound tripod—

"Leave the stupid fucking thing," I tell him.

"It's expensive," Alfred responds. "I need it."

"Whatever. Take it. It's stupid anyway," I tell Alfred. "And they don't know where we are. It was one shot."

"Leave it," Deon says. "Let's go."

"Just take the camera," Vanessa tells him.

Alfred grabs the camera off the tripod and packs it up.

We hurry down the stairs and out of the building, unseen. We make our way down the dark streets without a commie peep to be heard. Quick tonight, we are.

On Church Street, in the cover of darkness, a rifle sounds from the nearby depths. Alfred falls.

It came from a rooftop across Demonbreun. We fire upon it. Vanessa and Bobby go to Alfred while Deon and I fire into the distance. Vanessa and Bobby move Alfred to the alley across the street.

Shots ring out from other rooftops and the streets beside them. We all take cover. Deon and I shoot around the corner, but under fire, we have no possibility of aiming the shooters down.

"Get him back, now," Deon yells to Vanessa and Bobby. "We'll cover you."

Before Deon knows it, I'm gone. I run around the corner, back a block, then back up the street to the next corner.

I move behind a rubbish pile and aim downrange. I aim left toward the rooftops. I see one commie aiming their way. I pull the trigger, and he falls to the street below.

Deon lays down machine-gun fire up the rooftops, then begins shouting, "Go, go, go!"

Vanessa and Bobby move Alfred past me. Deon and I cover their escape. But is it too late for Alfred? Perhaps, but Bobby and Vanessa are surely out of harm's way.

It appears we've cleared the rooftops, but Deon and I proceed with caution as we make our way back to the library.

It turns out, Alfred's alright. The morphine helps. And later, when he's not alright, we'll just give him more morphine, and he'll be fine.

Heather tends to his wound. I don't know if she pulled the lead out and sowed him up or simply stuck gunpowder in there. I can't watch that kind of junk, not when it's an ally. It gives me the willies. But he's all bandaged up, and it looks like he'll live. Good. Not that I really like the guy, but he's a quality soldier. That's all that really matters anymore.

Vanessa's off busying herself with developing the stupid pictures Alfred was taking. At least it's easy to find a dark room here. You know, everywhere. She didn't have to go far. She's never very far away—not yet.

I'm getting more and more pessimistic about the world, about my love gone astray. Will I ever see her again? And if I do, is there any way I can make her change her dirty commie ways and be a human again?

"Will I ever look into those deep dark eyes again? Will she ever love me? Had she ever? Fuck her. Fuck her in her stupid fucking commie ass," I say to myself as I twist my way between thousands of hundred-thousand-word tomes upon tomes, with my best and only friend, ole Jackie-Boy.

"What the fuck, dude?" Deon asks as I walk off with my nectar.

"What?"

"You fucking shot a guy. Why would you shoot a guy?"

"Alfred's fine, dude. I was bored. He's not gonna die."

"It was a scouting mission."

"Whoops," I swoop my arm, then sip my nectar straight from the fountain.

Several rebels seem to have been sucked into the scene behind me without my knowledge. Upon noticing them, I can see why it's kind of intimidating to Deon.

Deon backs away and says, "You're getting weird. I hope you know that."

"I'm doing what needs to be done. For all of us."

"All of us? You sound like a fucking commie, dude."

"You sound like a fucking commie," I shoot back at Deon.

"You're a fucking commie, bitch," says a rebel, getting my back for some unknown reason.

"Yeah," more rebels agree.

Deon pauses, then walks away and says, "It's fucking weird, dude. It's fucking weird."

"You're fucking weird, dude," the rebels shout in unison.

"See, that's fucking weird, Harry," Deon declares, walking away.

30. Quest No. 2

WHEN ALL YOU WANT IN THIS world is love, but it's the only thing which truly evades you, which once you had, but they stole it, what would you do next?

Once I awaken and my stomach settles, I'm off for more. Again, I can smell several rebels following my footsteps as I walk my way alone across the boulevard in the waning hours of daylight. I can't help myself. I don't care if the sun's out. So-be it.

I walk dead center down 3rd Avenue up to Ash Street before it turns into Division. They don't seem to be expecting me, at least not the few little unprepared rat-guards who now lay dead in the street.

I aim west as several more rats pour out. I shoot one rat after the other rat. These poor bastards don't have any tanks or gunners. They're just little sitting rat-ducks, swimming in the pond, soon to be a deep red in the valley of the alleyway.

I will rip each of their commie souls from this plane of existence and send them to be burnt anew in the fires of each of the seven, nine, or however many fucking depths of hell there may happen to be.

Even if hell is only in the mind, they will feel every last fucking drop of it until their very being is transformed back through the light of God—where their every atom, cell, and electron will brim with blissful ecstasy as they're reborn in the holy spirit. But they've got a lot of pain to experience between now and then.

God has left this world. Though I am planning on sending every last damn commie in this city to him. I will have no help in the matter. It's up to me. God left me in charge here, in this rotten city. Or was it the devil? No, that couldn't be. The commies are the devil's playthings, not I. I'm simply playing on his playground, with his toys, and there's nothing that little cunt satan can do about it.

I'm not truly all alone. Someone's following me, be it the rebels or my platoon. I could walk through the streets unarmed, and not a commie could touch me. The angels are good, much better soldiers than I. I'm simply ravenous. There is nothing heavenly here. And nothing will suffice, nothing but my love, and my love is gone. Only thick red cold commie blood can fill this void I'm once again living in.

I continue walking along the boulevard. One rat drops then several more pop their heads out. What were once heavenly torpedos of lead raining down upon the commie scum become ordinary lead bullets. They do just as well in freeing the spirits of all those trapped in the commie flesh.

The wind off the passing commie rounds from the south is getting warm, so I hurry up and dive behind some basement entrance.

I hear more gunfire coming from behind me. It must be Deon. With their help or without, I'm on a mission. They can shoot me down five-thousand times, and still, I will pour molten lead down their fucking commie throats.

I can sense that the rats are gearing up for a real fight. Their alarms begin to sound, and I see them preparing to head my way off in the distance.

Good. Perhaps today is a good day to die.

With the daylight fighting to peek through the clouds, I see him, that little fucking bastard. He's been following me this whole fucking time. That's who it is. I thought it was the fucking rebels or the angels. But no, it's that little idiot. What the fuck is this brat doing? Shooting at the commies with his little twenty-two? He did get the one bastard, at least.

I understand his rage, but I can't let the fucking commies kill the little bastard. And perhaps, it's not the best day to die.

Little Oliver aims down through his sight, firing away. I take a step in front of his rifle, his finger on the trigger. He takes his eye from the scope and gives me a "You better get the fuck out of my way right this very second" look.

I storm to the little bastard, pick him up, and hurry east toward the railway tracks. Commies spray pussy pitter-pattering drooping lead rounds all around us. I hold the little bastard by the back of his jacket and dive over the tracks, tucking and rolling, trying not to squish or scrape Oliver's face on the gravel in the process.

We're only a little fucked. Commie rats surround the buildings facing the tracks in the Gulch. The bullets stop, so I peak up briefly until lead rains freely once again, piercing and skidding off the rail rocks.

"Yep, we're fucked," I figure, reaching my shottie over to spray buckshot their way.

I roll over a few turns, grab a grenade, pull the pin, and toss it to the sound of commie gibberish.

I lean up and aim through my irons. There's one, "Pop." And another.

I duck, then see little Oliver laying on his belly, firing shots with his little twenty-two. "Poof, poof, poof," it sounds.

I leap and dive at the little bastard, feeling the breeze from the passing bullet spray. I tackle Oliver and lay low beneath the tracks.

Yep, we're pretty fucked. I'm sure of it.

"Keep your fucking head down, kid," I yell. "Do you want to get shot?"

Oliver's eyes rage into mine, but he knows I'm right.

"On three," I tell him. "One."

I take a second grenade and pull the pin.

"Two," I pause, then toss the grenade. "Three. Run."

Oliver and I rise and dash towards downtown. Lead sprays around us until the grenade explodes to our six.

At that moment—again like heavenly lead torpedoing daggers—bullets pour from Deon, Vanessa, and Bobby's rifles.

I dive with little Oliver behind a burnt-out truck in the parking lot. The angel's heavenly fire isn't enough. The commies have two gunner trucks ready to storm the city, and they've spotted the platoon. They ring out fire upon them. Not good.

More gunfire rings out. This time, from the Demonbreun Street bridge behind us. It's the rebels, the dirty fucking
rebels. I knew I smelled them.

Thank fuck I did. Not that I trust the bastards, but at
least they're with us in our fight against the commie. And if
you're against the commie, we're on the same fucking team.

I aim down my scope while making sure Oliver doesn't
squirm away and get himself shot.

The gunner truck pulls up to 11th Avenue on McGavock
Street. I grab Oliver and run toward Union and Frist, behind
a few lines of cars.

The truck begins spraying 50 caliber rounds at us. If one
of those even grazes us, we're fucking done. I'm not trying to
get halved. The platoon and the rebels lay down as much
cover fire as they can, but it's not enough. Anytime one gunner gets shot down, there's another rat right there to take his
place.

But then, something magical happens, a rebel bastard
pops out on top of the building to our right with a rocket
launcher and flings a fiery metal cock-rocket right for the
commie truck gunner.

The back-blast flings the rebel bastard backwards. He
flies back and tumbles off the roof, not knowing the power he
was wielding. He appears to be alive, but it surely pains him.

We make it safely behind the building, but more commies are coming. There are always more fucking commies.

Oliver and I make an immediate retreat back northeast
towards the library. The platoon follows behind as the rebels
hold the line and get their injured buddy to safety.

Quite surprisingly, we all make it back in one piece.
Heather welcomes little Oliver with open arms, but the little
guy just walks right past her and grabs a peanut butter and
jelly sandwich from the breakfast table.

We all chow down on the PB&J's Heather prepared while she was stuck here worrying about Oliver and the others, perhaps even me. With that fucking look she always gives me, who the fuck even knows. I doubt even she does. Alfred's looking much better. I think he's already off the morphine. Bobby doesn't bother with a sandwich. He goes right for the bottle. Bobby here's on a bit of a downward spiral. He's enjoying the nectar just as much as I. At first, he was more of a pussy vodka drinker, but he has been turned onto the golden brown goodness over the last few days. It's not helping his spirits as much as I had hoped.

"Don't fail me now, Jackie Boy," I say to myself. "But never will the nectar fail I."

But Bobby, Bobby's always been a bit unstable, maybe the nectar is a little much for him, and he should go back to the pussy juice. Or he can just drink some rubbing alcohol. We've saved up plenty of that. Same shite in my view.

Plus, I don't want to fucking run out and have to scour the city for any remaining bottles that may be left un-shattered.

Maybe we can find a bar with as much nectar as I could ever need and just live there, underground. I could. Alone. Forever. Seal the exits. Nothing but golden flowing nectar until the very end.

That would be nice. But that's not realistic. I'll just fill Bobby's bottles with cheap bourbon. Fuck him. Not that bourbon's bad. It's just not quite like the Tennessee goodness I've grown so close to. It burns differently. I need to feel the fire in my chest.

The double doors of the Library swing open, and in walks a familiar rebel face. The rebel smiles. It's the same bastard I smashed in the teeth with the shotgun. No wonder one's chipped so unflatteringly.

"You," Chipped-Tooth says with a hint of vengeance.

"I thought you'd be long dead by now," I figure aloud.

"You wish," he responds quickly.

Then, a young blue-eyed rebel, younger than Bobby, introduces himself as Will.

"I want to show you something," says Will. "This way."

We look at each other suspiciously, then agree. The rebels stand aside and let us pass. There's an odd and thick feel to the air. It's tense yet welcoming, almost sucking us in down the long-familiar hall. The hall itself is almost alive and breathing in the thick moisture.

A trap? Better fucking not be.

The rebels seem to show me a strange amount of respect, especially after what happened last time I was here, with the whole triple 'homicide' thing. They must feel it too. Still, I'm ready to draw my pistol at the flick of a wrist.

We push through the halls as the rebel seas part. Even the rebels who tried to stand up to me before stand aside. It's almost as if they want to salute. What the fuck is their problem?

Young Will, leads us into a familiar candle-lit room, the long target practice hall of books. It's now filled with crates which are filled with pistols and rifles, grenades and ammo, knives, rockets, and explosives. It's a true treasure trove of weaponry. Better than gold in this world. Then there are boxes of wires and detonators and what-have-yous.

"This will be my room," I state to myself as my eyes pass over the goods with a glorious mischievousness.

"Where did you get all this?" I Vanessa asks.

"Some good guys in the TBI," Will says. "The police precinct, and some from the NG.

I open a crate which shines a golden majestic glow as its contents are revealed to me.

"Whatever you want, sir," the young blue-eyed rebel says. "It's on the house."

It's as if God himself is once again watching over us. And these men are his messengers, delivering us his holy grail of grand weaponry, allowing us to find freedom, defeat the commies, and begin civilization all over as it was always intended, truly free. But no. It can't be.

"Let us help you, sir," Will says with intent.

31. Splintering In The Dark

I DON'T SPEAK A WORD TO my disciples, which they've quickly become. At least that's what they're calling themselves; Will and the other twelve. These are no longer my thoughts. These are theirs. I'm no fucking chosen one.

I stay silent unless there's something I need from the disciples or a mission is ready to begin. But that's really up to little Oliver here, the prophet. For he has become the foreteller of myths for decades to come; if the little bastard child survives, which is doubtful.

I am only an instrument bringing God's righteousness upon the commie scum. God is speaking through me. Through me, the angels, and the disciples, God will strike down the wretched commie and inflict his righteous fear into every commie heart in these lands and over all of the Earth. We will crush the commie with all of God's mighty vengeance.

Then, she and I will shine on together on a hilltop, with our four children, raising fields of grain, greens, and goodies, with fresh wine and barley and hops, with cows for milk and cheese, my Jasmine and I.

I know she's safe. For whatever fate may befall me, I know she is still safely in the hands of God, and he will protect her from the commies. She's in their grasp, but God be damned himself if he lets anything happen to her.

"God?" I question myself inside. "There's no god here. She's not protected. They have her. They're doing unspeakable things to her. When they're done, and she's had enough little commie bastard children, they'll kill her. I can't save her. Who am I?"

"God," I respond internally after a deep breath. "If you can hear me, please keep my Jasmine safe. Do what you will with me, but please keep her safe. I beg of you, Lord."

"Hah," I laugh at myself. "Keep her safe? What's God going to do? God's gone. God left. He's not here anymore. Look at this fucking place. Look at that little bastard, Oliver. God's long fucking gone. Perhaps he's been gone. It's felt that way for a while. Perhaps he's over this place, with its repetitiveness."

"But it's home. God could never leave us. It's his creation. He's with her now, breathing life into and through her. He lives inside of her."

"The commies are living inside her now. Along with a little commie bastard child they implanted into her, in a grotesque orgy of fat old dirty commies fouling your woman."

"Ahh," I scream aloud, reaching my closed fists overhead, then bashing a triple-fist sized hole in the drywall.

"You're just the devil trying to lead me astray," I tell myself.

"Don't be cruel. I'm just showing you the truth. God's gone. See ya later. Aloha means goodbye."

"And hello," I smash the mirror with my fist.

The rebels show a look of concern as I stand here with blood dripping down my arm and a look that could slice through diamonds.

"You want to help?" I turn to ask of my disciples. "There is one thing you could help me with—"

I walk down the long dark hall towards the big long target practice room, which I have now taken as my chambers, as I said I would. Deon was right. This whole thing with the rebels is weird. But if they do my bidding, so be it.

Though it is odd and rather sick, and I don't much like it, not one bit, but I run with it. I need it. It feeds me. Perhaps in all the wrong ways, but it does feed me. We have things to do, many things. We're not going to let some silly morals or feel-good mentality get in our way. We have one mission in life now. To kill and maim every last fucking commie in the damn place.

Will, Bobby, and I, plus the disciples and other various rebels have spent the last couple of days together designing, wrapping, and then connecting wires to different explosives and detonators of all varying sizes, scopes, intensities, blast radiuses, and material densities.

Some are pure petrol bombs, some purely C-4. Some include added material, such as glass, nails, and ball bearings. Some are a healthy combination of all of the above, or even with some good ole napalm; just what the commies deserve.

But no civilian has ever deserved it—like our government had done in the past. America doesn't drop bombs. America gives hope. America quit being America long ago, which is the only reason the commie was able to do this to us in the first place. We allowed it. We were rotted out from the inside.

We were never supposed to be an empire. We were supposed to be free, a beacon of hope for all of the world, leading it by example into prosperity, not drowning it in bombs and unpayable debt to the invisible masters of the world, in usury, one of the greatest evils on the planet.

America has failed. But we will start over from the ashes. That's the only mission now—destroy the virus, and begin anew. We will force the invisible hand out of hiding and sever its grip on us. We will grow the world new and free.

Just look at us now. We're coming back to life through the darkness of it all. Or perhaps we're just helping to destroy it. We certainly aren't going to leave one safe place in this city for the commie to enter without burning from napalm or petrol, simply blasting into pieces, or at least getting a little shrapnel jammed up their asses.

Even little Oliver has begun to shadow me in our massive bomb-making operation. Oliver follows me like clockwork. He too, now a good little bomb-maker, much like I've become. Together we are changing the world, my little minion and me.

After I showed Oliver the ins and outs, he's become perhaps the best of us all, with those nimble little perfect bomb-making fingers.

This mission has been going for 48 sleepless hours straight, wiring and wiring until, "Boom!"

Where, in one of the other rooms, a careless rebel miswired a small C-4 igniter bomb, which was meant to ignite a larger petrol or napalm payload, or so the yells signify.

Luckily, the larger and more dangerous components sit safely next to me. We're also lucky that the thick fumes from napalm crafting didn't ignite in the explosion, which has left that poor rebel smooshed upside the wall, ceiling, and floor. I don't have to look. The sound told me everything I need to know.

After a short pause, I keep on with the wiring, as does little Oliver and the rest of my minions.

Now, into the third day. I can feel it. That look. I turn to see Heather with an almost new look, one of wondering. Then she gets closer and notices what we've been doing these last two and a half days and nights and what Oliver's nimble little fingers are helping us do. Her look of appreciation turns to horror and outrage.

She walks calmly over to little Oliver, "Hey, Oliver. Want to come with me? I'll make you a sandwich. There's pineapple juice."

Little Oliver sets his bomb and wiring kit down gently, gets up from the table, takes Heather's hand, and walks out of the room with her. She looks back at me with another new look I've never seen. Like I'm crazy or something.

"She's fucking crazy," I think, then realize. "She did just walk in to find an 8-year-old building bombs at four o'clock in the morning. Or sunrise, whenever it is."

He's just learning what he needs to survive in this world and to help to defeat the commie scum. But I get it, she wants him to stay innocent and safe, but he'll never be innocent. But safe, she can at least keep him safe, she hopes.

Alfred's happy the kid's out of the room too. He's not quite as comfortable with it as I am. Oliver's not an idiot. Any one of us has just as good of a chance of accidentally miswiring one of these things as he did.

Once Alfred had rested the first day after being shot, he began showing us how to make the good stuff. That, combined with the rebel's miscreant style, and my increasingly devious ingenuity, we might just have something here.

We're almost ready for our first true mission as a team, my disciples and I. Though Deon and Vanessa have been absent during all of this, my hope is that the angels will join us with their daggers of light.

Aside from helping us make bombs, Oliver's nimble little fingers have been up to something else. Every day, little Oliver draws piles of cartoons. He draws and draws. Quite morbid stuff. But we will use it. We will strike fear into the dead cold commie hearts with little Oliver's art.

The disciples, as they continue calling themselves—which I'm oddly getting more comfortable with—have set up an old printing press and are using bicycle power to print Oliver's cryptic art and messages. We're calling it The Free Nashville Press, delivering anti-commie messages directly to the rats, getting the papers to them in any way possible.

The printing press may become our most powerful weapon, "the pen." I allow Oliver to write most of the cryptic headlines, including the ones for his infamous cartoon series, "100 Ways To Kill A Commie."

The first of which, Cartoon #1, depicts a commie rat slid down a sharp pole, from the seat of his pants up through and out his skull, hung up like a flag. There has even been talk of turning some of Oliver's art into reality. The disciples begin plastering many of the cartoons up as murals across the city, anywhere the commie may tread.

The thirteen disciples will do most of the prophecy fulfillment. I'm busy planning. My mind runs wild in new ways in which to remove the commie strain from this world, which my disciples will fulfill, just as they will fulfill little Oliver's.

But mine, mine will have reason. Mine won't only strike fear into the commie heart. Mine will destroy the commie and take back our positions, and finally push the commie from this city. We will rip them apart as they flee, regardless of if I ever see that fucking commie whore again or not.

I quickly scroll down a letter to her, which she will surely see, being that I've given demands to have it printed in the next edition.

"My Jasmine, how could you? You were all that was good in this world. How could you allow the commie virus to rot your spirit and enslave you in wretched commie flesh? It can't be true, can it? You're so much better than that. Tell me you're no fucking commie, and we can still be together. Otherwise, you better get the fuck out of dodge because we're coming for all you commie bastards."

I'm fairly proud of this edition. The cartoon depicts me with my trusty buck knife in my teeth, dripping blood, as I hold three commie heads out dangling from my left hand, rifle in my right. Perhaps the disciples will plaster this one up for all to see, particularly Jasmine.

32. Traps

DEON STORMS INTO MY CORRIDOR with the newest copy of the Free Nashville Press. Alfred follows him in. Will and Bobby stand on my side.

"She's a Commie?" Deon asks demandingly. "And you knew?"

"Of course I knew," I respond. "I saw her."

"Saw her what?" asks Deon.

I pause, then let out, "Shoot Ken. She was literally holding the smoking gun."

"What the fuck, Harry? And you're just now telling us this? Fuck, man."

"How could I tell you? She was all I ever loved in this world. And now she's a fucking commie."

"I'm sorry," Deon says. "I know, man. But why don't you want to leave now?"

"I can't, Deon," I say. "I'm never leaving. There's nowhere to go."

I toss down photos from the scouting mission that the rebels had taken as Vanessa was developing them.

The images show the invaders closing in from all sides. The Gulch, Music Row, West End, Germantown. Tanks galore gather in Green Hills, ready to invade.

"Look. They're fucking everywhere. It's time we change things up a bit. You in or you out?"

"What the fuck, man?" Deon responds. "Why are you just showing us these?"

"Don't worry. It's all planned out."

I take Deon to show him the treasure trove of explosives. He knew we were up to something, but he didn't quite know the scale of it. Explosive devices line the bookshelves, hundreds of them.

It's time. Our mission, line the streets and buildings on the outskirts of downtown with masses of explosives. All the way from So-Bro, the Gulch, Music Row, and Germantown on in—anywhere the commie may enter and beyond. They'll be detonated by tripwire, battery-wired sensors, or old fashion mines.

Bobby and Will follow as I grab my things and walk towards the large double doors. Deon huddles with Alfred and Vanessa.

"It's time," I say, then walk outside.

The rest of my disciples follow suit.

"What are we doing?" Bobby questions me.

"We're protecting our city."

"Yeah. But without them?" Bobby asks.

And just then, Alfred, Deon, and Vanessa join us outside.

Deon approaches and says, "We'll help you. Just take it easy with this whole thing."

"What?" I ask. What the fuck's he talking about?

"Just be careful."

I almost laugh before I head off with Bobby, Will, the disciples, and other rebels. We're loaded with as many explosives as we can carry in our packs. The angels follow behind, surely second-guessing themselves.

Heather watches us leave with little Oliver held tight to her side. He fights to join, but it's no use.

We begin to approach Korean Veterans Boulevard. Start where it began, we figure, and work our way around.

And, of course, we must line the riverside with some of our more intriguing explosive contraptions.

This one's a pure mix of fun. I think little Oliver had a hand in its creation. At its core, C-4, of course, which is inside the core of a mini petrol tank. Outside of which, houses anything from broken glass, nails, razor blades, even diamonds. Add a little napalm on top, and you've got yourself a four-for.

We hide most of the explosives under driftwood and rubble strewn across the street. Some are spiderweb-like trip wires which I like. They're nearly undetectable until it's far too late.

"Commie-Be-Gone. No-More-Commie," I can see the hit songs now, B-grade commercial gold. "Commie-Go-Boom, Commie-Be-Damned, Damned-Commie. Boom-Commie-Boom-Boom."

A few rebels set this explosive. Another couple set this one. The disciples set a bunch. I set that one. Bobby sets a few. Will probably sets more than anyone. He's quick, but he's sure to die soon. It's quite a surprise to me that he's still around. And he's almost peppy about the situation. Maybe he's on something? I need some of that. Then I grasp the bottle and realize, no, I only need the gold, golden nectar.

Will can have whatever he's having. I've stopped caring about their opium and other drug habits after our first few missions together. Even if it makes them a little clumsy, like that dick who decided to blow half his body off by not paying attention to the process. They're pre-wired. Just a couple of steps, and they're planted. Be careful, guy.

The angels sit quietly perched. We can't see them, but we know they're there, watching over us.

Continuing our mission, we line the rest of the streets with trip mines of all sorts and sizes throughout the night.

Hours go by with no breaks until we're completely out of goodies.

The outer streets are now lined all the way from Germantown through the Gulch—Charlotte Avenue and south along the railroad, through 8th Avenue and SoBro—up and down the Cumberland River.

That's about four tons of C-4 loaded up and ready to blow. Not that I'm a mathematician or actually have any idea. That just sounds like a lot. And there's a damn lot of C-4 spread out across the city now. With plenty of petrol and napalm bombs to go with them.

For better or worse, there's no way in or out of downtown anymore. We're simply not going to let these fuckers in. The commies don't stand a fucking chance. I can't wait until they try attacking with a gaggle of commie bastards. That'll be fun to see.

And that's that.

And we could just wait.

But that's not mine, nor my disciple's style.

No, I don't trust them with my stuff or with Heather. But with a mission that involves scorching commies, sure. Blow the bastards straight to bits, chunks, and spaghetti splatter, chard to a crisp with a napalm glaze.

It's time for a little test—a taste. We set out to enrage the commie and make them attack. We head for the available rooftops and begin sniping their positions in the Gulch. We concentrate heavily on the rooftop bar of the newly owned Tamberline Hotel, where the officers are galavanting about with fine wine while their rats barely have enough cheese to keep from becoming skeletons. They sure are some skinny rat bastards.

After the first shot, the officers galavant no more. They duck away like cowards while they send their subordinates to the edge to act as human shields as the daggers rain forth.

On the streets below, we see their rats preparing. They're gathering in their trucks and in formation. We want them to advance. That's what this whole thing is about.

Deon, Alfred, and Vanessa wait patiently from their perch like we originally planned, but we can't help ourselves. They're sitting ducks, commie rat-ducks. It's all too easy, far too fucking easy. It's quite fun. Popping ticks, we call it. Will, Bobby, and I take out a few rats each before we let up.

The other disciples are close, almost too close. They mock the commies with machine-gun fire and mini handheld petrol bombs until they flee back across the tracks to lead the rats our way, being sure to watch their footsteps.

The commie forces begin storming our direction. There are at least sixty men and three gunner trucks. They approach confidently over the railroad tracks. Good. I'm glad they're confident. The glory will be that much greater. They're closing in.

The first row of commies makes it past the line, one truck, and a dozen men. The rest of the rats trail just behind, with the majority in the perfect position now.

Will whistles down to his fellow disciple on the street below, giving him a thumbs up.

Gunfire erupts as the commies begin firing at ghosts and whistling echoes.

The street-level rebel hides behind a stone wall and clicks an ignition switch. Will and Bobby drop below the short concrete roof wall.

I watch as the first C-4 bomb ignites the petrol bombs, which ignite the combo-bombs, which ignites the napalm.

I duck as the flames blast my way. Who knows what these particular bombs are filled with, but their contents are certainly whizzing overhead and clanking loudly against the cement.

The blast pushes through the wall, sending the disciple who detonated the bomb flying off. He lands several feet from where he began. He's rattled but mostly undamaged, it seems.

The commies scream gibberish, but an almost heavenly gibberish. They're speaking to God now. Perhaps the disciples are right. Perhaps he hasn't left this place. But no, if he were here, there would be no divine commie howls to praise and beg of him, for this invasion would have never taken place.

Not every rat down below is immediately blasted and maimed or burnt crispy with napalm. But they soon will be, after Will, Bobby, the angels, the disciples, and I finish them off.

But first, in the calm aftermath, we watch several burning rats stumble around like burning mummies. Their faces melt from the napalm fused to their dissolving skin. Into their organs, the napalm melts until they finally fall to the ground and melt like the wicked witch, where they'll burn for hours on end, perhaps the whole night through. The vultures won't even touch these rats.

After the brief pause, we begin to plaster lead daggers down upon the remaining commies from our various locations. They're almost dancing to the drumming bullet fire, searching for anything other than horror. But they will not find it, not in this life. They lost that chance the moment they arrived in this city.

Now, of course, they have to bring a fucking pussy tank out, the rat-fucks. So, we figure it's time to retreat back towards our base.

The tank won't dare enter our bomb-lined and reinforced fortress around the library and capital building. Though if it tries, good. It's most likely just showing face to keep us back. But we're not attacking. Not tonight. Not yet. We're just testing our defenses.

Later, we will attack. But for now, we head back to the damned library. It is starting to grow on me. Mostly due to the range room, basement printing press, and if I must guess, Heather. Still, there are much better places we could house.

I've had my eye particularly set on the capital building. It's a bit more vulnerable than the library to attack, but it also has a much better sniper's nest. Or I could just snipe from one of the various windows if given the need. Plus, the rooms are much nicer. Here, we're just kind of stuck. However, the booby-traps do make us feel much safer.

For now, we stay put. The others feel protected in the library, even with the rebels breathing down their necks, whom they're not particularly comfortable with. I don't blame them.

I'm even having a few second thoughts about my disciples, for one, the whole disciple thing. I'll admit that I was a little swayed for a moment. I've had my moments of weakness, good and bad, but it's a little much. I don't know God's plan. Could I be here for a reason? Sure. So could anyone. But that doesn't matter. That's not for me to know. Or for them. If I am, I am. If they are, they are. Same for anyone.

God's plan is not any of our fucking business. My only business is smashing the commie spirit, destroying the rot, and ripping the commie strain from this city.

There's always a commie lurking around somewhere. And that's why we must be vigilant. Wherever the commie strain appears, it must be plucked, or it will infect its fellow mates. And that's not something we can allow. Not anymore. Not after this. Not after Nashville.

In the future, we will hear stories of bravery in every city —some of them. Many of those stories will be buried in the rubble of the decimated cities, along with their fallen heroes. Will even ours survive? Will we ever make it out of this damned city? Will anyone? Doubtful.

That doesn't matter. Nor does God's plan. I'm here, and I will destroy the commie. That is all I know. And her—fucking, her—that fucking commie cunt.

It rages inside me. Goddamn her. How could she? My everything? My whole entire being was wrapped up in her. Now? Nothing. Pure nothingness. A void. We're living in the void. And the only way out is to fill it so full of cold commie blood that the void overflows, and we rise from it, and from this goddamned city.

She was my everything? And now? This? I'm reduced to this? Living like a dog in my own fucking city? The only hope left here is in the battle of the bottle and the bottom of the barrel. And we'll be out of the nectar soon.

I've scrounged through every bar, restaurant, and basement I could find. Pretty soon, I'm going to have to switch from the nectar to something far less palpable and enlightening. I have been stockpiling some supposedly fine bourbons just in case, but bourbon burns in your throat, not your chest. It's just not the same. And scotch? Scotch is far too smooth for wartime. I must burn. At least we've got plenty of lead.

33. New Free Nashville

I AWAKEN, KNEE DEEP IN the bottle, two flips over the moon, flopped down, sinking fast in the quicksand—

Heather walks over a glass of freshly boiled, then almost cooled water. Or is it coffee? It's hard to tell right now in the darkness; my tastebuds all but destroyed.

We're running low on bottled water, so we're tasked with filtering it. And to be sure it's free of the unholy, we burn the diseases out of it at a high enough temperature that nothing could survive it. Any traces of civilization have all but left this place, along with the music and sanitation.

Little Oliver has become quite the little bastard prince. He lets Heather and the disciples do everything for him, yet nothing. You can't touch the child, or he may just stab your hand with the knife he carries, which seems larger than he is. Who could blame him?

I allow Oliver all the freedom anyone could, but I also impart a touch of mine and Jasper's anti-commie wisdom on the little tyke, giving him a slight glint of guidance. "Commieland is a demon's playground, little one. But you already know that, don't you?"

Heather knows Oliver has his demons and that she can't free him. She can only feed him and shelter him. Her being there is enough. Every once in a while, the little bastard will cuddle up next to her. Rare, but it has happened a handful of times.

It seems everyone else is a little scared of the poor bastard. Maybe they should be. That little dude could snap in an instant and blow this whole place if he felt like it. We have it wired to blow. The entire city is pretty much ready to blow. If it wasn't for her, he'd probably do it. Why wouldn't he?

Heather's the only good thing for the kid, perhaps any of us. She's always motherly towards the little bastard, as motherly as he'll allow. Heather and Oliver both stay in my chambers now. There's plenty of room. I feel safer with her nearby, not for my sake, but for hers and his.

They're humanity's future, not I. They need to survive, or I may as well just lay down in the street at high noon and let the commie destroy me. For if humanity goes, I go. I nearly have. My humanity hangs on by a thread, but Heather is always there to sew it back up, damn her. I can't let anything happen to her.

Deon, Vanessa, Alfred, and Bobby are good, but they're not pure. We need a pure heart to keep us going. She is that pure heart.

Without Jasmine, I have grown a custom to having her around. There's no love between us, and there will never be. But I am beginning to understand that look. Perhaps I have even begun to give her a similar one¿

With Heather close, I keep my humanity close. Without her around, I could only imagine how far the disciples would lead me astray. They're vicious creatures. I'm glad they're on my side. I hope they don't turn on me. Though there is a Judas in the midst, somewhere. And if it's anyone, it's likely Chipped-Tooth. I've got my eye on him, as does Will.

Chipped-Tooth and mine's relationship hasn't improved much. I haven't had to shoot him yet, so that's a positive. Though, it is usually quite tense when he's around. It feels as if he literally wants to stab me in the back. That's why Will keeps a couple of disciples watching over him at all times.

As long as we have a mission, we're fine, for he is a warrior, a psycho, but a warrior-psycho. It's when the mission is over; that's when we have to worry about Chipped-Tooth.

"Just fucking try," I say and hope under my breath. "You half donkey-toothed pig-fucking bitch."

He won't dare. The disciples make sure of that. He's known by them as the fallen one. I only know him as Chipped-Tooth. I know none of their names except Will. I don't want to know. And Yancey, but that's not even his real name, so what's the use? They're all going to die soon anyway. Sometimes I hope we all do. It would be easier that way.

Will is the only one I really communicate with of the disciples. He does most of the conversing and delivering of orders to them, who then deliver the orders to any of the other rebels who may be involved in the day's mission.

I keep my distance from the others, even during the missions. We're usually separated into three or four groups: The rebels, disciples, the angels, then Will, Bobby, and myself. Plus, Oliver sometimes treks along with us.

Heather, nor I, can keep the little bastard from shadowing me on all of the missions with the cult. We have tried, but he's one stubborn bastard.

And yes, they're basically a fucking cult now. I knew it, and I never liked it, but the disciples are helping. I need their help. Though their brown cloaks don't help the matter, I certainly can't defeat the commies on my own. They do the dirty work. And with their assistance, we may just have a fucking shot. As long as Deon doesn't turn on me.

Deon really doesn't like the rebels or how they treat me as some kind of chosen leader. Still, the angels help greatly. Deon keeps the other angels on my side, regardless of how off-putting my behavior may be at times with the constant nectar supply and the disciples constantly in my shadows.

As the disciples see it, "I am the chosen one. And they, my disciples. With the angels, Deon, Vanessa, and Alfred always watching over us, raining God's lead-filled love down upon those that commit evil acts for evil men, for evil causes, commie causes."

But that's not how I see it, not anymore. Sure, I may speak that way to them, and maybe I started it, but I need them to follow me into the fire. So, I keep it up. We've got plans.

The angels basically just cover us on our missions now. They plant explosives from time to time, but they're not on the front lines. Neither are we. That's usually kept for the disciples, or more hopefully, random rebels we're free to sacrifice at a whim.

Not that the disciples mind a little self-sacrifice. In fact, one disciple, R.I.P., was on a mission, and he was supposed to jump, but he just stayed in the fucking C-4 wired petrol bomb of a truck as it hit its intended target, a makeshift commie roadblock. Jump, duck, and roll. It's not that difficult.

I can almost smell victory, but we must go on stabbing away at the commie spirit. Soon, they will be so degraded that they'll be too terrified to go on. Soon, they'll be too afraid to fire their guns. A little monkey glue deep in the barrel does a commie good. After you or the rat next to you lose a finger or an eye from a backfiring rifle, you're going to have a much harder time keeping your aim steady. The rumors in the paper alone will produce shaky trigger fingers.

Regardless of the physical difficulty, mentally, you're never going to want to touch another gun, but they're going to make you. They're fucking commies; that's what they do, regardless of the fear inside.

The commie machine-shell will power on until there is nothing left to power it with; until the very spirit inside has rotted out in total, and the commie shell has sucked it dry, and they just whittle, fall, and whisk away in the wind.

After this, they will fear us. Every one of them will fear us. In every town and city, they will get the word of what's been done here. And there will be those just like us in the other places, armed and ready, always vigilant. The commies don't stand a fucking chance in the long run. We will always persevere. Commies be damned. Thank God for the 2nd Amendment; and our forefathers.

34. Disaster Road

THE MISSIONS SEEM ENDLESS now. One mission sort of just fades into the next.

Then we hear it, almost like fireworks, but much more substantial and vibrational. We'll have our fun with the remaining gaggles of stragglers.

While the commies are in disarray, a few of the disciples go in for a closer look and come back with the perfect specimen, a commie commander, the one leading the raid. Now he himself will become a work of art. Little Oliver knows what to do with him. He always does.

This lucky rat is set to become Oliver's Cartoon #7/100. Every commie in the city will hear about it in myth, legend, or face to face one day very soon. That day is fast approaching for each and every commie bastard here.

The disciples hold the commie commander still while I confront the poor bastard over Jasmine and her whereabouts and this whole fucking commie nonsense.

"She stays with general Brosman," this pathetic commie rat says in broken English.

"Bring him to me," I demand.

"I can't bring him to you. That's impossible."

"Wrong answer," I say, then turn and walk away with little Oliver.

"I told you the truth," he yells.

"You're a goddamned commie," I tell him without looking back.

Oliver and I disappear to the commander's waning screams as the disciples go to work on that poor commie wretch. His cries, like angelic horns, communing with God himself. The sound of hammers, bones, and metal harmonize with his angelic wails. Maybe the disciples really are doing God's work. Perhaps, we all are. Perhaps, that's why he left us in this rat-fuck shell of a once-great and prosperous city.

The disciples sure don't mind fulfilling any and all of the sick little tasks Oliver prophesies in his cartoons. They enlarge what he draws, always placing them where they'd be visible to any incoming rats, often with "live" art dressed up right in front of the murals, where at just the right angle and distance, it looks like 3D art. This lucky commander will become one of those living murals.

The angels haven't exactly been on board with all that's been happening. I don't blame them. Deon, in particular, isn't too fond of the recent direction of little Oliver's street art, which now lines many of the buildings and alleyways around Broadway with ever more depraved acts to the dead commie rat-flesh and bones. He especially doesn't care for the "living art." Nor did he appreciate the scalps.

There were scalps, weren't there? Or have I been dreaming again? I hate when I dream. I don't like it much when I wake either. I'm not of too much care for either nowadays. However, the nectar helps with both.

If I do remember correctly, we've been making a commie mass grave right dead square in the middle of Broadway; heads only. We burn the bodies. We're not mad. We know the diseases commies carry. We're not going to risk it. But we have to send a message. Plus, it's Cartoon #9 in Little Oliver's "100 Ways To Kill A Commie" series. We must keep his predictions true.

I'm not around when any of that actually plays out and is strewn about as "living" street art. That's gross. But little Oliver is becoming quite the little creative. I'll give him that.

Most of his cartoons are far beyond even my taste. Heather's becoming less and less of a fan of any of it. But there is no controlling what that ever more maniacal-minded little boy does or draws. But she's always there for him, regardless of how morbid his little rascal brain becomes. She doesn't exactly appreciate the freedom I allow Oliver, but she knows he's no mere child. He does as he pleases.

"Be safe, Oliver," Heather always tells him before he follows us on a mission.

Little Oliver is a prophet painting prophecy on the walls, which my disciples and I almost always deliver upon. We will burn the commie filth together, little Oliver and I. Even the angels will have a golden hand in the matter——

Bobby, Will, and I lean against the red, tan, and gray-colored stone wall. The stones crumble below the tank treads on the road above, some seven or eight feet overhead.

"Oh fuck, please don't crush us," we surely hope, as if we have time to hope.

Bobby's praying. He should be. It's his turn. He's earning his stripes and overcoming his fear when close to the enemy. He has a long way to go with that, but perhaps this will be a real turning point for him.

Bobby reaches up, leaps, and slams his arm around, sticking the armed C-4 device onto the tank's tracks—we hope—close enough, surely. Gunshots ring out, splattering mud and concrete debris down upon us.

"Oh fuck, bad plant, bad plant," Bobby yells, then ducks for cover.

"Oh, shit," we all get down.

Gibberish is shouted by sixteen storming footsteps, then—

"BOOM!" the C-4 blows the tank, fully disabling it, plus all of the incoming commie feet. No more gunshots. No more gibberish. No more footsteps. No more commies. Bobby's really starting to come into his own.

The explosion has covered us in a mass of debris and smoke-darkened stone.

"Will? Will?" Bobby yells until he finds Will and pulls him out from under the rubble.

I dig my own left leg out. It's fine—fairly fine. I can walk —I believe.

Gunshots from more commie bastards ring out in the distance, but God's angels are with us, protecting us from on high. They always are. Not that they want to, but we are still on the same side. We just don't really hang out that much anymore.

Bobby and I carry Will from the rubble pile under the blown tank and dead commie orgy, safely back towards the library under cover of drumbeat fire.

Every tank we damage or destroy is a big win for us right now, and they're starting to pile up. The commies appear to be becoming quite fearful. We play up those fears. We don't even have to use real explosives every time.

This next night, when we know a commie invasion will be coming from the Gulch, we simply line the streets with fireworks and watch.

The moment the rats take one step across the little bridge, the sky lights up with booms and bursts and sparkles. You've never seen a group of grown men run away from danger quicker in your life.

The commander yells gibberish at his men to stop and keep advancing. But the "men" continue retreating. At which time, the commander pulls out his pistol and shoots several of his own men down. The rest of his rats stop cold.

But then Bobby lets it rip, slashing a lead-lined hole right through this commie commander's chest. He's not moving a peep. Too bad, though he could still make some swell "living" art.

Dead or alive, his men flee so damn fast that we don't even bother wasting rounds on them. Their fear will spread and continue spreading, and spread some more, through every one of their fucking worthless commie hearts.

She will hear of their fear. Perhaps the fear will dive deep into her very soul, opening a small portal for it to pass through to the surface, through her dead-cold commie heart. Then, perhaps her humanity will once again return, and her commie shell will burn and melt away, turning to ash.

For now, knowing the commie fears us so greatly is all I need to keep my optimism alive. Not that there's much optimism, nor is it in very good health, but we've come pretty far in destroying the commie faith. Therefore, my faith has increased, not in anything holy, but in at least keeping the city abreast for a while longer.

To complete the destruction of the commie spirit, we will have to begin advancing, not just defending. But we will have to watch our steps, not due to the commie presence in the city, but due to our massive trip bomb campaign throughout downtown. One wrong step and any number of us could go, "Boom."

Lucky for us, little Oliver has quite the memory. For without him, Bobby would have gone up in smoke just now. As Bobby was about to do a little cleanup, Oliver fired his little rifle as a warning shot. It only grazed Bobby.

Yeah, it was kind of a dick move for Oliver to shoot Bobby. But he did save his life, for if Bobby had picked up any piece of that particular pile of rubble, Bobby would have gone "Boom."

"And that's why you don't clean up the rubble," I mention as Bobby crawls back towards the Library.

"What the fuck, Oliver?" Bobby yells at the serious little boy.

Oliver doesn't say a word. He just flings the book he was reading onto the pile of rubbish that Bobby was bending down to pick up and "BOOM!"

Everyone dives for the ground, everyone but little Oliver. He just stands there as the dirt, dust, and debris overtake us all, including him.

Heather runs out, and there's little Oliver just standing amidst the smoke as the men come to their feet. Heather digs her way to him through the dust cloud.

"Come on, Oliver," she says. "You've had enough fun for one day. Let's get a sandwich, yeah?"

Oliver grabs her hand and follows her inside as the dust slowly begins to settle.

"What the fuck is wrong with that kid?" asks Bobby as he gets up off the ground, holding his flesh wound.

He doesn't need an answer, for we all know what the fuck's wrong with the kid.

"Go take care of that," I tell Bobby. "Will and I shall keep watch."

Bobby inspects his wound closer as he walks inside.

"I can't believe he shot him," Will says, then laughs. "That was awesome."

"I know," I almost chuckle. "Did you see Bobby's face?"

"I know. He was like, 'What the fuck, kid. You fucking shot me! Not cool, dude. Not cool.' But it was pretty fucking cool."

Lucky for Bobby, the kid only grazed his arm. Or is he just a bad shot? I'm pretty sure the kid knows where his anger should be targeted, so I'd say it was a good shot. Perhaps it's time for little Oliver to have an upgrade...

Oliver stands over the large wooden crate with zero excitement or anticipation for what may be to come. I flip the top off of the crate and pull out Oliver's very own perfectly sighted and silenced AR-15.

And what does little Oliver do? Does he smile? No. He just takes the rifle and handles it like a well-trained marine would. He'll be a good little fighter.

He's already right on target as he fires downrange at the commies he painted upon the bookshelf wall, plus the two little book rats Heather helped him build, which are being ripped to shreds as Oliver blasts away. The kick's less than one may expect. I'll save the .308 till he's eleven. He's already well versed in grenade theory—the kid can handle a .223.

35. Little Dino

THESE FUCKERS ARE ABOUT to get fucked more than any fuckers have ever been fucked throughout the history of fucking. Oh, these fuckers are going to pay!

We're getting good—almost too good. The explosives we make are getting quite fun; little creepy wiggly-eyed dolls from the 1950s, rolling napalm whiskey barrels, scooter bombs, C-4 sandwiches, pizza pies, and good-ole petrol bombs.

"C-4 and petrol bombs, them's my only friends."

Tonight, we're going for it. They've taken the Gulch, and we're not going to let that stand. We will humiliate, if not decimate, the enemy tonight. Tonight, they will wish they had never stepped foot on this entire planet. This will be our first true mission together.

I've spent much of the day training: shooting, doing pull-ups, and knifing punching bags held by willing disciples. They know I won't miss.

"It's fine. It's fine," the young disciple Yancey says. That's not his name. It's just what I call him because he looks like a Yancey, except for his shaved head. I imagine any real Yancey would have slightly longer surfer blonde hair. "I'm fine."

Yancey grabs the cut punching bag with his bleeding left hand and holds it tight. I continue stabbing away.

"Wait. Where the fuck is Bobby?" I ask stabbing and leaving the knife stuck. "It's time. Go get the others."

Yancey scurries off to round up the troops while wrapping his bloody hand.

We gather together in the main hall in four groups: myself, Bobby, Will, and little Oliver; the angels; the disciples; and the rebels.

We set out into the darkness, making our way near the train tracks which separate downtown from the Gulch.

Little Oliver, always the little fortune teller has just the perfect weapon to kick tonight off. Being a kid, he knows of all the new gadgets, and my disciples can find almost anything. And toys just happen to make the perfect little C-4 bombs. And these move—on their own—or with a remote.

Through my scope, I watch Oliver run across the train tracks lined with old rusted-out cargo railcars. He's around 11th Avenue, just past Demonbreun. He's not being a little idiot, for once. He's following the plan. He sets down a little dinosaur toy in the middle of the street and runs back our way.

A couple of commies saunter out onto the street and spout gibberish accusations against Oliver.

"Pop, Pop," gunshots sound, and little Oliver is freed from his so-called crimes as the two commies lay in lifeless sleep. The angels are with us this night.

Oliver runs back across the tracks to Heather, who waits below us. This is one mission even I won't allow Oliver on, but he did get to start it off, and he should be proud of that. Heather runs with Oliver back towards the library. Her path is well protected.

Little Dino has a mission. He is to begin it all. He's a brave little dinosaur.

"Start with a bang," isn't that the saying?

Little Dino wobbles his way slowly southward down 11th Avenue. It makes its way carefully up near the commie brigade stationed a block from the hotel where the rats nest. They shout gibberish at the toy and at each other in a great confusion.

They know it's coming. They know their two buddies are down. They've seen the signs little Oliver painted, and the gruesome cryptic messages he left the night before.

They saw the bloody one, of he, little Oliver, holding the chopped off blood dripping head of a commie by the helmet as he smiles; the dead commie body leaning back against the wall, spouting blood out of its neck, with the message, "Yum, commie blood's on the menu in the morrow."

Then, you hear it, like a symphony, little Dino goes "BOOM," rocking the entire street and splashing red commie matter thirty feet high.

Gunshots ring out like the climaxing crescendo of Stravinsky's "Ritual of Abduction," by a full symphony orchestra. Each different gun is timed and fired to an instrument, beginning the exact moment little Dino's mission completes; C-4 explosions for the timpani's, petrol bombs for the crashes.

I pull the pin of three grenades, composing as I slingshot them into the sky as the timpani smashes through the loudspeakers in the back of an old truck.

I watch God's lead rip through the flesh of the evil commies. These little rat-cunts duck and dive in vain from the heavenly leaded rainfall which pours down upon them like daggers from the almighty sky chariots which angel Deon, Vanessa, and Alfred ride in on—adorned with blissful white robes, with bright red scarves wrapped in ivy and roses—crowns of pure gold and jewels.

From the 8th Avenue SoBro hotels behind, the angels shoot their dagger-pointed arrows directly through the commie hearts, heads, faces, legs, knees, and toes.

My thirteen disciples set off the next various sets of explosives and continue to rain down machine fire, clearing the streets of any remaining commie life forms. It seems the rats have already retreated back to their nest in the Tamberline Hotel.

Without harm, the disciples steal a commie truck gunner and begin driving around in circles, pumping 50 caliber rounds into the first seven to ten floors of the Tamberline, ripping the rooms to shreds.

The mission tonight, already a success. It's such a success, that perhaps it's time to continue. Why stop now? It's time to finish them.

Bobby, Will, myself, and several disciples enter the brightly lit hotel to find nothing but fleshy ghosts of commies past. Of course, the commie bastards have giant generators for their own power needs, which we may have to commandeer, though I've grown fond of the darkness of night.

My disciples decide to drive the gunner truck straight into the hotel lobby, nearly crushing one of the disciples to death. He'll survive. After helping their buddy to his feet, they manage to take the 50 caliber gunner off the truck; they're pretty scrappy fellows. They drag it into the still-working elevator along with hundreds of rounds of ammo. Eight disciples ride the elevator from floor to floor, assumingly clearing each one of any visible commies, one stop at a time.

Various rebels remain outside, blowing up this and that, while the angels continue watching over us.

I run up the stairwell with Bobby and Will, plus four other disciples. We hear footsteps climbing down as fast as they can scurry, screaming gibberish at one another, praying to their commie leaders to save them, but who only force them to stand and fight us.

I toss a grenade up, bouncing it off the wall, just behind the poor rats. At least a few of their legs, arms, and heads are blown clean off as two of each come tumbling down.

We continue to rise, knowing the commie commander will be in the penthouse. He's our true target. We can't leave without him, and any good commie rat-master knows to use his position of power for luxury goods and services. What better luxury than the $5000 a night penthouse in one of Nashville's finest palaces?

More commies run into the stairwell to hide from the elevator gunner. That doesn't turn out so well for them either. Will, Bobby, and the disciples lay waste to them all before I even have a chance, freeing their spirits from the rotten commie flesh and mind. Tonight, our guns and bullets are the swords of God's light, slaying the evil invaders.

The commie fear grows stronger. You can feel it dripping as the sweat drops from this poor commander's face. I stand over him while his secretary's slit-throated body squirts warm rat-blood onto him. It blends with his own sweat, blood, and tears.

He begs for a fate of any other than the one befitting him. My disciples won't be kind. Bobby and I won't be watching, but his poor young little naked commie buddy in the corner will. Then, he will run, swim, and crawl to tell his commie brethren across the Cumberland what hath taken place here tonight.

It's always good to have an audience member in times like these, thus allowing the fear to continue to spread throughout the commie body, thus weakening it, destroying the virus itself with an ever greater virus, fear.

There's still a spirit in the commie machines. It's just stuck, trapped, and suffocating until God's angels and disciples release each one to his own personal hell to be chopped up, burnt, and devoured. Then to be spit back out and once again given the chance to prove they're no longer wretched little commies, to prove that they want free will and all that this life brings, without one drop of the commie strain having not been burnt or cut from his very being as he begs for forgiveness.

This commander's head will hang like a trophy, mocking the losers of this battle from a rope hanging in front of little Oliver's foretelling mural of this very scene. Forever the fortune teller, he.

The disciples swing a galant sword. I close my eyes and turn my head. The commander's body falls from the rooftop, his head held high in victory to rebel cheers. Too bad little Oliver isn't around to witness it. He would have gotten a kick out of it.

The child is important; that's certain. He might just be what wins this war for us. Not a sacrificial lamb to the slaughter, but as the fear-inducing nightmare he is becoming to each and every commie. The mere sight of a child will now most likely send even the bravest rat running in the opposite direction from the vision.

After the mission and mural's completion, we begin our journey back to the library. We're too low in numbers to leave any lasting guard in the Gulch. So instead, the disciples line its every street, building, and alleyway with "Commie-Go-Boom's."

Now, we celebrate; they can. I don't "celebrate."

36. Tales, Myths, & Legends

SINCE TAKING THE GULCH, things have been fairly quiet, other than a few rather enjoyable side missions. But those are for them, not for me. The nectar is my only release, as well as plotting.

The men are in better spirits now, perhaps because we don't have to worry as much about commie invasions—for now. Or perhaps it's their recent morphine resupply.

For said side missions, the disciples have mostly been bombing commie patrols and envoys. I've also had them run a few small missions on the east side, which they've come back from totally undetected—simply damaging a little hardware.

Much of our satisfaction comes from planting C-4 slash petrol bomb I.E.D.'s in commie vehicles or in positions we know they'll return to. Then, "snap, crackle, pop," and the entire entourage gets ripped into commie-burger meat, perfect to feed the hounds. They've been feeding on commies for weeks, which brings us to cartoon #37, "Ain't Nothing But A Hound dog," which willfully shows the hounds ripping multiple wide-eyed commies into pieces and devouring them.

Now, little Oliver is no Picasso, but he is becoming quite the little Scott Adams. They're a little rougher and more imperfect, but I feel like that adds to the effect; almost trippy-like but always foreboding.

He's our own little Nostradomous but far more accurate in his predictions. The disciples nearly always display the "living" artwork prominently within a day or two of printing—whenever they get the chance. One day, we will use that to our advantage.

Oliver pops out these cartoons fast, sometimes five or ten in a day. #44 depicts a commie wobbling zombie-like back towards the commie-pound with his eyeballs hanging out of their sockets, strapped to the brim with a C-4 vest. You do the math. Given our track record, a commie is bound to live out this grotesque scene in the very near future. All we have to do is print it, which is what Will and the others are doing as we speak.

You feel the fear more and more in the hearts of the commies when they attack now. It's palpable, moist, damp like a swamp. They're in dread. The fear campaign is working—every sound a monster—a monster around every corner—every step a bomb awaits.

Squirlier than squirrels, the rats have become. Officers yell at them to continue onward, into the unknown hells which surely await them upon the downtown shoreline, but as they disperse from the commie boats, they are laid to rest within a few moments.

The officers are afraid now. They should be. They're usually the ones depicted in little Oliver's foretellings, so it's understandable. They have mostly stopped going on the missions, or keep guards with them at all times, whenever they do.

Of course, that's who the angels are almost always sure to devour when given half the chance.

Deon, Vanessa, and Alfred have begun to mostly do their own thing, though they don't mind sniping when we have a good mission, and certainly not when trouble is brewing.

The angels want the same thing, to end the wretched reign of the commie virus in this city, in this world. We all do. Common commie enemies create strange bedfellows.

Just look at Chipped-Tooth, Yancey, and me. It's a miracle either of them are still alive. I wouldn't trust either in anything other than killing and maiming commie scum-suckers. But in that, yeah, I trust the fuck out of these two dirtbags.

Since the big mission in the Gulch, the disciples have been getting a little restless. They're ready for bigger and grander assignments, but we're just not yet ready to go full East. So, I give them some simple missions. I even let them sort out a few missions themselves, to work out their recklessness.

On the current so-called reckless mission that I decide to join, the commies capture prophet Oliver and begin to haul him back towards their patrol boat.

Three of the commie's drop. One commie holds Oliver captive with a knife to his neck until a bullet plops right through his forehead. His fourteen other comrades drop just the same.

Left standing alone is little blood-splattered Oliver, who walks back our way with a look of success on his little unwavering face. Deon, Alfred, and the gang continue to snipe rats across the river, protecting little Oliver, who just almost blew the whole plan. Perhaps I should stop taking the little bastard on missions, especially when he or I haven't planned it.

The one rat who is left unharmed runs back towards his boat. Before he can make it, shots ring out in his path, decimating the boat. He starts swimming back across the water. We let him go. But unlucky for he, his comrades aren't very welcoming. They mow him down before he even makes it a tenth of the way to shore.

They don't want to let any more fear into their men, so it seems they just remove the fearful ones now. The generals themselves are perhaps the most fearful now. One of Oliver's recent releases is just for them. And we don't fail often. Plus, Will and a few of the rebels recorded a song just for General Brosman, titled "Cut You Up Into Pieces (Feed You To The Crocs)."

That's another thing that many of us thought was a little too reckless, particularly Alfred. The disciples decided to take crocodiles from the zoo and bring them into the mix. All of the zoo animals have been released into the wild. The crocs now roam the Cumberland shorelines.

Why? I ask. Because they thought it would be funny, and also to strike even more fear into the commies. Plus, they knew the animals were starving. So yes, reports of Jaguar attacks have been passed around the rebel ranks. How they made it down to the zoo and back unnoticed, I know not. The same luck can't be said of those rebels who tried to escape the city by vehicle, only to be blown away before even getting to music row.

The Komodo dragons are probably the worst of the bunch, which were brought here for a summer exhibit. Let's hope they don't propagate themselves into a natural existing species in America; if there's any America left once all is said and done.

After returning with the blood-splattered Oliver, Bobby and I sit in my chambers sharing the nectar, plans of commie blood and dreaming of a future free of all things commie. We discovered a whole new stockpile of the golden goodness in the Gulch, so I don't mind sharing. Heather sits nearby, watching over little Oliver.

Bobby is perhaps becoming my only friend in this wretched place. It's strange how that happens, but sometimes it's the ones you never expect, who you become the closest to. Perhaps even starting as enemies, as Bobby and I certainly had.

Now, here we are, actually bonding. I didn't often bond with dudes in normal life, let alone during wartime. At least he doesn't have the urge to "share" like some of the others. I'm not into "sharing."

All of a sudden, a knock bangs on the door, and in steps Will, Chipped-Tooth, and Yancey, followed by the other ten disciples.

What do they want? I hadn't spoken to them in days, it seems. Perhaps Will, but certainly none of the others.

"The disciples seek your guidance, sir," Will tells me.

"You don't need my guidance," I inform him. "I'll tell you when it's ready."

"We will follow you through the depths of hell, sir," one skin-headed disciple tells me, bowing in his brown cloak.

"Cut that shit out," I tell him. "It's creepy."

"What can we do, sir?" Yancey asks.

"Let me get some rest."

"But, what's our mission, sir?" Debouchy asks—whoever the fuck that is. "What's the greater plan?"

"I don't know," I tell them all, hugging the bottle. "Just do whatever the fuck you want. When it's ready, it will be ready, and you'll know."

This is probably the wrong response, as these idiots just go off and decide their own mission. These fools obviously do need guidance, but Bobby, the nectar, and I aren't in the mood. Neither is Will, who decides to stick around to partake in the nectar and weave stories of commie mishaps and rat blood, which are somewhat entertaining.

"Tina Marx, 64," Will says. "Kansas City, Missouri: About three minutes past curfew on August 14th. Tina thought she would be rewarded for being a good rat sympathizer, but as soon as she brought her niece Holly to the roadblock for trying to sneak off to see her boyfriend, the commies put one right through Tina's forehead. But they didn't kill Holly. They did something much worse—"

"Here's one," Will continues. "Did you hear about the guy who locked thirty kids in his basement in East Nashville, doing who knows what to them? And when the commies found out, they rewarded him with a position in their citizen Rat-Core, which is in charge of training the children to be good little soulless commies?"

"Are these true?" Bobby or I ask. The nectar has my mind in blurs this eve.

"I'm pretty sure. I'm thinking of putting them in a book," Will says. "Maybe little Oliver here can do the artwork. Think you could do that? Do a little artwork for my book, Oliver?"

Oliver says nothing. He just shakes his head, "Yes," then begins to draw with his favorite blood-colored crayon. It's a deeper red than the normal red. The guy knows his stuff. Heather watches over him as the fellas and I continue pouring nectar down our gizzards.

We probably should have continued our advancement immediately. But Jackie Boy and I aren't quite ready. Plus, Deon, Vanessa, and Alfred need a little more convincing before we attack the, at minimum, five-thousand commie strong compound—more like ten to twenty.

I have more planning to do, the best of which always comes when I'm knee-deep in the golden-sphere. I want it to be just right. The nectar will be of great help in that.

If I even mention a single detail to them, the disciples would be gung ho and basically drag me right into it. So, these plans are made in secret, to be kept secret. Deon's the only one trustworthy enough, and he thinks I'm just plain mad for even considering it. I told him it will work. Dangerous, yes. But not impossible. And if successful, we could all but destroy the commie virus in this entire fucking city.

Of course, I have my other motives. Deon knows that. But destroying the very core of the commie compound, and ripping the commie strain from this city, is quite the motivator in itself.

Deon knows there is much more to the plan. And he knows what she has become. He knows I would be risking everything. But he also knows that I have to and that perhaps, we all must risk everything. We already are. Why not go all the way?

Of course, I have to risk it. I must see her once more, regardless of if it will be the last or not. I have to look her in the eye to see if any of that good and that love still exist inside of her or if it has fully rotted in the filth of the cold-blooded commie shell.

What fucking luck I have.

As we sit, Will weaves another tale for us while we sip what's left from this bottle, "In last week's installment of Antifa Tales 101, little Jonnie Tucker and his big-time Antifa pals thought they were real big boys when they went up against one Grayson Briggs."

Will goes on, "Mr. Briggs was a quiet guy who kept mostly to himself, but when eight Antifa's attacked him, he was dead quiet. By that, I mean, within forty-five seconds, every one of those Antifa bullies was dropped into a pool of his own red and brown. It turns out they weren't such big boys after all."

Will continues, "This was even after the men in black—aka, commie pussies in black—knew the commie invaders didn't want them. But still, they tried to be good little communist sympathizers. But the people left in this city were not putting up with it, so they didn't last long. Not long at all. Too bad Mr. Briggs isn't here with us now, R.I.P."

As we relax in the chambers, an ominous vibration begins to take effect. From the sound of things, the disciples had decided it was time to up the antics. The sound of explosions rattle handfuls of books off the shelves. It would seem a bit eerie if we weren't so used to it.

Will, Bobby, and I quickly load up our arsenals and exit the chamber doors, leaving Heather and Oliver safely behind.

Several disciples come running inside to the main lobby laughing their asses off. They're beginning to get a little reckless, even to my standards.

It appears they've brought back a fucking commie brigade with them, the dumb bastards. If they didn't know where we are, they will now—or will they?

No, will be the answer to that as they don't stay for long —their souls do not. Those poor bastards never knew what hit them; I'm not even sure.

The explosions shake the city's very foundation. I guess that's what all the chuckling was about. Outside looks and sounds like pure armageddon, once again.

The commies know we are small in number. But they also know we have quite the arsenal and that we are rather fearless in comparison to their rat soldiers, who have rightfully become giant floppy vaginas—rat-vaginas.

I feel almost sorry for the commies now. They don't want to be here any more than us, but that doesn't stop me one bit when it comes to freeing every last rotting rat-soul I come into contact with. It only makes me stronger, knowing that I'm really just doing them a favor.

It's almost an insult to rats, comparing commies to them, but so be it. We're talking sewer rats with red demon eyes, not the cute ones you can buy at a pet shop or find in your ceiling.

37. Dangerously Good

I FIND DEON DOWN THE hall and admit to him, "Okay, you're right. It is fucking weird now."

"Yeah, it's fucking weird," Deon says. "It's always been weird."

"I know, but can we maybe go somewhere else now? Say, the capital?

"We're safe here, Harry. I know it's not the ideal living situation for anyone. But it's the only thing we've got."

"I'm just afraid they might do something."

The whole cult aspect of the disciples is getting weird for everyone, especially the angels. It's weird enough for me, their chosen one. I can only imagine what Heather thinks. At least she's safe. They won't dare allow harm to come to their queen. Though, their bowing down to her and Oliver every time they pass is becoming a bit much.

Alfred fucking hates the disciples, and really, all of the rebels. He is always on guard. These rebel militia clowns have no order or leadership. They have me, but I'm not one for control—only during missions. They have free reign otherwise.

Alfred's over it. He's the only one that would ever say anything to them. And today, they deserve a talking to. Lord knows I'm not going to say anything. I do my best to avoid them altogether, other than Will. I just enjoy seeing well-laid plans fulfilled, and the disciples are dangerously good at that.

"What do you all think you're doing?" Alfred asks the disciples.

"What's it look like?" Chipped-Tooth sputters, his tooth slightly whistling.

"Get them the fuck out of here," Alfred demands.

"Why don't you make us?" Yancey responds as footsteps surround Alfred.

I can't see any of this, but I can hear it. And I'm not so sure I like what I'm hearing.

"It's sick," Alfred says. "We're not living like this. It will draw attention to us."

"Perhaps we need a new centerpiece?" Chipped-Tooth begs the question to Alfred.

The other disciples move in closer, or so the sounds indicate.

"Back the fuck off," Alfred demands.

I hear sounds of scuffling, so I hurry to my feet, grab my rifle, and rush to the front.

The disciples hold Alfred down while Yancey and Chipped-Tooth wrap a noose around his neck and stuff month-old socks in his mouth.

"Hey," I say casually, as I notice several dead commies hanging.

"Sir?" Yancey asks. "What shall we do with the traitor?"

I say nothing, but with a slight smile and a whimper of a laugh, I slowly lift my AR and slam its butt into Yancey's pussy-ass mouth. He's now surely better off than Chipped-Tooth, in his once trademarked look.

No disciple dares stand in my way, especially Chipped-Tooth. I give Yancey one more strong whack to the mouth, leveling him to the floor.

Will steps up, "Surely that's enough, sir."

I look Alfred in the eyes. We both know things have gone way too far, and it's time to end any delinquencies.

I flip my rifle around and pop Yancey twice in the chest. The disciples back away. Will and Bobby stand behind me, frozen. Alfred removes the noose from his neck.

"What the fuck?" Alfred says while backing away. "You didn't have to shoot him."

"Yes, I did," I state, staring down Chipped-Tooth. "So that nothing like this ever happens again."

Vanessa and Deon run out. Heather holds little Oliver's eyes shut as they stand behind them inside the main hall.

"Alfred?" Vanessa worries as she sees him with the noose in hand.

"What happened?" Deon asks as I walk away and off to my chambers, past Heather and Oliver.

"Pack your supplies," I say. "We're leaving."

"We can't leave," responds Alfred. "You saw the photos."

"We're not leaving the city," I tell him.

"Where are we going?" asks Heather, following closely behind with Oliver.

"Where we should have been this whole time," I respond.

I assume Deon, Vanessa, and perhaps Bobby and Will help Alfred to his feet and out of the hall. But I can't be so sure, though it's silent to my six.

I enter the long narrow hall and start to fill as many bags, packs, and sacks with as much ammo, magazines, and explosives as I can carry. There's always more here if we ever do need to resupply. They won't stand in my way. I'm still their chosen one, and I still need them for the mission. But I'm not living under the same fucking roof as these lunatics anymore.

Once darkness falls, little Oliver, Heather, Bobby, and I meet Deon, Alfred, and Vanessa near the large double doors. Will and the disciples stand behind us on the stairwell to the second floor.

"But sir?" Will asks. "What shall we do?"

"I don't care," I say, standing between the others and the door.

"But sir?"

"Just keep up the good work, and when we're ready for you, we'll call on you."

"We'll be ready when you need us, sir," Will says. "Always."

The other disciples and rebels don't look so sure, not so sure at all. I feel a great divide opening between Will and myself, and we're at least hallway friends. The looks some of the others give me are, I'll just say, a little less pleasant.

With great precaution, fully alert to any commie rat stench, we head off into the night. Deon and I lead the others northward through the darkness.

It's a quiet night, but at any moment, we know an attack could occur, or a sniper could aim any one of us down. For some reason, that feels more plausible now, with this great divide growing. Or the disciples may just shoot us all in the back for turning on them. They are a little bit fucking crazy. Who wouldn't be?

"You're going to fucking regret this," Chipped-Tooth says, standing at the front of the library with Will and the other twelve disciples. "What about the prophecies?"

I'll give the disciples one thing; they are persistent. There is always a new rebel to take the place of any disciple who is laid to waste. They've already initiated a new member to take Yancey's place, shaved his head, and slapped on a new cloak. The other rebels who are left aren't much of men. Well, perhaps too much of men. They aren't the friendly, let's hang out and have a drink kind of men. These are men teetering on the lines of sanity and pure madness. They can be quite cruel. Many of the disciples can be. I've been a touch cruel. War is cruel.

Some of the rebels and disciples deserve to burn in this fucking city. But I will use them for our final mission. And if a success, this whole thing can be turned on its head. Even they may come through this as changed men.

This was never the plan. Escape was the plan. But now, my mind is spotting connections it has never noticed before. It senses what to do and where to do it next.

Through this whole fucking bloody thing, I am changed forever. But if there's one thing this fucking war has done, it's brought my genius out. A mad genius? Perhaps. But a genius nonetheless. Little Oliver has been a great help in all of this. Having him around, I've been able to see things differently.

Everyone has a bit of genius inside, buried somewhere. Some people use it. Some let it go to waste. I was letting mine go to waste. But now, I am forced to use it.

This war has forced me into a mad brilliance, and I will have my moment. She and I will stand eye to eye. She can escape with me and give up her evil cold dead hearted commie ways and live freely again with me, or she can stay and burn with the rest of them. She gets one second chance, and it's a fucking biggie. If this plan actually succeeds, she won't have much of a fucking choice but to come with me.

Up ahead, we see the capital. We walk past the theater and quickly make our way across the street. We hurry up the stairs out front. Heather carries Oliver while Deon, Vanessa, and Alfred lead the way. Bobby follows me.

Before I even make it up the final staircase, Alfred has the door open, and we're in. Home sweet home. Finally, we'll be able to live in a little luxury.

The inside of the capital is pretty much untouched. There's very minimal damage from the surrounding carnage. Nothing structural, simply cosmetic, along with the cryptic messages and graffiti left from citizens long since gone, fled, or dead.

Best of all, and why I always had my eye on the place, the tower still stands, which has always been of utmost importance to someone with a keen eye such as myself. I want a three-sixty-degree panorama of my surroundings. I want to be able to snipe three-thousand commies down in a thirty-minute window. Unlikely? Sure. But I will give it my best damn shot.

I've been here once. And if I remember correctly, I go up these steps, then all the way back, and I'm in the grand office suite, which shall be mine. I can't remember if it's for the governor, a congressman, or what, but I can't complain; much better.

Heather and Oliver follow me in. I have much planning to do, and although I want the space to myself, I must keep them safe. Plus, I may need the little bastard's drawing skills shortly.

The others stay in the same room, including Bobby. I guess there is safety in numbers. I need my space, and little Oliver needs his, where he can draw in peace and be watched over and cared for by Heather while I watch over her.

After getting settled, we set up alarm bells and steam whistles to detect any breaches. We have some great views of the scenery, perfect for commie detection. The punch-packing explosives we'll line our surroundings with shortly will be of extra deterrence.

38. Capital Punishment

ONCE THE NECTAR AND I settle into the new room, our mind is working overtime, in pure brilliance. No one will know of its genius until the plan goes fully into action. And this is only the beginning.

I cover the white walls, massive stone columns, and marble floors with black permanent marker. I scrawl the plan out from front to back, from outline to manuscript.

I must've spent the last sixteen and a half hours spelling out the plan like a maniacal poem of destruction and victory. However, before I really have the chance to dig into the whole thing and expand it into something even remotely real, a golden shimmer begins to shine outside in the pitch-black darkness. Must be the moon.

The shimmer appears to get larger. Shadows begin to appear. We're not expecting visitors.

Heather enters my chambers holding Oliver. We don't need to say anything to each other. She just gives me that look, but even more worried than normal. She needs my help. Everyone does. This is my problem after all.

The liquid glow makes its way up the grassy hill from the north. It becomes obvious that it's the disciples and their rebel friends. They carry torches and a large wooden cross.

Will and Chipped-Tooth lead the party while the disciples plant the cross into the earth halfway up the hillside.

Deon, Vanessa, Alfred, and Bobby storm in.

The disciple's light the cross afire on the lawn below.

"Goddamnit, Harry," says Deon.

Vanessa and Alfred aim their rifles downrange at the disciples.

I lower their weapons.

"I'll take care of it," I tell them calmly. "I should have never let it go so far. But I'll take care of it."

"You fucking better take care of it," Alfred says. "They're going to get us fucking slaughtered."

When I turn to exit, Heather grabs my arm and looks into my eyes, "Be careful."

I shake her grip off without a word and walk out, unarmed. The platoon stays behind as I make my way down the stairs and out onto the back lawn.

All of the rebels and disciples stand, hooded in brown robes with fiery reflections dancing red in their cultish eyes.

"What say thee, oh chosen one? Have ye forsaken us? Are we not good enough in thou eyes?" asks Chipped-Tooth proudly.

I walk up to Will in front of the burning cross, "Let's discuss this in private."

"Unacceptable," Will responds loudly. "You're either with us, or you're against us. You lead us, or we'll have no choice but to—"

"Don't you see?" I command my men. "I do need your help. It's not complete, but I have a plan. And I need all of you. It will be risky, and I need time and space to plot it out. But if you follow me on this mission, through the depths of commie hell, we may just come out the other side to freedom."

The disciple's eyes turn from a glaring murderous tone to glory and excitement, with hoots and hollers.

"Tell us your plan, chosen one," Chipped-Tooth demands.

"In three nights, it will begin," I tell them. "Just wait, and I will bring the plan to you on that day. Do you agree?"

"But we don't know the plan," Chipped-Tooth says. "How can we trust you?"

"If you do not agree to the terms, just kill me now," I tell them.

Chipped-Tooth cocks then raises his pistol at me.

"Yes," Will lowers Chipped-Tooth's revolver. "We agree to the terms."

A shot rings out, and Chipped-Tooth plops to the ground like a flipped pancake. The torches scatter and drop. The disciples and rebels take up arms and run for cover. I dash up the hill for the capital. Will follows me, dragging Chipped-Tooth along with the help of another rebel. His rifle drags behind him, slung to his shoulder. The disciples spread out and defend.

I'm unsure where the bullets are coming from, but Deon and the others begin to lay down fire from above.

A few dozen commies decide to storm up the lawn behind us. It's not their lucky day. I don't even have to fire a shot. I don't even have a weapon. I figure if the disciples really wanted me dead, there would be nothing I could do about it—I wasn't expecting all of this.

They got a few of us, and Chipped-Tooth doesn't look so grand, but these fucking commies don't stand a chance. All of the firing our way seems to stop. I walk back out into the open and onto the hill. I watch commie after commie drop like flies.

I simply stand here in the light of the cross, and instead of feeling like an unholy act, the burning cross seems to allow for the holy to enter this world through it. God's fire is on our side.

I turn to see Deon, Vanessa, and Alfred in the tower of the capital, firing round after glorious round into the commie brigade, who collapse from the piercing lead rainfall.

Not a single one of these commies wants to be on that hill, and for good fucking reason. Within the next twenty minutes, every single one of those bastards will burn under the cross. The disciples will drag them under the fire and pour gasoline on them. Even the wounded must burn. We can no longer hold any punches. This is war.

Word will surely return, and not another commie will dare storm this damn hill. The only thing we may have to worry about after this will be artillery. They had stopped shelling weeks ago, though it could spring up at any moment. And just then, wouldn't you fucking know it, not artillery no, a fucking chommie appears overhead, about 200 yards away. From the commie-chopper, out pours dozens of special-op commies. "Eww, I'm scared."

They do look a little bit more special than the rats we have been facing, but they're out in open land while we've fully barricaded ourselves amongst the pillars and walls.

I run, dive, and grab Chipped-Tooth's rifle, then hide behind a giant column and scope downrange. The commie special-ops do bring heavy fire, but it's the chommie that's causing us problems. It's already downed several more rebels and is ripping our cover to shreds. Wood and cement debris blizzard us. We must down it.

I dash for the rear entrance and skip through several 50 caliber rounds that plaster the wall inches away from me. I smash my way in and run full speed up the steps towards my chambers.

"Stay down," I yell at Heather.

Out runs little Oliver with his rifle rearing to go. He attempts to run by me, but I scoop him up and carry him back to Heather.

"Oliver," I set him down and look the little guy in the eyes. "I need you to stay strong, okay. I need you to stay here and protect Heather. Can you do that? I believe in you, Oliver."

"Okay," Oliver says with a searing vengeance raging inside. He tilts his head down and walks back into the room with Heather and his rifle, which is bigger than he is. He carries the AR-15 high and proud.

"Thank you," Heather mouths at me silently. Not that I could hear her if she said it aloud, being deafened again by the gunshots.

I rush to my chambers, grab my AR-10, and sight the chommie through the window. This bird's mine. However, it drifts around and out of my vision towards Victory Park to the south.

I run down the hall to the front of the building. I exit onto the balcony, staring dead-eyed at the rat pilot.

I aim the pilot down and pull. The bullet splatters a one-inch mark into the windshield, but it doesn't breakthrough. I shoot a second round. Then quickly a third, and a fourth.

The pilot smiles at me with his crooked rat-teeth. His gunner begins to bring the muzzle up and over my way, blasting rounds ever closer. I dive, but it's too late. If just two or three more rounds had gone through that thing, I would be, at just this very second, inside out, fully shredded.

I stand up calmly and a bit confused. The gunner jerks at his overheated weapon. The pilot's rat-tooth smile turns from confident to frantically terrified. He yells at the gunner, but the gun's jammed. And it's hot.

I aim down the pilot. I aim him down again. The glass holds strong. He yells and yells at his gunner as he takes evasive maneuvers. To my dismay, it appears the gunner has removed the jam and is fully reloaded.

The pilot's confident smile returns. I pull the trigger right as the gunner has me dead in his sights once more. He squeezes the trigger.

I can feel the airstream jet by the right side of my neck.

The chommie jerks back—the pilot's brains drip from the chair and ceiling onto his no longer smiling rat-toothed face.

The commie-chopper, aside from flinging backwards and momentarily upwards, has begun a firm descent towards Victory Park and the Military Museum. How fucking convenient.

The gunner's erratic shooting stops as he tries in vain to steady the chopper, but leaps out at the last second. I can't see if he survives the landing. The flash from the chopper's crash blurs that out. I'm now more concerned with the immediate threat, or so I thought.

Special-ops my ass. Without their little chopper, these pussies are no better than the rest. They do have armor on, which makes them a little bit more formidable than their non-special rat comrades, but not formidable enough.

They fire up at me, but I'm able to quickly take out two from my superior vantage point. The rebels and angels take care of the rest. As I said, when we're on a mission, we're dynamite. It's that whole when the mission's over part that gets to us.

Will comes out from behind a giant pillar and looks up at me, "It's beautiful, isn't it?"

"When it's done," I tell him. "Burn them all."

"Yes, sir," Will salutes, then begins to gather his men.

I return to my chambers to tell Heather of the good news and to grab a celebratory bottle to share as goodwill with my disciples; make that two.

From my chambers, I see the disciples and rebels walking down the hill, firing at the petrified commies who drop their arms to surrender. But there will be no surrendering today. Perhaps it would be different if this was a fair fight, or it were a day sooner. But we're outnumbered by man and machine, 1,000 to one, and 1,000 to none.

Plus, where would we keep them? It's their fucking fault that the disciples must burn the rest of the living rats alive. We have no other choice. The disciples and rebels drag them up the hill by their commie necks and hair with a few gentle stabs to begin the festivities.

I walk outside calmly, once again unarmed. I hand Will and Chipped-Tooth a handle each. Chipped-Tooth isn't sure what to think. He stands with Will's help, bleeding from the gut-shot.

"Take care of them, and I will take care of the plan," I tell my disciples in the burning night. "In three nights, we take back what's ours."

The disciples and rebels nod as they begin to fulfill my wishes on the grounds below, splashing the dead and living rats with ten gallons of gasoline before tossing the canister into the flames.

I walk back into the capital to their gibberish wails and sizzling moans. There's no need to look.

I head up to my chambers to continue plotting the mission in full, step by step, with all of the moving pieces coming together in perfect, if not maddening harmony, or so I hope.

Upon entering my chambers, Heather hugs me tightly. I have no time for pleasantries. I brush her off and make my way to a vacant wall to continue inking the plan. She understands.

It's strange—I don't even miss my old life. I've adjusted to this one. It's all I know. The love is gone.

It's only now—only war—blood—plotting—destruction.

Is there any city in our country not under siege at this very moment? In this world? We still don't even know who the fuck these commie rats are. I'm not sure we'll ever know. History has a way of obscuring itself. But one dead commie's just as good as another.

39. The Plot

AFTER TWO DAYS AND NIGHTS in my new chambers, the room is covered with mission actions, attack points, explosion sites, plus all of the in-between steps with precise timing.

It's to be my greatest masterpiece. I'll have to give little Oliver some of the credit, for he drew many of the actions out. I did the planning and all of the important stuff, but that little bastard is spot on with the commie blood that will be flowing through the streets once the plan succeeds flawlessly with not a single casualty on our side, minus a rebel, disciple, or two.

It's time to let Deon see it. Then he will understand. Then he will agree to go on the mission with me, even if it be our last, for he will understand. It's our only shot, and I know damn sure my old pal Deon will be up for it once he sees its excellence.

Deon will convince the others. No one else can see the full plan, except for Oliver, of course. And Heather, who has earned more trust than any of the others. There's not a scent of commie on her.

No one else can be trusted. If Jasmine can turn commie on me, any of these other bastards can, except for Deon. There is not a drop of commie in that man, nor in Oliver. But the others, I can't be totally sure.

Bobby is certainly frightened enough to be a rat, but only under threat of extreme torture, physical or psychological.

I don't know what Vanessa's always up to or thinking about. She speaks less than I do. And that's fucking saying something. But she is a brave warrior, our own Michelle Rodriguez.

Alfred? Fuck Alfred. He is no commie. I just don't want him to see it. I don't want to hear his opinion. I don't want to hear anyone's opinion.

Now Deon? He's a man who could take this kind of masterful planning to the grave. And I must show him, or the others would never join.

"Hey buddy," I stand observing my masterpiece on the white walls, furniture, and colossal columns, mixed with Oliver's doodles in blood-red. "Why don't you go get uncle Deon for me and bring him in here? And just him, okay?"

Little Oliver sets down his blood-red marker, stands astutely, and exits the massively oversized room.

I wait proudly.

Oliver leads Deon in. He looks at my walls of wonder with a distraught look of worry.

"What the fuck is this?" Deon asks.

"Isn't it perfect?" I confess.

"Is this what you've been doing in here these last few days?"

"It's my greatest masterpiece."

"Are you truly insane, Harry?"

"You haven't even seen it yet. Look around you. There's no other way."

I walk around the room, showing him mission point after mission point, after schematic, after fact.

"Here," I say, showing him the plan all laid out. "See? And here—but wait. This is when it starts to get good."

"Um-hmm. Okay," Deon begins to understand.

"And just when you thought it couldn't get any better," I lead and motion to the finale with my arms. "Where it all comes together."

"What about this little part?" Deon points to an area of the plan covered up by an oversized palm plant, which has somehow survived thanks to a bottle of water stuck upside down in it.

"Don't worry about that," I assure him. "I've got that covered."

"If you say so," Deon says. "And that?"

"What? The tank?"

"Yeah—the tank."

"Don't worry about the tank. We'll get to the tank when we get to the tank."

"It says right here," Deon points. "Deon and Harry commandeer enemy tank and—"

"It's cool. Just take it all in."

"Have you ever driven a tank, Harry?"

"I don't know. Have you? We'll figure it; read a book or whatever in the library. We'll need more supplies anyway. And we must inform them of their part of the plan so they can prepare."

"Wait?" Deon questions firmly. "They're coming?"

"Of course," I tell him. "Final mission. They're the little dicks."

"Dicks? I thought those were rockets?"

"No, like cause they're dicks. And I didn't want anyone to know that we're going to work with those guys again. They're kind of crazy."

"I know they're fucking crazy," Deon assures me. "I've been telling you that since they started following you around like fucking psychos."

"Yeah," I respond with a kill shot. "But we need them. The plan doesn't work without them. And it is my masterpiece. They'll be our pawns. Come on Deon, what do you say? One final mission before we blow this fucking town?"

"Okay, Harry," Deon agrees. "I'll see if I can get the others on board and—"

"My man," I interrupt.

"Just get some fucking sleep, will you?" Deon says while trying to take my bottle of nectar that's been glued to my left hand this whole shebang. He's unsuccessful.

I don't think he was even trying because I'm six or seven sheets to the wind, and I'm pretty sure he's been sober this whole fucking time.

How does he fucking stand it? All this blood and desecration? The stink, the rubble, the burning, the lead, and this fucking heat? I'm used to it now, but lord knows I miss my glorious A/C unit, the Astro-Cool 3000. Oh, how I miss you, my friend. You brought waves of coolness over she and I as we danced under the sheets.

I've been feeling a lot better since I began on my masterpiece, some forty-eight hours and thirty-seven minutes ago. Not that I'm keeping count, but that fucking coo-coo-clock 'coos' every fucking thirty minutes, so it's hard to fucking miss it. I've wanted to smash it to bits, but I'm saving my rage. I'm too deep into the plan to waste the few seconds it would lose me smashing it.

I don't need any fucking sleep. Not with a mind functioning as highly as mine is. Perhaps the disciples were onto something. I am feeling almost supernatural. But no, I need to give that shit a rest.

This isn't about me. It's about freedom. It's about the people who are still trapped in East Nashville. It's about the freedom-loving people all throughout the world. If all goes as planned, we may once again be able to live freely and peacefully. But whatever goes as planned?

Part Three

40. *Before Sunrise*

FINALLY—IT'S TIME—OUR ONE true mission. Will it be their blood pouring through the Cumberland River, or will it be ours?

We gather on the front steps of the Capital. Deon, Vanessa, Alfred, and I stand prepared. Will and Bobby stand guard next to Heather and little Oliver.

"If I don't make it back, look up to Deon and Alfred," I tell Oliver. "They're good men. I know you've been through something terrible that no child should ever see, but we love you, Oliver. You're a good kid. Heather will look after you while we're gone, along with Bobby and Will. Do as Heather tells you, okay?"

Oliver shakes, "Yes."

Heather hugs me tightly. I allow it for once. The touch of humanity she welds may be the last I feel in this life. She kisses my cheek as I turn away.

"I don't want you to go," Heather tells me.

"I have to. When I come back, we'll leave this God-forsaken place."

"But what if you don't?" Heather worries with the look to end all looks.

"You'll be fine. The others will watch over you."

"You're the only one I can trust."

"That's not true."

"Yes, it is. And if you do make it to her, how do you know she won't do to you what she did to Ken?"

"Because we love each other."

Heather hugs me with a very tight bear grip.

"Promise me you'll come back?" her tone says more than words ever could.

"Okay. I'll come back."

"Do you promise?"

"Okay, yes. I promise."

She lets go of me and holds tightly onto little Oliver.

"Take good care of them," I tell Bobby and Will. "Thank you."

"I will, Harry," Bobby says. "Good luck."

"I don't see why I can't go," Will says. "You know I can help."

"If you want to help," I tell him. "Protect her and the child with your life."

"Okay," Will says. "Yes, sir."

"Alright," says Bobby. "Go get those commie bastards."

Deon, Vanessa, Alfred, and I head off on our grandest mission.

The disciples are on their own, but they know their part of the plan. And they know the times. Our recently procured mechanical watches are synchronized. Everyone knows only their part of the plan, except for Deon and myself.

If the disciple's mission is going as planned, diversions will be set all around, before it even begins. Everyone should be ready and waiting for sunrise to fully set in. It's beautiful. They surely won't be prepared. We've never taken any real action during the daylight. They're more vulnerable than ever; we're more determined.

41. Them or Us

THE SUN BEGINS TO RISE while Deon, Vanessa, Alfred, and I armor up with the vests Alfred has decided to equip us with, finally. Surely they could have helped earlier,

'Alfred.' We begin our long walk to the patrol boat, each haul-
ing a large pack full of armaments.

"Thank you all," I tell them. "I know I haven't been the
easiest to get along with. And if this is it, I love you all."

"What?" Deon is flabbergasted.

"Don't make me say it again," I demand.

"Alright, man," Deon says. "I love you too, brother. May
God be with us."

I grab Deon's far shoulder and give him a hug as we
walk along.

"Just don't do anything stupid," Alfred says to my left.

I simply smile at Alfred and raise my eyebrows in excited
anticipation.

Of course, I'm excited. This is my masterpiece in action,
coming to full fruition.

"Quit smiling," Alfred says. "It's not funny. This is fucking dangerous."

"I know," I respond smirkingly.

"But he's right," Vanessa says with half a smile. "It's
been an honor serving with you all. Now let's take these
commie bastards out once and for all."

"Alright," I say with a crooked enthusiasm as we make
our way up towards Jefferson Street and down the river bank.

I uncover the hidden boat, which is filled with C-4,
petrol bombs, and thousands of rounds of ammo. Plus, the
50 caliber gunner we retained from the Gulch winnings.

"What the fuck, Harry?" Deon ponders as he looks into
the bomb-filled patrol boat.

"What?" I ask.

"Think this might be a little overkill?" Deon asks.

"Nope," I respond dead-fucking serious.

Deon just huffs and shakes his ever more fro'd out head
and bearded face. Now that's a bastard I respect.

We wait for the moment…

We watch our watches…

Until finally, the time has arrived.

"Ten. Nine. Eight… Two. One."

We put on our ripped t-shirt masks to help with what's coming. Nothing happens. Has something gone wrong? I check my watch. I tap it four times.

A small boom sounds off from south of Five-Points. It poofs a little puff of smoke.

Deon gives me a "what-the-fuck?" look, lowering his mask.

I shrug at him.

When suddenly, "BOOM! BOOM!"

The air is ruptured with huge, ripping, thunderous roars, "BOOM!"

It's a crashing, a collapse of epically grand proportions, a mesmerizing loudness. The tallest building downtown collapses behind us at near free-fall speed. The ground rumbles below as the steel and concrete crash down.

A huge wall of dirt and smoke engulfs us and the entire city. It spreads out past Five-Points in East Nashville and south past Green Hills.

We quickly shove the ticking-time boat into the river and hop in.

The commies don't stand a fucking chance. They can't see us, at least. And right now, that's all that matters as we propel the boat southward along our side of the shoreline.

More explosions erupt in the distance, vaguely brightening the thick, smokey, dirt-filled repugnant air. The air has been repugnant ever since the rats arrived. This morning, it's thicker than it has ever been. Visibility is zero.

Through the blind thickness, we begin to cross. I drive the boat quietly onto the muddy shoreline, right next to the commie's main armed vehicle storage center, just south of the stadium.

Alfred and Vanessa hop out, aiming through the thick air for any possible commies.

Deon and I attach a long chain to the front of the boat with a large S-hook, then drag the chain towards the stockyard and hook it to a red-marked commie truck.

Explosions continue to rock the surrounding areas, still mostly diversions. The disciples haven't even started their true mission, but so far today they have not let me down—nor the rebels, who do most of the diversions.

"Best of luck everyone," Deon says. "Let's make these bastards hurt."

Deon and Vanessa hug each other quite hugely. They look each other in the eyes deeply, confidently reassuring the other.

"We'll see you soon, mates," Alfred says. "Good luck, Harry."

"Thanks," I say. "Thank you all. May the Lord be with you."

They give me a suspicion-filled look, but they're in agreement. I guess they just don't figure me for a man of God.

He won't let us down. Not today. Not after all of this.

Vanessa and Alfred hop into the truck and get it running.

Deon and I find and procure the tank that the disciples marked for us with a red stripe. He's right. We've never driven a tank before, but soon we will get the hang of it—just have to get it started.

I don't have any idea how, but I manage to get the damn thing running. Or was it Deon? Neither of us can be sure as we question each other with surprised glances.

Now the controls—no clue. We do get it moving. Bumpy and slow, yes, but we're moving. And we just need it running and waiting.

Deon and I climb out of the tank, hop down, and run to the boat. We grab several petrol and C-4 bombs each. Alfred mans the 50 caliber gunner in the back of the truck while Vanessa pulls the fully bomb-loaded boat in tow. It skids out of the water and onto the pavement.

Vanessa stops and gets out to un-attach the hook from the boat, which is in a near-perfect position by the armament storage facility. They've got to keep all their tank shells and 50 cal rounds somewhere. This looks like the spot.

Vanessa and Alfred hop out and begins transporting the guns and ammo from the boat to the truck.

Gunfire erupts as Deon and I run about, placing bombs under every tank and gunner in sight. Alfred leaps back into the back of the truck and hammers the smoke camouflaged enemies with the 50 cal. Vanessa fires away beside the cab.

Deon and I sprint back to the boat for more explosives, then back to pack them under tank treads.

Deon hurries to grab the bucket that's filled with quick-drying monkey-glue balloons. He stuffs them in tank nozzles and pops them while I continue placing C-4 on the treads. We could be overlapping some, but that's fine. Though commie tanks blowing themselves up is quite the image.

Several commies continue to fire blindly into the smoke and dust, which still hangs heavy over the air.

Vanessa and Alfred continue to cover us.

Who knows why the commies thought leaving their valuables this close to the shoreline was a good idea, but I'm not complaining. I guess they weren't expecting us.

We've now successfully planted some sort of explosive on or monkey-glued almost ninety percent of the vehicles, for a total of at least forty-five.

After mission A's completion—the bombs are set and ready—Deon and I run back towards the boat.

Alfred fires the respective 50 caliber gunner upon the incoming invisible rats, surely shredding the lot of them.

While Alfred's firing north towards the stadium, I spot a commie climbing onto our running tank.

"Vanessa," I shout, pointing to the tank.

Vanessa looks out and shoots several shots at the commie fuck with her handgun, finally dropping the bastard. I hurriedly search for the detonator in the patrol boat, as does Deon.

"Well?" Deon asks. "Did you bring it?"

"Of course, I brought it. I think."

"You think? This is your plan, Harry."

"Um—here it is," I grab the device and dash past the truck to the tank. "Let's go."

Deon follows right behind while denouncing me, "Idiot."

We get to the tank and begin climbing on top.

Several commies appear through the smoke. I aim my pistol their way. They spot me, but it's too late. Alfred mows down the three of them, then a fourth and a fifth without pause. I can't even squeeze the trigger before they are plastered to pieces on the pavement. The 50 caliber rounds punch fist-sized holes through their commie rat-guts.

Deon hops in the tank. I hop in behind him and take the reigns. I do my best to drive the damn thing, but these controls are getting the best of me.

"Do you want to switch?" Deon asks.

"I've got it," I say as I shoot out a blast to the northeast, smashing through a building. I see a couple of commies flung off the roof like G.I. Commie-Joes.

The tank's monitor shows heat signatures, so we can really see the two commies flip and flop through the smoke-filled air. No wonder that fucking tank that almost splattered Ken and I wasn't hindered by all of the smoke.

Deon's gunner also reads heat signatures, which is sure to be helpful during our immediate advance through the dust-filled air.

Too bad everything's in gibberish, or this might be easy, though I manage to trudge the tank on down the road, up Shelby Avenue—left through the neighborhoods.

After moving clear of the soon-to-be commie equipment graveyard, we ignite what is surely the largest explosion we've experienced this entire summer.

The sky behind us erupts. An extreme heatwave blows overhead.

I would almost assume that Alfred and Vanessa got scorched, but they've managed to survive it, though their hair may be a little singed, particularly Alfred's. They continue trekking behind us in the gunner truck.

Now that I've slightly gotten the hang of this fucking thing, we head straight for the commie headquarters, right dead in the heart of Five-Points—new fucking Broadway. We turn right down Woodland street, straight towards the dead-cold commie heart center.

There are no civilians here, aside from her, only rats for the slaughter. Though we can't see far in the smoke with our naked eyes, we see rats atop many roofs and balconies through the monitors.

We begin to tear into the buildings. The rats scatter. I shoot a blast through the midsection of one building while Deon serves out 50 caliber lead pies into the street and lower levels of the buildings.

Upon a roof to the left sit three men with what appear to be anti-tank rocket launchers. Luckily, they're in plain view, and they are not prepared. The smoke is too thick for their eyes, but not ours.

One rat fires, one runs, one freezes. The shell's impact blasts the building's top off. Each rat is sent flying in opposite directions to its certain demise.

We blast the casinos on new Broadway to bits. This is where these fucking commies live, the rat-fucks. Commies-go-boom, commies-go-splat, left and right.

We continue our slow descent into commie hell. Menacingly, the buildings begin to surround us, closer and closer.

The disciples and rebels continue to wreak havoc all around. The smoke and dust thicken as the explosions creep ever closer to Five-Points.

A few commies on the street shoot their machine guns at us, but they do nothing. Deon quickly diffuses the situation.

Deon mows down every rat he finds in the street. The best is when one of the 50 cal rounds blasts off a commie leg, and the commie falls like a half-dead rat, yet squirms like a bloody slug—rat-slug. Their slug-like bodies crawl to their final resting place.

42. The Stadium

ALFRED AND VANESSA SHOULD be to their objective by now. The disciples better be there waiting.

This may be the most important aspect of the whole fucking mission, one I had to gloss over, as no one could know about it. Nobody did, not fully.

This isn't about me. It's about freedom. And as it turns out, it's also about the thousands of citizens trapped in that fucking commie-camp.

We hoped the stories were just myths. We never saw anyone, except for the one who leaped from the top, smashing to the ground while the guards laughed. They stopped laughing when we let fire rain down on them like ghouls, slashing their commie flesh with burning lead from across the river. Their laughter turned into bloody gibberish screams.

We just thought they were having a little commie fun, forcing the poor bastard to jump. But no, he jumped to escape. It was just far too high.

The space underneath the stadium could house 10,000 people easily. Barbed wire surrounds the whole thing. A few dozen guards stand by at any moment.

It's certainly a difficult myth to swallow but there had been signs everywhere—including actual messages asking for help written in blood on the upper levels, which the commies quickly covered.

We didn't want to believe that civilians were trapped there, and we never truly knew for sure, nor the massive scope of it; not until we saw the pictures the disciples were able to procure.

We saw the kids. Then we knew. I wasn't a fan of how they got to us, nor the depths they traveled, but once disciple #7 pulled them out, we knew. We all knew. Why else would Vanessa or Alfred agree to this? Let alone, Deon? That's what they're really in this fight for.

I knew it was true this whole time. We all did. We just didn't want to think about it. We didn't want to think that our friends or neighbors could be trapped in there. We hadn't been in contact with anyone from East Nashville this whole time. And what could we do?

We know what they were doing. We had intel. Alfred did. They were doing what commies always do, what only a commie could do, what commies have done throughout the twentieth century.

Lord knows what the fuck they're doing with the young children; thousands more just like little Oliver. Hopefully, no other had seen what Oliver had, but fat chance of that in Commie-Ville.

We all knew it was true. Now, there is no more doubt. And if this mission is truly a success, every last single one of those civilians will be freed, many of which will choose to help us in our mission to fully take back East Nashville and drive the scum from this city.

The disciples have surely planted the devices under the smoke-filled clouds by now, ready to distract and destroy. Also, to blast a twenty-by-twenty-foot hole in the southeast side of the stadium, forging the perfect exit.

Then, Vanessa, Alfred, and several disciples will enter and free them all, opening the door to the light.

Chipped-Tooth will man the 50 cal gunner. He's still injured, but there was no way he was missing the fight of a lifetime, nor would I allow it. The rest of the disciples and some rebels should be spread out by now to deal with any commie fucks who dare block the civilian's escape.

Alfred and Vanessa will lead the thousands of citizens from the stadium, and they will all run north, to freedom, to their homes, their cars, or steal cars, and escape.

They will take all of the city buses that have survived, and they will disappear into the hills of the free states, which Tennessee will surely be once this is all over. The evacuation from the city must be swift, but we can sure use the help of the healthier civilians. There should be hundreds of rifles and handguns laid out waiting for them.

Deon and I continue our destruction unobstructed—commie blood's a'splattering. The streets are all but vacant of living dead-hearted commies. A vague splatting of machine-gun fire bounces off our steal beast. Deon quickly batters down their location.

Most of Five-Points is now up in flames. I fire and blast the buildings surrounding the main headquarters, the Vandemore, perhaps the fanciest casino resort in the entire southeast. The rats don't dare peak their ugly fucking commie faces out of the windows.

I know where her fucking room is, if Oliver and the disciple's intel is any good, which it is. Her room's close to that blast, and it probably shook her, but it didn't harm her. The Vandemore will remain mostly unscathed. Dozens of explosions blast into the sky around the stadium. We get a fair view through the 360-degree tank cameras.

Now the mission is truly moving forward as planned, my masterpiece in action. But I can't feel it yet. It's time to pay my love a visit. I won't feel anything until I see her and look her dead in the fucking eyes.

If I see even a shred of commie in her beautiful fucking soul, I will smack that fucking commie right out of her. I will wake her up and bring her back to life, to freedom. Then I will love her with everything I am. I will heal her. I will bring her with me, no matter how much she fights me, and we will escape together as the sun sets and we're far from this wretched place.

Then, once this is all truly over, we will come back and rebuild this once beautiful city. In time, the flowers will bloom, and the birds will sing. Out of the putridness, life will flourish here once more.

Now it's time. And there it is. The clear path lights itself for me.

Smoke fills even more of every inch of air now, offering the perfect cover for Deon and I. We escape the tank chambers and make our way through the thick drifting air.

The tank explodes to our six. We couldn't just leave it sitting there for the rats.

Deon and I walk down Woodland Street, which is now mostly blown out Honky Tonks, sports betting bars, and burning casinos. Perhaps the old charm is now returning after vanishing from its foray into truly being Nash Vegas. So, I'm actually feeling rather accomplished, destroying something tragic to make way for something beautiful again.

We'll have to rebuild the whole fucking thing anyway; why not bring down the whole fucking house?

Commie fucks begin to appear through the denseness, dozens of them, but we drop each one with our heavenly leaded daggers of love. Today, we are their reckoning. Today, we are angels of death, freeing the commies of their rotted tormented flesh which entraps their very souls.

Their fear leaves them vulnerable. Their shaking hands struggle to aim us down. It feels as if God himself is directing mine and Deon's movements, defenses, and offenses, laying them down to rest in perfect rhythm and harmony.

Most of the rats aren't even coming for us. They're simply running from their posts, retreating to who-knows-where.

Every time one of these commie fucks pops his rat-snout out of the thick smoke, Deon or I smoke them, blast them down, or jab our knives through their necks. There is no coming back from that, and it leaves them more time to think about what they've done in this life. Even a commie knows truth upon death's doorstep.

The commies deserve to suffer the greatest of sufferings. It's their moment. Face to face with death, they gasp as the blood fills their every breath, until that final moment of suffocation.

What a beautiful moment it must be for each and every commie bastard we throat fuck with our heavenly daggers. They go from spouting gibberish, to spouting blood, to speaking directly to God himself. If that's not beautiful, I don't know what is, not in this world. It's the only truth any of these commie fucks will ever know again.

Nothing will be as beautiful again, not until I hold her and help each commie bastard who stands between her and me meet their maker.

Today, I will know for sure. When I look into her eyes, I will know.

Deon and I walk through the smoke, popping the fleeing commies with our pistols, rifles, and my sawed-off. Don't ever let some fucking politician tell you the Second Amendment is outdated. The commie virus can pop up anywhere, at any time, and we must be prepared. That's why we're going to rip it off the face of this earth and out by every last fucking root. My shotgun blast leaves a dinner plate hole in this poor fleeing cunt's guts.

The rats keep coming, but they are rather terrified, every single one of them. Most aren't even attacking, they're fleeing. They can't see a thing through this smoke, but a few of them do obey their overlords and come out firing. They're almost just as easy. The wind's blowing in their faces, glittering their eyes with dust.

The look on this poor commie's fucking face is priceless. He appears through the smoke and sees my pistol staring him square in the eye. Dust and smoke breeze off him like a fluffy cloud.

This is one lucky rat. I only clip him, but he's down, and his gun drops away. I walk over to the poor fucking bastard as he reaches for his gun. He's a little off-balance with his burnt-out jaw. The gun's barely out of his reach.

I stand above this dark-haired commie fuck as he tries his best to cover his face from the gun. I shove the barrel into his dirty commie fucking mouth and "Pop!"

But it wasn't me. I felt the bullet wiz by my face. A commie drops five feet behind me.

"Thanks," I tell Deon.

"What are you waiting for?" Deon asks as this commie bastard squirms and squirms beneath me, mumbling gibberish as he deep throats my thick hot metal barrel.

"Pop!" the gun sounds and the rat quits squirming.

"I guess it's not his lucky day," I say in a low heroic tone. Deon shakes his head, "Let's go, dude."

We continue on as the thick smoke dances off our weapons like fractals. Good thing Alfred hooked us up with flash suppressors. These bastards can't see us, but we can sure see the flash of any commie firing through the smoke, allowing us to lay them to rest pretty easily, or at least down for a good nap.

Through the dusty smoke, there it is, the commie fucking compound headquarters, the Vandemore, alive in all its gaudy casino resort glory; gold, copper, and maroon; shiny, decadent, and drab.

She's in there, right above where the little coffee shop used to be, right in the middle of Five-Points. We have to be careful now.

"Wait till I get my fucking hands on that fucking officer who turned her," I mutter to myself in waiting. "Just fucking wait, you fucking commie rat-fuck-bastard."

"You alright, Harry?" Deon asks.

"Yeah," I tell him. "Let's do this."

"After you," Deon holds out his rifled hand.

43. Gibberish

KNOWING THERE WILL BE at least a couple dozen rats inside, if not hundreds, we head through the thick smoke to the front of the Vandemore Resort and Casino. It rises from the ashes of the burning city. The lights pour out wispy red, pink, and gold neon cloud bursts, which hang in the rich smokey air.

The building has a set of smashed double doors on each side of the revolving doors. I take the left side, Deon goes right. We lean back against the marble walls. I signal Deon.

We grab two grenades each, then count together silently, "one, two——"

We toss all four grenades in through the blown-out doors, one after the other, in all directions.

Gibberish spouts out and about until, "Boom! Boom-Boom! Boom!"

Deon and I grab one more grenade each, pull the pins, and toss.

Faint, gibberish screams are heard as the rats scurry for their lives—those who are still able.

"Go!" I yell and storm through the left door, Deon through the right, as the grenades explode. The Vandemore lobby is as smoke-filled as outside.

Giant red-carpeted stairwells wind up each side of the circular room to the center like a fu manchu. We skip the red-light casino in the back and storm to the stairs on the right side of the front desk.

Deon's armed with his submachine gun and 1911. I've got my 9mm and sawed-off shotgun—rifles on our backs.

We make our way up the hot, damp, and humid stairwell, halfway to the second floor. We hear faint gibberish. The commies prepare from the second-floor entry.

"Good thing we brought a lot of these," I pull out my fourth grenade, pull the pin, wind up, and fling a wicked submarine screwball up the wall. It winds its way speedily around and up near the fearful commies. It reminds me that I've still got a bit of a hole in my shoulder, but the adrenaline's too heavy to sweat it.

Deon and I storm up the stairs, blasting through the red-liquid smokey air. Blood splatters out of the grayness from the blast, momentarily bringing light to the darkness. Deon lays the survivors down with his 100-round clip while I blast away with my semi-auto sawed-off.

We enter the second-floor hallway and watch as the only three commies standing pause, turn, drop their weapons, and RUN!

"No commies left behind," I think aloud as I pop two in the back. Deon sprays down the third, perhaps all three. Who can be sure? And what's it matter? "Every dead commie's a good commie."

"You've got that right, brother," Deon agrees.

We make our way to the fire escape stairwell at the back of the hall. Fully reloaded, we enter. The sounds of footsteps clatter up the metal stairs above like scared little mice.

A commanding voice shouts gibberish at his men. The footsteps stop, then fearfully turn. The feet slowly begin to make their way back down the stairwell.

I fire one shot up their way, and these pussy commies storm back up the stairs until "Pop."

A limp, dead commie flops his bloodied broken neck down the steps. Several live rats follow—stuck between a heartless commander and the bringers of bloodshed, Deon and I. Their fear is thicker than the smokey air itself.

"Shh…" Deon whispers.

A commie boot appears carefully around the corner.

"Pop," Deon shoots the rat in the foot with his 1911. He falls down our way, then covers his face. Deon pops him twice, through the hands and face.

Another commie appears into view, he fires. I blast him back with my shottie, but Deon's down. He's hit.

I take his submachine gun, reach it around the stairwell turn, and spray twenty rounds.

I kneel down to Deon.

"Oww," he moans, pulling off his life-saving vest as he catches his breath.

A grenade floats and bounces down our way. I kick the bastard, but I'm not sure which way it went.

"BOOM," the grenade blasts down the flight of stairs behind us. It's warm, but we're fine.

We look each other in the eyes. There's no time for losing. I pull Deon up, and he flops his plate carrier to the ground, then takes his "subby" back.

Lucky for us, the commies are too cheap to buy their rat-soldiers any armor. Otherwise, this day would have been a little bit more difficult.

Being tired of this little game, I pull out another grenade, but Deon stops me. I guess he believes it to be his turn, so he grabs one, pulls the pin, pauses, then throws the grenade straight up between the shaft.

The grenade reaches its apex but doesn't burst. It begins to fall back our way.

"Oh shit," Deon shouts as we hit the ground.

The grenade explodes a couple of flights above us. Good thing he's got an arm on him.

"Gibberish?" the commander spouts in a wild outcry, questioning if a single "man" is left to protect him.

Not one of his rats answers in any spoken language. Their bodies bang loudly as they plummet downward, clanging against the metal stairs, echoing through the even smokier corridor.

Deon and I stand, then begin making our way upward, faster and faster.

Only four footsteps are heard now besides our own. Two commies hustle their way up above. In vain, I sure hope.

We hear more rats waiting for us on the ninth or tenth floor. They shout down, hoping for a response from their comrades, but all is quiet now.

"Hey, you commie fucks," I shout up the stairs. "We're coming for you."

They respond with the usual frantic gibberish. If they want any chance at continuing in this life, they better just leap out of the fucking window because today is not a day to stand in my way, nor Deon's.

With half of our mission complete and having destroyed the majority of the commie compound and their heavy machinery, the rats better damn well know that they don't stand much of a fucking chance here. Not while they stand between my love and I. Commie or not, I will heal her and set her free. We're close.

To the sound of it, the grenades tossed by both Deon and I take care of the stairwell guards. My shotgun's empty, so I drop it behind and ready my pistol.

We make our way up slowly to the top floor. The path is clear. Not a fucking commie in sight, not in one piece.

All is quiet, but suspecting something isn't quite right, I kick the door to the hall open.

Machine gun fire pours into the metal door, ricocheting lead all around with loud cracks, tings, and thuds.

"Well," I think aloud, pull out the nectar from my pack and go to take a swig, but Deon grabs it away.

We lock eyes fiercely, but he's got a point. Deon rips off a piece of his shirt, shoves it into my glorious nectar bottle, and lights the fuse.

I look at him like he's insane. But I understand. We are low on explosives. Plus, there must be a minimum of eight rats waiting to pump lead into us the moment we step foot into the hall.

Fuck these commie fucks.

Deon kicks the door open and tosses the molotov fountain of youth around the door with his left hand, then plops onto the ground, peaks out, and fires away.

"Gibberish," they spout as the molotov bursts and commies alight.

I leap across the hall and take cover, then peak out and drop the commie nearest.

Several ignited rats hit the ground and roll but without much success. Deon and I rain glorious lead down upon the remaining commie wretches.

The two of us make our way through the burning rats, firing at any slight movement. There isn't much left, aside from the one still burning alive.

There it is; the long hall leading to a large wooden door at the end. That must be it, where all of the magic in the universe awaits.

Is she really on the other side of that door? Am I about to see my love again? My stomach churns with butterflies and whiskey pains. Is she really where little Oliver and all of the disciple's intel told me she was? Still? With that officer? What has he done to her? How was he able to warp her mind?

She was so true and free and beautiful, only to turn wretched, sick, and diseased. Can I turn her back? Can I free her? Will she willfully escape with me, or must I force her hand?

44. Dreadfully Majestic

DEON AND I SMASH THROUGH the penthouse door, and there she is, her and only her. My Jasmine. My love. My light. My sun. My glory. My heart. I melt in her presence. I'm stunned. She stands there in full-on commie rat garb with a .45 in her right hand.

Without a flinch, Jasmine shoots Deon in the gut.

"Oww. Eh… You commie bitch," Deon says with a painful-sounding jest as he goes down bleeding.

Jasmine and I aim fiercely at each other, looking deep into each other's eyes. She's afraid. She's hurting. What have they done to her? How could she do this? To Deon? Our friend? What is wrong with this fucking woman?

Is there any good left in her? Is there any good left that wants to escape the commie prison? Is she so deeply trapped within the confines of the cold dead commie heart that she'll never be able to escape?

Jasmine and my eyes remain locked in this sickeningly majestic moment. Magical despite all of the fire, smoke, putridness, the war all around, and her cold dead heart.

Deon is bleeding out on the ground next to me.

"What are you waiting for?" Deon asks.

"I'm sorry, brother," I say to Deon. "We'll get you out of here."

"Hah," Jasmine provokes, then shoots Deon a second, then a third time, while spouting gibberish—possibly a fourth and fifth.

I fire into the wall a foot from her head. We aim at each other between the eyes.

I get down on one knee next to Deon and hold his bloody hand, still aiming her down.

"I'm sorry," I tell him once more.

"Get them out of the city," Deon says as dark red liquid pumps from his mouth. His eyes fall back as his spirit leaves his now limp body.

"Rest in peace, Deon Hardaway," I say, then stand and aim heavy at Jasmine—eye to eye—gun to gun.

A commie officer—him—general Brosman, walks in from the bath behind her.

"Well, well, well," Brosman says, then slowly raises his pistol.

"Wait," she turns to him.

"Brosman?" I question angrily as he smiles.

I turn my pistol and pop the general straight through the head.

"Harry!" Jasmine screams with a wretched scowl, then with an even more scowling squeal. "Harry! What is wrong with you? He was a great man."

"He's a fucking commie," I respond. "You just killed one of the best and bravest men who's ever lived. My friend."

"He's my friend," she explains fiercely. "He helped me. He kept me safe. I loved him."

"Love?" I question. "We were in love."

"This is bigger than us," Jasmine explains. "It's for the cause."

"What cause?"

"The greater good."

"This is the greater good?"

Jasmine shakes, "Yes."

"What about us?"

"What about us?" she snarls.

"I loved you with every drop of my heart and spirit. You were the only thing I ever wanted in this life."

"This isn't about us, Harry! There are bigger things in the world than you and I."

"What about love?"

"I do love you, Harry."

"No, you do not. You have no idea what you're doing."

"Yes, I do. Things are going to be wonderful once this is all over. You have no vision, Harry."

"What did they do to you?"

"Nothing. This was my decision long ago."

"Long ago? What does that mean?"

"Do you think that this just happened? All of a sudden?"

"Just put the gun down and come with me. We can make a home somewhere far away from all of this and start a family."

She laughs, "A family? With you? Rebel scum?"

Jasmine pulls the trigger. Time stops. My eyes close—waiting for the end—there she is—but it's not her—perhaps it never truly was?

The gun clicks. She's out. She pulls the trigger again. This time I don't flinch.

"What are you going to do?" she laughs. "Shoot me?"

I stare into her cold, deadened eyes.

It takes every ounce of my willpower not to end her. My index finger flinches on the trigger of the increasingly heavy pistol.

"Well?" she mocks. "You're not going to do anything. You're a little pussy just like you've always been. And you want me to start a family with you? Please."

"How could this happen to you? We were so happy."

"Why do you think I went home that day?" Jasmine asks with her deep ever-darkening eyes. "Do you think I just forgot my computer? Do you think they just happened to know where I was when I "escaped?" Or did I perhaps swallow a GPS tracker to inform them of your locations before going back home with my new family?"

"I want to rip your fucking heart out. But you can keep it."

"Gibberish, gibberish, gibberish," this commie cunt spouts in a vile venom-spitting outburst.

I walk to her. She goes for Brosman's gun, but I grab her and smack the fuck out of her once beautiful and loving face. She turns her cheek back and spits blood at me. I begin to drag her towards the large solid redwood door.

"Let's go."

"Get your fucking hands off of me," Jasmine spits fire at me.

I grab Deon's submachine gun, plus his extra magazines, then drag Jasmine through the door.

Pounding footsteps come bouncing up the metal stairs near the other end of the smokey hall. The open flames burn hot, so we move swiftly.

I'm glad the fucking rats are coming. It's they or I. And it's not fucking me. Not when I'm this close.

The smell of the rat bastards wafts out from the stairwell. I know they're close. I grab my second to last grenade, crack the door, and toss it down the stairs.

The grenade explodes, maiming probably a half dozen commies. I pull Jasmine behind me into the stairwell corridor. Smoke fills every inch of the dreadfully humid sauna.

"Gibberish, gibberish, gibberish," several frightened and injured commies spatter. Jasmine spatters back a warning until I shut her mouth.

Through the smoke, a rat appears, "Pop."

A second rat, "Pop," a third. "Pop."

Jasmine tries to stop me, but it's no fucking use.

As I reach for my final grenade, a fourth rat appears through the smoke. I shove Jasmine into him. They tumble down the stairs. I follow and pop him right through the skull.

Jasmine grabs his gun and turns it my way. I smack it from her cold commie hand.

I pull the pin on my last grenade and toss it off the wall, bouncing it down the next level of stairs.

"Gibberish," I hear right before the rat screams turn to fire and blood-curdled wails.

Now it really is time to flee. The fire engulfs the floor above us, soon to spread below.

I drag Jasmine behind me, against her every will. I spray Uzi fire at the last few remaining rats, who are now mostly fleeing. They drop like flies, flopping down to sounds of cracking and plopping.

"Let me go," Jasmine demands.

We make it down the fire escape with no more incidents and out into the second-floor hall.

I drag Jasmine to the elegant staircase, where we had once passionately made out, and down to the main lobby. There's not a live rat in sight.

45. Blood In The Streets

I DRAG JASMINE OUT OF THE front entrance. Thousands of civilians run free through the smokey street, skin and bones and sickly.

The plan has worked. The citizens are free. And with the weapons stash that Vanessa, Alfred, and the disciples brought, many are helping take out the remaining commies.

They show no mercy. The rats don't deserve any. That's why they don't receive any. Every one of these bastards participated in bringing hell on earth to this land. Now they're getting what has been coming to them all along. These men, women, and even children are angry. They're starving and ill. The vengeance will bring them new life.

I drag Jasmine along westward. In an alley through the smokey air, I see a gaggle of commies lining up civilians to execute them.

I drag Jasmine towards them, then swing her to the ground in front of me. I spot Alfred and Vanessa in the line through a gap in the fog.

"Alfred!" I shout and flip my AR around, then begin to mow down the unsuspecting commies right as they begin their execution.

My chest all but explodes. I drop, searching for my breath. One lucky rat bastard nearly pierced my armor. It feels like a fifteen-pound bowling ball smashed right into my chest, crushing my lungs.

"Harry!" Vanessa yells, then quickly snaps the rat bastard's neck who shot me, then pops the last couple rats from the firing line. She then turns to find Alfred bleeding out and drops to his side.

I flop my vest off, and my breath returns, though sunken. I stand to walk her way.

Jasmine rises with her back turned to me. I grab her left arm with my right hand.

She spins and slashes my right shoulder with a serrated knife, then disappears like a puff of smoke. It's much thicker behind me.

"Harry!" Vanessa yells.

"Wait there," I tell her.

I storm after Jasmine through the thick air.

I can't see her through the smoke and dust, but I'm onto her.

I feel a sharp pain as a knife breezes by and slices the same arm.

Then again, from my right, she slices me a third time, passing silently through the thick air.

"Give it up, Jasmine," I tell her. "It's over."

She again swoops by. She slashes my back, but this time, I trip her up. She falls.

I grab her by the ankle as she tries and tries to cut me, but my violent pulls throw her off.

Jasmine winds up and swings directly for my heart. I catch her arm, then shove her down and straddle her.

I slam her hand against the ground over and over. She spits and spouts gibberish insults in my face. The knife drops from her hand. I fling it away from her.

I begin choking her with my right hand while my left holds her hands into the ground above her head.

She keeps spitting at me. I release her neck and smack her.

"Calm down, Jasmine," I tell her. "It's over. Give it up already."

"This is how you treat the woman you love?" Jasmine spits in my face. "You pussy."

I smack her with the back of my hand again. Blood drips from her lip.

"You're not the woman I loved," I tell her. "She's gone. But I'm going to get her back."

"Hah," she spits. "Good luck."

During this exchange, Jasmine manages to grab my knife off my belt and jabs it directly into my left side. I drop and roll over to my right. She gets up and starts to run. I grab her right ankle and hold her tight. I pull her in and myself towards her.

I pin her down, both of her hands. She continues spouting gibberish and spitting blood in my face with her vile mouth.

"May God have mercy on your soul," I tell her.

"God?" she laughs. "You? Talking about God? Now, that's rich."

"Why do you think we won this war?"

"You think you've won?" she responds. "You haven't won anything. This is everywhere. It's the great revolution. There's no stopping it."

"We just did," I tell her.

"Is that what you think?" she asks, laughing as I slam her head into the pavement.

We lock eyes deeply. I tried to save her. It's all I wanted. But she has given me no choice.

I pull the knife from my side. It feels far worse than the initial stabbing. I open my eyes, and we look directly and deeply into each other's eyes, into each other's very souls. Her's is buried so deeply that it will never return to the surface in this life.

"Gibberish, gibberish, gibberish," Jasmine spouts in the vilest accent I've ever heard. It's disgusting coming from such a once beautiful and amazing woman.

I look her in the eyes. They've fully turned. There's a machine-esque hate in them now and only hate. Everything I've ever known or loved is dead. She's all I ever wanted. Now I know I'll never have her.

Commies can't love. And she's a commie rat now. She's the worst of them all. She gave up everything—love—the very thing which binds this universe, this life, together. She has given it all away to be a lifeless, brainless, commie rat-cunt.

She deserves it more than any other commie before her. She had it all. She let them take it from her. She let them penetrate her and steal her from God. The strongest woman I had ever known turned into the weakest, the coldest.

Her flesh has rotted before my eyes. It's the devil's trick. She let satan himself penetrate her with the commie filth which now pours through her veins. A total repulsion. Cold. Cold and dead. Forever dead and cold. The beauty in her heart has died.

I do all I can do for Jasmine. I set her free. I jab the knife through the front of her throat. Her gibberish shouts turn to gasps, to gurgling, to a pitiful yet beautiful moaning.

I can see it. Her eyes turn almost immediately. They turn from commie hate to a remembrance and back to love. Here she is again. She is free once more, her spirit alive and glorious. She sees me again. She's returning to God, to where she came from. If only there were another way.

Blood pours out of her neck and mouth, but her spirit is freed, and her forgotten love returns with all its glory.

I let go of her arms and touch her softening face. She reaches up and touches mine. She caresses it instead of scratching at it.

Tears drip from both of our eyes.

Time stands completely still. I pull her up and put my forehead against hers. God himself is here with us. He's with her. All his light and glory shine upon her, freeing her. All of her sins wash away.

In this moment, she is truly beautiful and glorious again. Her heart beats heavy. She gasps for the air she'll never again breathe. Her eyes show a love that I hadn't seen since the morning before this all began. Her heart has been freed by God's love.

"I love you, my Jasmine," I tell her softly. "I'll forever miss you, my love. I'm sorry it had to be this way. You're truly a glorious soul. Never forget that. I'll always love you."

A glorious love shines in her eyes as her beautiful face softens even more. She begins to crack a smile as my tears meld with hers on her cheek.

I kiss her forehead, and she goes limp in my arms. Her body lightens. I can feel her spirit dance out of her body and back to God, to heaven, to the light and the love.

A bliss vibrates up through my wearied cells as tears pour from my eyes. I gently lay her head and body down to rest. My stomach turns.

"I'm sorry, my love," I say to the heavens. "May you be free again and love again. I hope to see you again one day. Goodbye, love."

I turn away from my Jasmine's body and hurl out all of the demons.

I don't know if it's from my actions, her commie putridness leaving her body, or this wretchedness that surrounds us all, but my insides are all but pouring out of me. Thankfully, her spirit has left this putrid place, and she won't have to see any more of this. She's returning home, to her true home, a home far beyond any that I could have ever given her.

"I will always love you, Jasmine."

46. The Death Of Me

TODAY—TODAY, I DIED—that life.

Today I'm born anew, merely fifteen seconds ago. Perhaps Jasmine was always a commie rat, and I just never knew it. But no, they stole her from me. They stole her from herself. There was no getting her back. The dark red stain on my shirt proves it.

Commies will destroy everything to turn mankind into machine-like cattle, just so they can control every facet of civilization. It's as if they're playing a video game, and all we are is a push of a button.

That's what they want from us. And it's the one thing they'll never get, not from the free ones. Forever free, we will be.

I don't want to leave her body's side, but she's no longer here. She's with God now. She's at peace. The free people of Nashville are finding theirs.

Gunfire comes into focus as time reawakens. The sound bounces and echoes off the newly minted rubble of East Nashville.

It's not the commies anymore. It's the citizens of Free Nashville. They're letting God's heavenly fire rain down upon the godless commie scum with all of their vengeance, God's vengeance.

Some citizens flee as quickly as they can. Many stick around and advance upon every last commie conclave with a rage that won't soon be forgotten.

Have we won? Is it all over? Are we free now? Will this world ever truly be free again?

This war is far from over. Jasmine was right. But this battle is ending. Nashville is freed, and New Nashville will rise from the ashes and be great once again, years from now.

Perhaps there are a few commie conclaves left in Germantown, Brentwood, and Franklin. But soon, they too will be destroyed. They've lost this city, and they're not getting it back.

How have the other city's faired? Certainly not all as well as we have. But perhaps there really are those who withstood the initial invasion. Perhaps, the rumors are true? Perhaps, "Don't Mess With Texas?"

Dallas was the place where we nearly lost our freedom over half a century ago when they assassinated one of the only great presidents in the past century. Now, will Dallas be the place where we will regain our freedom? Or will Charleston? New Orleans?

We've heard rumors about these places, where the commies never stood a chance. Soon, we will see. And if true, freedom will spread like a wildfire, like pollen, like water flowing down the mountain in spring from the melting snow.

We will devour the commie, and God's love will shine here again. It will wash over the entire planet and free us all.

It wasn't I who saved this city. It was all of us. It was God. We became brave and triumphant through his power. Others will hear of what happened in this city, and others will follow.

Perhaps there is a long war ahead of us, and it may take even more out of us, but our humanity will remain. Lord knows we're not staying here—not now. But we will return, and we will rebuild. New Nashville will thrive again. We all will, free from the commie scum.

Just as I'm letting go of my lost love's lifeless body, a commie fuck sneaks behind me with a hatchet, ready to chop me in half.

He swings, but I could smell the fucking commie rat-stench coming. Plus, his awkward footsteps were hard to miss. I turn and pop him twice in the chest. The hatchet swings out of his hand and just nicks my left shoulder.

I catch him and give him the shush signal, then pop him twice more through the belly or chest. I can't be sure. His body drops heavy.

I stand, once again realizing the pain where blood pours out of my side and arm as I leave my Jasmine's side forever.

I make my way painfully towards Vanessa. She's with Alfred, holding his hand.

"Vanessa?" I ask. "Is he okay?"

She looks at me with tears in her eyes, fighting them as hard as she can. She's a soldier, but soldiers are allowed to cry, especially on days like today.

"Alfred?" I question. "We'll get you home."

"Home?" Alfred says with what feels like his last breath. "You know there's no such thing as home any longer."

"There will be," I say and fall to my knees beside him. "And you're coming with us. Come on, buddy."

Alfred tries to speak, but blood fills his lungs. He gasps.

"We've got to go," Vanessa says, then turns to Alfred and smacks his face. "Alfred? Alfred?"

It's too late for him. Vanessa pauses a brief moment, takes a deep breath, hugs Alfred, then shuts his eyes.

"Where is Deon?" she asks through salty tears.

I shake my head somberly, "It's my fault."

"What?" Vanessa slams me against the ground.

"I'm sorry."

"Well, where is she?" Vanessa asks, holding tightly to my collar.

I shake my head. Words no longer mean a thing. She understands. Our tears both fall.

"Harry?" Vanessa worries, wiping her eyes. "You're shot."

"No, I'm not," I inform her.

"Then what's that red stuff?" she asks.

"Blood—my blood."

"Yeah, you're bleeding. You're shot."

"I'm not shot."

"What happened?"

"She stabbed me," I say casually. "It's not that bad."

Vanessa's eyes widen, "Let's go." She stands and helps me to my feet. "Are you sure you're okay?"

"It's fine. I don't really even feel it."

"Cause you're in shock. Wait a little while. Can you walk?"

"I made it this far, didn't I?" I say as we begin making our way back to the river. The pain keeps my pace much slower than normal, but steadily we progress back towards the river.

Firing blindly through the smoke, a commie rat appears. Over my shoulder, Vanessa fires two rounds right through his chest. I would thank her, but if ever there was a time not to convey our emotions, this is it. We press onward as my mind drifts.

I hath no more revenge left. I could just walk lifeless into the water to drown or be slaughtered for all I care, but my new honed instincts kick in, and I depopulate the world of two more commies along the riverside.

Vanessa and I push a patrol boat into the water and jet-set back to downtown. Shots rain around us, piercing the water in a quiet beauty.

They can't see us through the smokey dust-filled air, but they can surely hear us. The shots are a touch close for comfort.

I drive as Vanessa sprays the casino by the stadium, their last remaining stronghold, where the civilians and rebels should be storming any minute.

The engine roars towards the quickly approaching coastline. There's no slowing down. I ram the boat onto shore. It slides twenty feet up the river bank until we both flip off upon the abrupt stop.

After a few moments, I come to in a puddle just below a lip which protects me from the gunfire. Mud fills and packs my bloody wounds.

Am I dead? No. That would be too easy.

I get up and jet west. I climb the crumbling three-foot-tall stairs up to the street above. I hit the ground and fall forward.

"What was that?" I wonder.

Someone grabs me and drags me away from the incoming fire.

"Blood? Why is there blood?" I journey inward. "Peculiar."

"Harry? Harry?" a strong female voice repeats. "You're hit, but it's just a flesh wound. Let's go."

I hazelly see Vanessa reach for my hand. She helps me up, and onward we push.

A blast of some sort smashes a nearby building. We both fall, though both conscious, it seems.

Vanessa grabs me again and helps me to my feet. We make our way free of the gunfire and continue through the ever-thickening debris and rubble.

As we walk back towards the capital, my side begins to throb piercingly. But thanks to the concussion and ongoing shock, I can't feel much of the pain. Soon, that may be different.

"Where's my nectar when I need it?" I wonder aloud.

"We'll just get you some morphine," Vanessa says.

47. *Piercing Into View*

THROUGH THE DUST AND SMOKE, the capital pierces into view. Vanessa hurries up the steps and swings the door open. The smokey air swirls into a swift whirlwind.

With each step I take, my body aches deeper from the mud-filled slices in my side and arm, and whatever this new burning pain is in my thigh.

Heather runs out to the steps. She stops. There it is, that same fucking look; just fucking look at it. I've never seen anything more fucking annoying in my life. Surely, I have not.

Nevertheless, it's a look I never want to stop seeing.

"Are you okay?" asks Heather. "I was so worried about you."

"You were?" I ask.

"Yes. What would I do without you?" Heather asks.

She runs down the steps. Twelve steps away, she pauses. She looks at my wounds.

We look deeply into each other's eyes. She takes off her jacket and walks my way. I walk to her.

Had she known all along? She runs to me. A lightness comes over me. A satisfying tingling flows through; not the pins and needles, which is all I've been feeling, but a warm gentle caress. How had I never seen it before? The way she's always looked at me—how she's looking at me now.

I finally know what it means. I thought I understood it, but no. Now I feel it. It's her breath, her steadiness, her depth, the infinince of her all, her sorrow, and her love. The true face of an angel. Absolute beauty and goodness.

The smokey light dances off her golden hair and skin. Those beautiful full and moist lips; her smile and concern for me, which speaks thousands of words in a hundred and one languages; the brightness in her sparkling blue eyes, in her whole being.

I walk her way. She runs. She leaps into my arms. I catch her. I can hardly breathe. I feel at home for the first time since before the war.

I move in and kiss her glistening full wet lips. They feel as if they could suck my life force from me, but instead, they feed me pure energy, freedom, and bliss. They suck out all of the sorrow. It feels as if love itself is pouring out of her and flowing between us, yet with all of the sorrow in the world, but it's no longer sorrow.

All of the aching, the pain, the fear, she's transforming it. She's receiving it and changing it into good. She is the alchemist.

"I need you," I look deeply into her eyes and tell her. "I've always needed you."

"What about her?" Heather asks.

"She's gone," I say, surely revealing my guilt.

"It's okay, Harry," she assures me.

She continues sucking my lips with a fiery passion while pressuring her jacket against my wounded side, pulling me in.

"We've got to go," I tell her.

"Tonight?" she asks.

"Yes."

"You're wounded," she says softly. "You need to rest."

"Just pack it."

"Are you sure?"

"Yes. We must go now."

"Okay," she says, shakes yes, then kisses me.

The world is still burning, but with her, that doesn't matter. She is breathing new life back into the world. The flowers will bloom again. I must get her to safety; and the child.

Perhaps I knew it all along, but the other was in my way. Now, I see it. She has been the only decent and good thing in this place all of this time. She has held my heart and soul.

She has kept me from falling into the deep abyss. She's been there to pull me out every time I was at the precipice.

Those lips. Those eyes. The sparkle. The love. The energy. The feeling. She and I. Heather; my Heather. She is my true lioness.

She unlocks her lips from mine and pulls me along. We walk slowly up the capital stairs through the smokey haze.

The remaining disciples stand aside as the stoop seems to widen and the skies lower and darken above us.

Dirty, bruised, and bloodied, I follow Heather inside.

It feels surreal; nothing but this eternal moment, our destiny fulfilled. Now to live in peace in the mountains and hills, by the rivers and springs.

Or to fight on? Not I. My fight is finished. The others can do as they please. I have new priorities.

We're going to make it our own now. We will carve our own paths and create our own existence, allowing only laws which will never neglect our freedom; God's law.

The world as we know it is over. Now it's up to us. We will start anew, she and I; Heather, who God has always shown through. I was just a fool not to recognize it before. But I was under a spell—just a spell. I felt it, so it was real. But not like this. This is true depth. This is everything.

This is the "I'll never be able to leave this person again in all of eternity kind of love." My every fiber knows it.

Maybe that's what I had thought about Jasmine, but with her, I had to force it. Even before the war. I always had to try, to change, to be different, to be what she wanted, to not upset her.

With Heather, all I ever have to be is natural; the good and the bad; the rage, the love, the fear, the daring; the love of God; the fear of God and death, and what will become of me upon that fateful day.

She accepts all of me, and she's seen my absolute worst. She knows that deep down I am, if not good, I'm at least not bad. And she, she is all good, only good, forever and always good. She's the heart of love itself; the mother, the child, the lover, the nurturer. She's risen above all others.

She and I can nurture each other. It's in both of us. She may not have seen that part of me yet, but she will. If we make it out of this damned city, she will.

48. Will

THE EIGHT DISCIPLES REMAINING part like a bloody sea as Heather and I enter the capital. The world squeezes tighter, the ceiling shrinks in, and the door shuts.

The disciples close in around us in a wide circle, watching us ominously, as always. It's over. I have no more orders for them.

Bobby, Will, and little Oliver greet us inside the circle. Vanessa's already off preparing. She knows it's now or never. She always knows.

"Thank you, Bobby," I say. "Thank you. It's over. Is the truck ready?"

"Almost," Bobby says, holding a large duffle bag. "I'll pull into position."

"We did it, sir," Will says. "We will be kings in New Nashville. You will be, sir. We will be your knights in shining armor. Legends, we will all be. Tales will be told."

"We're leaving, Will," I inform him. "But thank you. Thank you all. We could have never done this without each of you."

"You can't leave, sir," Will states.

"Yes, I can. It's over," I say, then head for the stairs with Heather and Oliver.

"What about us?" Will and the crowd follows.

"Stay if you want," I stop and turn on the stairs. "But there's nothing left here."

"It's Friday, sir. One last hurrah?"

"No. It's over, Will. If you're smart, you'll leave too. You all will."

"But, sir," Will interjects with a fresh bottle of nectar he pushes my way.

I reject the honorable gift. I'm cutting back. Plus, I have all I need already loaded in the truck.

"Keep it," I tell him. "It's yours."

"The nectar?" Will questions himself, staring at the dark golden brown glowing bottle in the candlelight.

"We're leaving," I end it. "Everyone pack what you can."

"Okay, sir," Will says, then walks away with the nectar. The other seven disciples follow, including Chipped-Tooth.

Bobby and Vanessa finish gathering supplies while Heather opens my sliced denim jacket. She cuts my bloodied white t-shirt apart to access my bloody side.

"This is going to—" Heather says right before she pours rubbing alcohol on my wounds to my uncharacteristic howls and heavy deep painful breaths. "Hurt."

Now I feel it. I feel it pulsating now as she empties the bottle, cleaning out the mud. What happened to the morphine? Heather packs my wounds, then wraps me with gauze.

She then helps gather Oliver's belongings and hurries a jacket on him. Once we're safely out of the city, she can sow me up. The dust is beginning to settle. We must be off soon and leave this whole tragedy behind us. We can't wait for nightfall.

Heather helps me to my feet as I moan and groan. We grab our things and exit the chambers. Little Oliver follows with his backpack and rifle. He takes Heather's hand.

We walk down the stairs into the lobby to find the disciples holding Vanessa by the arms, circled around her like

hungry wolves. A few disciples close in behind and grab
Heather and Oliver before I can react. The disciples force us
down with Vanessa and circle around us.

"Let them go," I demand.

"We can't do that, sir," Will answers. "I told you, we
can't allow you to leave."

"Get your hands off of her," I raise my gun to the disciple who holds Heather hostage.

Will walks over and lowers my pistol, "It's how it has to
be, Harry. We're starting a new golden revolution in the city.
You'll see. You will rule over it all. You are our king, sire.
Long live King Harry!"

"Here here, hail King Harry," the disciples regurgitate
proudly.

"Just take me," I tell them. "Let them go. They need to
get out of the city."

"But don't you see, sir?" Will says. "They are our
future."

"See the child?" Will continues, holding little Oliver's
face like a puppet. "The prophet. See the queen? Your queen,
sir? Our queen. You said it yourself, sir."

Will touches Heather's arm lightly and almost shivers in
delight.

"Not like this, Will," I tell him. "You have to listen to me.
We'll come back and rebuild. But we need to leave for a little
while."

"But we won, sir." Chipped-Tooth proclaims.

"You can't go," Will says.

"Watch me," I say, then walk towards Heather and notice Bobby peeking in from the window out front.

"Sorry about this, sir," Will says as he swings my own
pistol into my jaw.

I guess there is a stopping me. But I certainly didn't think it would be Will. If anyone, I figured it would be Chipped-Tooth.

As I fall back, I see Bobby raise his gun through the window but drops it back below. I hit heavy on the floor.

It feels like several minutes have passed here in the void, on this cold marble, but from the looks of things, it's only been a few seconds.

"You think you can take her from me?" I question, then stand to my feet, checking my jaw. "That will never be the case. You all should know that."

Heather's worried and fearful look remains strong. She locks eyes with mine. She trusts me, but she knows the woes of this warring world. She knows better than to believe in positive outcomes, regardless of how much she trusts me.

Bobby peaks in through the window. We lock eyes and signal "go."

Will notices me looking, sees Bobby, and shouts, "Stop him."

Bobby shoots the disciple holding Oliver and fires some more. Oliver dives in hiding.

"What are you waiting for?" Will shouts. "Go."

I dash towards Heather, nod my head, and she ducks heavily. The disciple holding her reaches his gun out. I stiff-arm the bastard in the throat, then dip under his shoulder and take control of his handgun. He fights me for it.

Heather gives him a good hard bite, giving me control over the gun. I flip him over and pop him in the chest with his own weapon.

Vanessa fights off the two men holding her captive, giving me time to shoot one of the bastards. The other lets go and shoves Vanessa towards me, then runs off for cover.

Will turns my way. Bobby shoots him in the back. Gunfire erupts from every which way.

A gun fires behind me, and a disciple drops, grazing my legs. I turn and see Heather breathing heavily, holding the smoking gun. Little Oliver runs to her. She scoops him up and moves towards the front.

Vanessa grabs a fallen pistol, takes the limping Will by the throat, rises, and drags him in a headlock towards the exit. She fires at the Chipped-Tooth and the three other disciples who fire at us from the pews.

Heather and Oliver are out the door. Vanessa follows behind, firing, pulling Will along. We take cover behind the thick walls.

I look down and see Bobby bleeding out on the front stoop, "Bobby?"

"Go," Bobby coughs. "Just go."

"We're taking you," I tell him. "You'll be alright."

Vanessa looks at me, knowing it's of no use.

Still, I try to pick Bobby up, but he's in too much excruciating pain, or so his screams seem to signify. I lay him back down as Vanessa continues to cover us.

"Just go, Harry," Bobby commands. "Get them out of here."

"Thank you, Bobby," I say as I kneel and grab his hand. "And though I walk through the valley of death, I shall fear no evil. For thine is the kingdom, the power, the glory. Amen."

"Go," Bobby demands. "Go."

"You're a good friend, Bobby."

I let go of his hand and grab Heather's. We run with Oliver towards the truck waiting on the street below.

Vanessa leaves Will bleeding out next to Bobby. She bends down, forehead to forehead with Bobby, then hurries to follow us.

"We could have had everything, Harry," Will yells in certain vain. "Why?"

"We will have everything," I yell back. "Just not here. Not yet."

"We could have been kings here, sir," Will shouts. "The kings of New Nashville."

The disciples start to fire upon us from the front door. Vanessa hops in to drive. Heather hops in the back, keeping low while buckling Oliver up, then herself. I climb into the passenger seat, grab my rifle, and lay down cover fire into the front of the capital.

"Go," I tell Vanessa.

"Where are the keys?" Vanessa asks, searching wildly.

"Bobby," we think aloud in unison.

I hop out of the truck, aiming my rifle at the doorway, firing round after round. The disciples scurry back inside for cover. I hurry carefully back towards Bobby.

"Bobby?" I whisper shout from the stoop below.

Bobby slowly turns his head back my way.

"Key, Bobby," I say. "Keys."

Bobby reaches slowly into his pocket and pulls out the key. He tries his best to toss it back to me, but his arm goes limp as Chipped-Tooth shoots Bobby in the chest, then storms out the door.

"You dirty rotten fucking chipped-tooth bitch," I say. "I thought you were already fucking dead."

"Heroes don't die," Chipped-Tooth says as he raises his gun in an odd but quick flipping motion and fires.

I blast lead into and through Chipped-Tooth's chest on repeat. He misses his chance by inches. He falls to his knees, then over to his left side, straight down onto his face. He was a wily little bastard. I'll give him that.

I grab Bobby's limp yet still pulsing hand, take the keys, then rush towards the truck.

I toss Vanessa the keys from twenty yards away. She leaps and catches them, then starts the engine. I hop in, and she takes off. I fire away at the capital as we begin to leave this hollowed-out city behind.

Heather ducks and holds Oliver down. I hold her hand tightly yet calmly, hoping to reassure her. Vanessa speeds along, winding her way out of the city, westward and south towards the Heartland, or wherever we may land. An island far away, perhaps?

Will the music ever return to Nashville? I can almost hear it now as the deafness in my ears begins to wane and the skyline begins to shrink in the rearview.

49. The Path Ahead

WE MAKE IT OUT OF DOWNTOWN without incident, forging our own path southwest through the neighborhood streets of Belle Meade so as to avoid any leftover rats in Green Hills, Brentwood, or Franklin.

I keep my eyes alert for any damn commie who may hop out of the woodwork on the route ahead. However, the streets seem perfectly clear of the bastards. Odd, considering I was planning on having to use any assortment of the plethora of grenades and explosives I have in the pack at my feet. There are some lucky rats out there today.

The sun begins to set as we pass through rich historic neighborhoods filled with giant estates which still stand proudly. From behind us, hellfire begins to rain down from the skies upon what's left of the city and any remaining rats, rebels, or lost wandering souls.

I hope all of the citizens made it out in time. But I don't want to think about that. I just want to get to where we're headed. I'm hoping Bobby was already gone before he could see it, but not Will. I hope Will is witness to his prophecy blowing up before his eyes, for he is no prophet, only little Oliver.

It's rather beautiful watching the city burn through the side-view mirror. Light from the bombs burst through the golden smoke and clouds, haloing forth.

I turn to look. My breath is taken away by Heather's extraordinariness, her calm brave glow, and purity while the world burns around her. She's the loving center of the universe, fully blossomed and benevolent.

Holding her hand, I am holding the world itself, creation itself. It keeps me whole and keeps my entire being from breaking into one-hundred billion bits and dissolving away. She is why the world exists, the woman, the receiver of life, the giver of life.

She is the light of the world, all the light there ever was or will be again. God is living inside of her, giving out blessings to little Oliver and myself, and all things around, the air itself.

She holds me. The child holds her, and she the child. The earth is shaking, but we plow forth on our path. This isn't the easiest drive with plenty of fallen trees, burnt-out cars, and other rubble crowding the streets, but we've made it free of the smoke and ash of the burning city.

Fireballs rise higher in the rearview inferno. Are we simply trapped between empires raging it out in the final battle of mankind? That no longer matters for us. We're together, and we're starting over.

The last four months took a toll on us all, but we made it, the few of us. We're filled with anguish and pain, but also honor and glory, and now finally, some real hope.

We want safety. We want peace. Something we thought we may never know again, which only the hills and forests can bring now. She and I will make it to a new home. We will live on the land. We will be free and love each other truly.

Heather nor I say a word. We don't need to. Holding hands, touching, we are free. Not a soul says a word as we speed south.

I look back, and Heather's eyes say everything, her hopeful yet fearful look. She hasn't once turned to look behind. She knows our future is ahead of us, not behind. The past is gone. It will be decades before the city's back to its glory. And that doesn't matter.

Love and peace are on the horizon ahead. It's rising again. It's flowing through Heather, and through me, through all of us.

Vanessa drives on through Belle Meade, down highway 100, to Pasquo down Natchez Trace, as the golden burning glow slowly shrinks on the horizon behind us.

All that's left of the city must be burning now, all the way from Music row through the Gulch, Broadway, and Germantown. There can't be a thing left alive there, not a fucking rat. Not after that.

Commie jets continue to drop hellfire from above. It looks more like heat lightning from this distance. I'm not even upset that they're finishing off the city. It needs to burn fully so as to smoke the rats and the filth out. I'm pretty sure that Oliver agrees. I guess in their mind, if they can't have it, nobody can—just like a fucking commie.

Vanessa pulls into a gas station. One which doesn't inspire confidence with the several dead and pecked at bodies, but so far, no commies; no anyone—living. It's vacant, along with the road we've traversed.

I fill up the tank with my AR slung to my chest by siphoning fuel from the stranded vehicles.

Vanessa clears the station, then shatters the glass door and escorts Heather and Oliver inside. While they're inside, Vanessa searches stranded vehicles and dead bodies for keys. There are about seven possibilities. Only two are worth considering. She gets lucky with one which is nearly filled up. We both fill up several five-gallon gas tanks, so we don't have to stop in the open again.

Heather and Oliver hurry out to the truck with snacks and drinks as we refueling.

After wishing Vanessa luck and saying our thanks and goodbyes, I drive off in the large black matte truck. We head West in the dark of night. We pray that crossing the Mississippi will be our only real obstacle.

Vanessa heads off southward. I believe she plans to head down to New Orleans. I almost remember her saying something about family there. I imagine she'll rejoin the fight. She's indicated that.

Heather sits in the passenger seat. Oliver's buckled up tightly in the back with headphones on and playlists from Heather's phone, which she was finally able to charge. Turning it on has weighed heavily on her heart. Holding my hand, she calms her breath.

The road is wide and clear. A calmness fills the humid southern air.

A light appears behind us. Headlights.

I turn our lights off, and with our taped rear lights, perhaps they haven't spotted us, but they're closing in fast.

Our truck hits something in the darkness but plows forward.

Spotlights shine upon us.

Heather holds my hand tightly.

Gunshots fire. We duck. I reach my handgun out and spray several rounds to our rear.

"Grenade," I say to Heather. "Toss a grenade."

She throws a green-bomber behind us. The explosion devoirs the road behind the vehicle. A second green-bomber does the same. They're too close—getting closer.

"Hold the wheel," I tell Heather, then turn the head-lights back on.

"Okay," Heather says, then grabs the wheel. "Stay down, Oliver."

"You got it?" I ask.

She shakes, "yes," as she weaves through the obstacles of the bumpy road.

I reach behind the seats, into a rucksack, and pull out a bottle of nectar. Just what I need.

"Really?" Heather asks. "Now?"

They're getting dangerously close to our bumper.

I just look at her with a sly crooked half-smile. Then I rip off some of my shirt fabric and stuff the fuze into the bottle of goodness. I check my pockets.

"Matches," I say. "Check the glove box."

Heather hangs onto the wheel with one hand, barely keeping the boat steady as she searches.

The commie-mobile rams into our bumper.

I fire several more shots their way. They're still shooting at us.

Heather hands me the book of matches, "Here."

The first doesn't spark. The second does, and the flame ignites. I put it to the fuse.

The rat bastards bump us a second time, and a spit of fire erupts from the bottle, landing on the dash, burning. I contain the fire, keeping an eye on the lit fuse.

They begin pulling up hastily beside us, maybe three feet between us. I lean out the window and sling the molotov, then fire away. The bottle shatters on the edge of the passenger door, flinging nectar fire through the open window, alighting the dirty rat bastards.

"Harry," Heather says, worried.

I look forward to see a sudden tree obstacle in the road. Heather and I both steer the truck to the right and barely scrape it. She lets go of the reigns and holds tightly to my thigh.

I grab her hand and hold it firmly as the commie-mobile crashes headfirst into the giant fallen tree. Two of the fiery rats fling thirty feet through the windshield. I don't know what happened to the other rats, but their fates are no better.

Heather and I share a quick monumental stare, then focus on the road ahead.

Little Oliver just sits there with his headphones on, drawing, actively unaware of the chaos of the moment as the blazing horizon disappears behind us into the deep night sky.

50. The Beginning

AFTER SPENDING THE COLD and hungry winter in a small dug-out hut, spring has finally sprung, sprouting flowers, wild berries, and various edible plants in abundance.

In our search for a new home, we were able to pick up Heather's parents from their country home in Arkansas, along with various tools, kerosine tanks, canned goods, and other necessities. They helped Heather lead us here deep into the Ozark's, near a place she used to come to as a child, where we live hidden amongst the thickly wooded hills, away from all of the blood, chaos, and tragedy. We're miles from any road or trail, far away from the towns and cities.

Winter was harsh. But we survived. Who knows how long this war will last. But we will withstand it. Vanessa has surely continued the good fight. My only fight now is to love, protect, and care for my family and the woman I love.

I will love Heather until the day I die and beyond. She is my true everything. There is nothing I wouldn't do to keep her safe. She's my only duty now. If anyone dares bring a fight to us, I will lay all of the vengeance in the world upon them. Our new home will be well hidden with a grass roof, dug deeply into the wooded hillside.

When we're not planting and mending the crops scattered in the meadows, her father and I spend the days building the cabin. Much of that time is spent digging and reinforcing the roof so that it doesn't cave in on us while we're digging. It's coming along; structurally. We hope to dig a well once the cabin is done, but a stream flows nearby on most days. After filtering it, the water tastes fine. We're able to snag a few fish out of it from time to time, which we cook on a small gas grill.

Heather's happy to have her parents around. I pray my folks are fine, but I may never know. Their small town may be untouched, but there's no way to reach them.

Along with the cooking and foraging, Heather's mother helps with little Oliver. Having her mother around has brought a greater peace to Heather's heart, though the pain she feels will never go away.

Little Oliver grows bigger by the day. His drawings have become a little more peaceful, yet a savage rages inside of him. A vengeance burns deep within the little man. Heather keeps him calm as best she can. May the child find peace one day; may we all.

We'll do our best with the child, but who knows the dark places he'll go in this life. Heather and I will watch over him and try to keep him from falling too far astray. Perhaps God still has a few miracles up his sleeve.

My only mission in life now is to raise a family with my lioness, the strongest-hearted, most kind and motherly woman I've ever known. Of course, she is. She has to be. She lost a child at the start of all of this, her little girl. She was devastated, as anyone would be. She was only four. She was Heather's entire world.

Even through all of her pain, Heather is still giving life to the world. Her very being brightens it. Every moment we share feels completely alive, full of pleasure as well as pain. While still somber from everything that took place, our love grows deeper by the moment.

She and I are starting our own family now. Heather's pregnant with our very own child. She's expecting a little angel in four months.

I will keep her safe. And the child. We will survive this.

We'll stay hidden here for as long as it takes.

Free and alive, her beauty shines in the wide-open world beneath the tree cover on the hillside. She and I lay together in the grass, eating fresh blackberries, holding the very universe in our arms as we hold each other and the wonder growing inside of her.

We've found our home.

Epilogue

IN THE END, PERHAPS IT WAS the commie himself who set us free. Maybe we needed this wake-up call. Perhaps, we had to lose it all to see how great this thing is—how great it can be again—free of constraints and petty laws—living on the land—living by the only law, God's law, the golden law.

I believe Jasper may have even become proud of the anti-commie I've become, that we've all become. The last fucking thing any American left alive wants now, in this world, is communism. It has shown its true face here. Once again, the face of pure evil. A total lack of humanity, a machine-esque existence with no free will—an existence we will never accept.

We will burn their institutions to the ground, as they have burnt our cities.

We're all Americans now, all patriots. They thought this war would destroy us, but it has only made us stronger. It has united us all as one again, against the commie virus, the enemy of all humanity.

The bullshit left-right paradigm has broken. The truth is now known, will be known, and forever known. The ones who brought this upon us will never again have a chance to weld power over us. If they don't hand over the reins willingly, we will take it from them with all the force of the universe, of God, of man, woman, and animal. We will thrive again and live freely. New technologies will set us free, not control us.

Human drama will always remain. Love and hate will fluctuate. But together, we will overcome the gravest threat humanity has ever faced —the money men, central banks, secret societies, intelligence agencies, the media, the lies, the commies. We will shine light into the darkness, and we will be set free.

It's already happening, no matter how grim it may appear.

For all of those who have fallen, may God bless their souls. For those of you who still remain, may nothing of this fate ever fall upon you or your lands again. Live in peace with your brothers and sisters, and keep a vigilant eye for any commie rat bastards who may appear, any authoritarian.

Bless you, in your efforts.

May no living creature ever have to go through this kind of tragedy again.

ABOUT THE AUTHOR

HAROLD MACK

Dune buggy enthusiast
Collector of ancient artifacts
Stock market crusader
Blissfully informed
Non-surfing surfer dude
Played "What I Got" on stage with the
lead guitarist of Train, Jimmy Stafford.
Almost died snowboarding in the Alps
Fuji shooter
No kids that he knows of
Doesn't own a llama

Made in the USA
Coppell, TX
06 December 2021